THE WANDERER

HENRI ALAIN-FOURNIER *was born on October 3, 1886 in the French village of Chapelle-d'Angellon, the son of a schoolmaster. He was killed during the First World War at St. Rémy on September 22, 1914, at the age of twenty-eight.*

THE WANDERER *was Fournier's only completed novel. Another,* Colombe Blanchet, *unfinished at the time of his death, was included in a collection of his short pieces,* Miracles, *published in 1924, with an introduction by Jacques Rivière. Four volumes of Fournier's correspondence with Rivière were brought out in 1928.*

THE WANDERER *was published in France in 1912 under the title* Le Grand Meaulnes. *The first English and American editions appeared in 1928.*

ALAIN-FOURNIER

Translated by Françoise Delisle
Introduction by Fredrika Blair

The Wanderer

(LE GRAND MEAULNES)

DOUBLEDAY ANCHOR BOOKS

DOUBLEDAY & COMPANY, INC., GARDEN CITY, NEW YORK

CONTENTS

PART I

Chapter 1   The Boarder   19
Chapter 2   After Four O'Clock   27
Chapter 3   I Haunted a Basket-Maker's Shop   30
Chapter 4   The Escape   34
Chapter 5   The Cart Comes Back   38
Chapter 6   Some One Knocks at the Window   42
Chapter 7   The Silk Waistcoat   47
Chapter 8   The Adventure   53
Chapter 9   A Halt   56
Chapter 10 The Sheepfold   60
Chapter 11 The Mysterious Manor   63
Chapter 12 Wellington's Room   68
Chapter 13 The Strange Festival   72
Chapter 14 The Strange
            Festival (Continuation)   76
Chapter 15 The Meeting   81
Chapter 16 Frantz de Galais   89
Chapter 17 The Strange Festival (End)   94

PART II

Chapter 1   The Great Game   101
Chapter 2   We Fall into an Ambush   106
Chapter 3   The Bohemian at School   110

Chapter 4   Which Deals with the Mysterious
               Manor   116
Chapter 5   The Man in Sand-Shoes   121
Chapter 6   A Quarrel Behind the Scenes   125
Chapter 7   The Bohemian Takes Off
               His Bandage   129
Chapter 8   The Police   132
Chapter 9   In Search of the Lost Trail   135
Chapter 10 Washing-Day   142
Chapter 11 I Betray Him   146
Chapter 12 The Three Letters from Meaulnes 151

PART III

Chapter 1   Bathing   159
Chapter 2   At Florentin's   165
Chapter 3   The Ghost   174
Chapter 4   Great News   181
Chapter 5   The Country Outing   187
Chapter 6   The Country Outing (End)   193
Chapter 7   The Wedding Day   200
Chapter 8   Frantz's Call   203
Chapter 9   Happy People   208
Chapter 10 Frantz's House   213
Chapter 11 A Talk in the Rain   220
Chapter 12 The Burden   225
Chapter 13 The Composition Test Book   232
Chapter 14 The Secret   235
Chapter 15 The Secret (Continued)   241
Chapter 16 The Secret (Concluded)   247

EPILOGUE   251

INTRODUCTION

Thirty years ago Henri Alain-Fournier was killed on the battlefields of France—presumed killed, rather, for his body was never found. He was twenty-eight years old, and his early death cut short a career which was already more than 'promising' though he had only published one book. This was the novel *Le Grand Meaulnes*, in English called *The Wanderer*. He had also written some poems and short stories, later to appear under the title *Miracles*, and had begun work on a second novel, *Colombe Blanchet*. But it is on his first book that his reputation rests. Though slow in obtaining popularity in France, from the first *Le Grand Meaulnes* deeply impressed such critics as Julien Benda, Edmond Jaloux, and the poet Charles Péguy, and by 1929 it had run into sixty-nine editions. In this country, after a modest start, it has fared increasingly well. It first appeared in 1928 with a preface by Havelock Ellis and enjoyed a favorable reception by the critics. The book went out of print but was soon reissued by New Directions. Since then the demand has been so steady as to justify the present edition.

Le Grand Meaulnes is the story of the strange adventure which begins when the student Augustin Meaulnes borrows a horse and wagon without permis-

sion, and drives off to the station to meet the grandparents of his friend Seurel. Meaulnes becomes lost, and
after wandering for a day and a night in the forest, he
comes across a driveway where the dust has been swept
in 'great regular circles, as it was swept at his home before holidays.' He follows the road and comes to a half-
ruined manor. Lanterns have been hung in the gaping
windows, and peasants and children, wearing the costumes of three generations ago, are dining on long
trestle tables. Meaulnes learns from one of the guests
that the son of the house, a headstrong and fanciful
young man, is bringing home his fiancée, and this celebration has been arranged to please the young couple.
The next day the guests go for a boat ride on the lake,
although it is winter, and Meaulnes is placed next to a
beautiful girl whom he discovers to be the sister of the
young man. But the boat ride ends, and still the guests
of honor have not appeared. Finally the young man ar-
rives alone. His fiancée has refused to come with him.
The party breaks up, and in the confusion Meaulnes is
unable to say good-bye to his new friend. A farmer offers
to drive him part of the way back, Meaulnes accepts,
falls asleep, and when he returns to the school, he is
unable to find out where he has been. The efforts of
Meaulnes and Seurel to rediscover the 'lost château'
where the young girl lives form the chief part of the
story.

That is roughly the plot of Le Grand Meaulnes, but
a summary cannot convey the quality of the book. Fournier, like Flaubert, seems to have tested his prose by
reading it aloud; in any case, it possesses a music and a
simplicity which recall Sainte Julien l'Hospitalier; it is
at once mysterious and sober. The small town, the school
of Sainte Agathe, and the surrounding countryside are
described with the liveliness and the fidelity of things
long known; and yet in the very process of being described they are somehow transformed by hints and pre-

monitions of events to come. Fournier once said that he
meant to 'insert the marvelous into reality,' and in *Le
Grand Meaulnes* the commonplace and the strange are
inextricably mixed. The fight in the snow at night, di-
rected by the gypsy with the bandaged head, nevertheless remains a fight among schoolboys who can be
recognized 'by their muffled voices and their manner of
attacking.' And the most fantastic episodes become cred-
ible through the sharpness of his observations. Fournier
knows how to evoke the sight and smell of a place by a
few precise details: the classroom in winter, with the
odor of 'herrings frying on the stove, and of the singed
wool of those who, on coming in, had warmed themselves
too close.' His account of the amusements at school, the
excitement of the boys at the prospect of driving to the
station for Seurel's grandparents, Seurel's initial feeling
of pleasure when the classroom is used as a laundry ('at
the first moment—I was still so young—I considered this
novelty as a holiday') makes us understand, better than
any explanations could, how restricted and uneventful
life in the village was. And constantly, though Fournier
uses only simple, concrete words, he manages to suggest
something more intangible: solitude, the wonder which
children feel at an icy morning. He speaks of the students
arriving at school with eyes 'still dazzled from having
crossed fields of hoar-frost, from looking on frozen ponds,
and thickets from which hares ran'; or of the winter
landscape through which Meaulnes drove: 'Once more
it was the vast frozen countryside, without incident or
distraction; only from time to time a magpie, frightened
by the cart, would fly up, to perch farther off on a head-
less elm.' In all these descriptions there is an awareness
of the mystery which underlies commonplace happenings.

It is perhaps this feeling of mystery, that all created
things whether great or small are worthy of interest,
which enables Fournier to make so prosaic a figure as

the 'methodical housewife' Millie so charming. He shows
us Millie trying on her made-over hat with a mixture of
coquetry and self-consciousness; or even while she is in-
specting the new house and complaining that their furniture will never fit, gently wiping the grimy face of her
little boy. But it is in the understanding of children that
he excels. He has caught the very mood of youth, the
restlessness, the anxiety, the tremendous hopes, and the
melancholy of that period when 'we believed that happiness was near, and that one had but to set forth in order
to find it.' Seurel, with his hero worship of his older
friend; Meaulnes himself, proud and solitary, unable to
keep from wounding the girl he loves—almost as a precaution—because he cannot believe that joy will last,
have been drawn from firsthand experience. Even when
he is at the height of his fortune Meaulnes is incapable
of trusting in his good luck. 'Meaulnes felt in himself
that slight anguish which seizes you at the end of too-
happy days.' Beneath his rejoicing, he has always a sense
of guilt; an uninvited guest at the celebration, he thinks:
'"All the same, there must be people in the world who
would forgive me." And he imagines old people, grandparents who are convinced beforehand that everything
you do is good.' Yet he and Seurel, in between their
planning and their disappointments, are still young
enough to play violent games in the courtyard, and to
enjoy mystery for its own sake. ' "Be my friends," said
the gypsy. He added . . . "Swear that you will answer
when I call you—when I call you this way" (and he let
out a strange sort of cry: Hou-ou!) "Meaulnes, you swear
first!" And we swore, for like the children that we were,
everything that was more serious and solemn than usual
delighted us.'

Fournier's work grows out of the impressionist-sym-
bolist tradition. I have used the two words together because symbolism and impressionism were overlapping
tendencies. It was not, however, the symbolist masters,

Rimbaud, Verlaine, and Mallarmé, who made the deepest impression on Fournier, though he was later to know and admire their poetry; it was rather the lesser poets, Laforgue, Jammes, and Henri de Régnier, who awakened his literary enthusiasm. While he was in school he wrote a number of pieces in the symbolist manner, and was accordingly cast down when Gide remarked that it was 'no longer the moment to write prose poems.' Yet Fournier later became dissatisfied with symbolism. Many of its devices seemed to him obscure or artificial. For example, in *Pelléas and Mélisande*, Maeterlinck, in order to give Mélisande an other-worldly quality, has her say that she does not know where she comes from. Fournier would not have used such a mechanical device. Whatever mystery he suggests must arise by inference rather than by statement, and in natural surroundings. Besides this, symbolism did not always harmonize with his belief in simplicity of style and his interest in humble people. The novel *Marie Claire*, by Marguerite Audoux, with its grave majestic peasants, gave him the impetus he needed to start off in another direction. But his style never lost the imprint of symbolism; his later work realizes his aim at nineteen when he confided to his friend Rivière: 'For the time being, I would rather follow Laforgue, but in writing *a novel*. That's contradictory; it would no longer be so if one presented life with its characters, and the novel with its characters, as only dreams which meet."

In some respects *Le Grand Meaulnes* resembles Kafka's fantasy, *The Castle*. Both are allegories. *The Castle* is an allegorical account of the search for heaven, and *Le Grand Meaulnes* of the search for happiness. In both of them there is the same combination of dreamlike vision and everyday detail. But there the resemblance ceases. In *Le Grand Meaulnes* most of the action is initiated by the characters; whereas in *The Castle* the characters submit to the action; they move about in a

state of uneasy somnambulism. But the chief difference
between the two books lies in the way the allegory is
handled. In *The Castle* the allegory is much more open,
and the characters, because they are symbols, are not
fully developed. Meaulnes and Seurel, on the contrary,
are living people, and the fantastic adventures in which
they are engaged in no way alter their basic reality. In
this connection it is interesting to read what Fournier
wrote about Ibsen's *Master Builder*. 'I should like the
simple life of the characters, and that of the symbols
to be more mixed. I should like their lives to be sym-
bolical, and not them.'

Fournier was, as we may guess from this, a conscious
craftsman. Though he thought too much analysis was
bad for writing ('All things have only been known to me
by the impression they have left on my heart. Therefore
I have not tried to distinguish them'), yet from the first
he had a clear conception of what he should work for in
art. To his friend Jacques Rivière, who, worried because
Fournier had always liked simple, touching stories, had
warned him against falling into sentimentality, Fournier
replied, 'I think that sentimentality is above all sloppy
writing—doing things too fast, in the easy way.' And
Fournier was right. His adolescents are not sentimental
because he knows too much about them. By the time
he was twenty he had decided: 'My credo in art:—childhood. To be able to reproduce it without any childishness, with its depth which touches mysteries. My future
book will be perhaps an imperceptible perpetual shifting back and forth between dream and reality—"dream"
understood as the immense and imprecise childish life
hovering over the other, and ceaselessly put into motion
by echoes of the first.' For him, fantasy is a method of
arriving at truth. Realism, in excluding emotions and
associations, and limiting itself to describing an external
reality which is the same for everybody, can only express
a partial truth. 'I don't see how we ever could have been

taken in by such a crude theory.' Just as we feel Poe's *Tales* to be true, in spite of their supernatural elements, because they depict the horror of which the human mind is capable, so the strange adventure which befell Meaulnes is a true account, though not a literal one, of the pride and longing of youth.

Fournier gives this indication of his aim in writing: 'It is . . . of that world at the same time past and desired, mysteriously mingled with the world of my life, mysteriously suggested by it, that I wish to speak. . . . Nevertheless, I do not think that it is the sole mystery of one will, one divinity, but rather of a life remembered with my past life, of a landscape which the actual landscape makes me desire. I shan't find, like Gide, words on the actual landscape which suggest the mystery, instead I'll describe *the other mysterious landscape.*'

'The other landscape'—the phrase is characteristic. There is through all Fournier's writing a feeling of homesickness for some other place, and a consciousness, even in joyful moments, of the shortness of joy, which transforms the fields, houses, and people that Fournier describes, giving them a heightened intensity and poignance. Another young man felt the same nostalgia:

> *Aye, in the very temple of Delight*
> *Veiled Melancholy hath her sov'reign shrine . . .*

Evidently Fournier recognized their kinship, for he said, in a letter to Rivière, 'You understand, my book is the story by Keats: *"Certain of them met Antigone in another existence, and no human love will be able to satisfy them."*' As well as this nostalgia, there is the counter feeling that everything is possible, that the lost manor can be found, that the student has only to tell the young chatelaine his love and she will accept him. It is the intensity of emotion behind Fournier's descriptions, rather than the descriptions, in themselves direct and realistic, which gives the landscape its immaterial, dreamlike quality.

As, according to Fournier, the dream has its basis in reality, so *Le Grand Meaulnes* is based on Fournier's experience. His father, like Seurel's, was a schoolteacher, his uncle Florent kept a store in Nancy like Uncle Florentin in the book, the country he describes is the country of his childhood. And the unknown beloved whom Fournier called 'Slender Waist' served as his model for Yvonne de Galais, the young mistress of the manor; her dress, her appearance, and the few words they exchanged all tally with the dress, appearance, and words of the real girl. Fournier met the real girl in a park, and though she was reserved, and probably of a higher social position than he, he managed to engage her in conversation. He tells of their meeting in a letter to Rivière: 'It would not be enough to call her "elegant." Purity is the word which suits her best, her dress, her great chestnut-colored coat, her body which I have never imagined, as well as her face. . . . Our encounter was extraordinarily mysterious. "Ah!" we said, "we know each other better than if we knew who the other was." And it was strangely true. She said, "We are children; we have done a foolish thing." So great was her candor and our happiness that one could not have guessed what foolish thing she meant: not a word of love had yet been spoken.' They saw each other several times, then she disappeared, and when finally after many efforts he discovered her address, it was only to learn with despair that she had since been married. Though Fournier fell in love again, to the end of his life he believed that she was the only woman who could have made him happy.

Fournier's attitude toward women was a curious one. It is certainly not usual for a young man to spend so many years longing for someone he knows to be unobtainable. But the social conventions of that period made it difficult for a young man to know any respectable girl at all well; moreover his family was not rich, so in all probability the girls he could have had were not of an education or a class to have satisfied him. He gives some hint of this when he exclaims: 'I hope with all my heart that "Slender Waist" is poor!' But besides this, there was in Fournier's character a fastidiousness, coupled with an inability to overlook faults in those he loved, which must have made him hard to please for long. In a letter to his sister Isabelle, writing about the poet Laforgue, he remarks: 'He loved a girl, he had loved girls . . . and yet when the moment came to tell his love he could not forget all the silly things they say, and which She might have said. . . . His irony came from hiding his emotion. . . . It seems to me I know him like a brother.' Rivière later wrote about him in words which would have applied equally well to Meaulnes: 'For Fournier, the moment of the most complete privation is also the moment of interior fulfillment. His suffering, which is real, should not deceive us. Fournier only finds himself and his powers in the moment when he feels empty of everything which he needs. He feels seized at once with despair and audacity; instead of resigning anything, he requires everything. Knowing perfectly well that he will not obtain it, he demands a treasure, which is his due.' It is difficult not to suspect that Fournier fell in love with Slender Waist precisely because she was unobtainable, and he therefore ran no risk of disillusionment.

What is Fournier's place in literature? It is hard to judge any writer who has been cut off before maturity; one must guard against either overestimating him because of his tragic death, or judging his work as one would judge the work of a man of fifty. *Miracles*, having been written before *Le Grand Meaulnes*, is of little use in helping us to determine what Fournier's later books would have been like. It does show, however, that in spite of his sensitivity and obvious literary gifts, poetry was not Fournier's most congenial medium. The stories

included, notably '*Le Miracle des dames du village*' and
'*Le Miracle de la fermière*' (both of which had appeared
in magazines during the author's lifetime), succeed far
better, being written in that simple yet magical style
which Fournier was to perfect in his novel. But the evi-
dence of *La Grand Meaulnes* itself, the mastery of its
prose and its psychological insight, proves that his talent
was no flash in the pan. Fournier has not the range of a
Flaubert or a Hugo; he may be more justly compared
to a writer like Poe, whose field was narrower but whose
genius was no less real. It is certain that as an interpreter
of youth, of the sadness and hopes and wonder of childhood, Fournier has few rivals. He has the vision of a poet
and the impartiality of those medieval illuminators of
Books of Hours who show peasants binding sheaves and
the Virgin in the clouds above them, both with the same
air of miraculous bright clarity.

FREDRIKA BLAIR

Part I

chapter 1. THE BOARDER

He arrived at our home on a Sunday of November,
189. . . I still say 'our home,' although the house no
longer belongs to us. We left that part of the country
nearly fifteen years ago and shall certainly never go back
to it.

We were living in the building of the Higher Elementary Classes at Sainte-Agathe's School. My father, whom
I was in the habit of calling M. Seurel as did other
pupils, was head of the Middle School and also of the
Higher Elementary classes where pupils worked for
the preliminary teacher's examination. Mother taught
the infants.

At the extreme end of the small town a long red house
with five glass doors and a Virginia creeper upon its
walls; an immense courtyard with shelters, a wash-
house and a huge gateway, on the side looking towards
the village; on the north side, a small gate opening on the
road leading to the station three kilometres off; on
the south, at the back of the house, fields, gardens,
meadows joining the outskirts . . . such is the simple
plan of this dwelling where I spent the most troubled

but the most happy days of my life—the house from
which we launched our adventures and to which they
returned to break themselves like waves on a bare rock.

At the time of some new 'appointments,' a whim of
fate, due to some inspector or to the Prefect, had led us
there. Towards the end of the summer holidays, a long
time ago, a peasant cart, preceding our household goods,
deposited my mother and myself before the little rusty
gate. Urchins who were stealing peaches in the garden
silently escaped through holes in the hedge. . . . My
mother, whom we used to call Millie and who was the
most methodical housekeeper I ever knew, had at once
gone into the rooms full of dusty straw, and had de-
clared with much consternation—as was her custom at
each 'removal'—that our furniture would never fit in a
house so badly built. . . . She had come out to impart
her trouble to me. While speaking she had, with her
handkerchief, gently wiped my face blackened by the
journey. Then she had gone back to consider what doors
and windows would have to be blocked to make the
place habitable. . . . As for me, wearing a big straw hat
with streamers, I was left alone on the gravel of that
strange playground, waiting for her, prying shyly around
the well and under the cart-shed.

Thus to-day I picture our arrival. For as soon as I
wish to bring back the distant memory of that first evening when I waited in our playground at Sainte-Agathe,
at once it is another kind of waiting which I recall, at
once I see myself again, both hands pressed to the bars
of the front gate, anxiously watching for some one who
will soon come down the High Street. If I try to imagine
that first night which I must have spent in my attic,
amidst the lumber-rooms on the upper storey, I recall
other nights; I am no longer alone in that room; a tall,
restless, and friendly shadow moves along its walls and
walks to and fro. And that quiet countryside—the school,
old Father Martin's field, with its three walnut trees,

the garden daily invaded on the stroke of four by women paying calls—all this is, in my memory, forever stirred and transformed by the presence of him who upset all our youth and whose sudden flight even did not leave us in peace.

Yet we had already been ten years in that district when Meaulnes arrived.

I was fifteen. It was a cold Sunday of November, the first day of autumn to make one think of winter. All day Millie had waited for the station omnibus to bring her a hat for the bad weather. That morning she missed Mass, and right up to the sermon, from my place in the choir with the other children, I looked anxiously towards the door to see her come to church wearing her new hat.

In the afternoon, I had to go to vespers alone. 'Anyhow,' she said to comfort me, brushing my little suit with her hand, 'even if it had come, this precious hat, I should have had to spend my Sunday making it up again.'

This is how our winter Sundays were often spent. In the early morning Father went off to some misty pond to jack-fish from a boat, and Mother retired till nightfall into her dark bedroom, to remake her simple dresses. She shut herself up in that way for fear some lady visitor, as poor as herself and as proud, might surprise her at the job. As for me, vespers over, I waited, reading in the cold dining-room, until she opened the door to show me how she was getting on.

That Sunday, a little excitement in front of the church kept me out-of-doors after vespers. A christening, under the porch, had attracted a crowd of urchins. In the square a few villagers had put on their firemen's jackets and piled their arms;[1] stiff and stamping their feet with cold,

---

[1]French firemen carry rifles during drill, although the custom is now dying out in towns.

they were listening to Boujardon, the corporal, losing himself in theory. . . .

The christening bells stopped suddenly, like festive chimes at a mistaken time and place. Boujardon and his men, rifles slung over their shoulders, dragged off the fire engine at a slow trot, and I saw them disappear at the first turning, followed by four silent urchins, crushing under their heavy boots the twigs on the frozen road, down which I dared not follow them.

In the village the only place left alive was the Café Daniel, from which I heard the murmurs of the drinkers' talk rise and fall, and hugging the low wall of the big playground which separated our house from the village, I came, rather anxious at being late, to the small gate.

It was ajar and I saw at once that something unusual was happening.

In fact, there stood, outside the dining-room door—the nearest of the five glass doors opening on the playground—a grey-headed woman, leaning forward and trying to look through the curtains. She was small and wore a black old-fashioned velvet bonnet. Her face was thin and refined, but worn with anxiety, and, at sight of her, I do not know what misgiving made me stand still on the first step, in front of the gate.

'My goodness, where's he gone!' she was muttering to herself. 'He was with me a moment ago. He must have gone all round the house already. Perhaps he's run away . . .'

And after each sentence she gave three barely perceptible little taps on the window-pane.

No one came to let in the unknown visitor. Without any doubt Millie had received her hat from the station, and, hearing nothing, at the end of the red bedroom, before a bed bestrewed with old ribbons and uncurled feathers, she was stitching, undoing, and remaking her modest headgear. In fact, as soon as I came into the dining-room, followed closely by the visitor, Mother appeared with both her hands to her head, holding wires, ribbons, and feathers which were not yet perfectly secured.

She smiled at me, from blue eyes tired with working till dusk, and exclaimed: 'Look! I was waiting to show you . . .'

But noticing that woman sitting in the big armchair at the other end of the room, she stopped, disconcerted. She quickly removed her hat, and during the whole scene that followed, held it against her breast, inside out, like a nest resting in the bend of her right arm.

The woman with the old-fashioned bonnet had begun to explain herself. She held between her knees an umbrella and a leather handbag, slightly nodding her head the while, and clicking her tongue as do village women when paying a call. She had regained full assurance, and when she spoke of her son she even assumed a superior and mysterious manner which puzzled us.

They had both driven from La Ferté d'Angillon, fourteen kilometres from Sainte-Agathe. Herself a widow— and very rich, as she gave us to understand—she had lost the younger of her two children, a boy called Antoine, who had suddenly died one evening, on returning from school, after bathing with his brother in a dirty pond. She had decided to let Augustin, the elder boy, board with us, that he might take the Higher Course.

And forthwith she began to praise this boarder whom she was bringing us. I could no longer recognise the grey-headed woman whom, only a minute ago, I had seen stooping in front of the door, with the piteous and haggard bearing of a hen who has lost the wildest chick in her brood.

What she was relating with admiration about her son was surprising enough; he loved doing things to please her, he had often gone along the river-bank for miles barelegged, to bring her wild ducks' and moor hens' eggs hidden amongst the reeds . . . He could set nets . . .

The other night, he had found a pheasant caught in a snare, in the wood . . .

I, who hardly dared to enter the house if I had torn my overall, looked at Millie with astonishment.

But Mother was no longer listening. She even motioned to the woman to be quiet; and putting down her 'nest' on the table with great care, she got up silently as if to take some one by surprise . . .

Above us, indeed, in a box-room where the blackened remains of the last fourteenth of July fireworks were piled up, an unknown step trod confidently to and fro, shaking the ceiling, crossed the huge dark lumber-rooms of the upper storey and passed at last towards the unused assistant masters' rooms, where lime tree leaves were put to dry and apples to ripen.

'A little while ago,' said Millie in a low voice, 'I heard that noise in the rooms downstairs; I thought it was you, François, come back . . .'

No one answered. We stood, the three of us, with beating hearts; then the attic door which led to the kitchen was heard to open; some one came down, crossed the kitchen, and appeared in the dim entrance of the dining-room.

'Why! It is you, Augustin!' said the visitor.

He was a tall boy of seventeen, or thereabout. At first, as night was falling, I saw only his peasant felt hat, pushed to the back of his head, and his black overall[1]

----

[1]This is the traditional black overall worn by the French schoolchildren in Alain-Fournier's youth and still to be seen in villages, though it is not so much worn in towns. This detail, and others so typically French, must not deceive the reader as to the age of the schoolboys in the book. It should be borne in mind that most of the main characters in the book, amongst the boys, are youths whose ages vary from between sixteen to past eighteen. It was the custom for boys of that age to wear the black overall.

tightly belted in the fashion of schoolboys. I could see, too, that he was smiling . . .

He saw me, and before any one had had time to demand an explanation: 'Aren't you coming into the playground?' he asked.

I hesitated for a moment. Then, as Millie did not keep me back, I took up my cap and went towards him. We left by the kitchen door and went into the yard under the shelter where darkness was already gathering. In the dim evening light I watched, as I walked, his sharp-featured face with its straight nose and downy lip.

'Look,' said he, 'I found this in your box-rooms. You couldn't have looked at these things.'

He was holding in his hand a little wheel of blackened wood; a string of partly burnt squibs was twisted round it; evidently a Catherine wheel from the fireworks display on the fourteenth of July.

'Two of them didn't go off. We will set them alight,' said he, in the tone of voice of one who hopes to make better finds later on.

He threw his hat to the ground, and I saw that his hair was cropped like a peasant's. He showed me two squib lighters with their paper tapers which the flame had singed, before going out. He stuck the axle of the wheel into the sand and—to my astonishment, as such things were strictly forbidden me—pulled out of his pocket a box of matches. Bending down with care, he lighted the squib. Then, taking hold of my hand, he quickly drew me back.

A moment later, as she came out of the door with Meaulnes' mother after having discussed and settled the boarding fees, my mother saw two sheaves of red-and-white stars rising up under the shelter, hissing like bellows. For a moment's space she caught a glimpse of me as I stood in this magic light, holding by the hand the tall strange boy and showing no fear . . .

Once again, she dared not say anything.

And that evening, at dinner, there sat at our table a silent guest who ate with lowered head, paying no attention to the three pairs of eyes fixed upon him.

chapter 2

AFTER FOUR O'CLOCK

Until then I had never loafed about in the streets with the other village boys. An affection of the hip from which I had suffered up to this year 189 . . had made me nervous and wretched. I still see myself chasing the nimble schoolboys in the alleys round our home, hopping wretchedly on one leg. . . .

So I was seldom allowed to go out, and I recall that Millie, who was very proud of me, more than once brought me home and boxed my ears for having been caught hopping thus with some village urchins.

The arrival of Augustin Meaulnes, at the very time of my cure, marked the beginning of a new life.

Before his coming, a dreary evening of loneliness began for me when lessons were over at four. Father was in the habit of carrying into the dining-room grate the fire remaining in the classroom stove; and, little by little, the last boys who had lingered behind left the chilled building, thick with clouds of smoke. There were still a few games, some galloping races in the playground, then night came; the two pupils who had swept the classroom fetched their hoods and cloaks, and with their baskets under their arms went away quickly, leaving the big gate open. . . .

Then, as long as there was a ray of light, I stopped in the record-room at the town hall, with its dead flies and posters that flapped in the draught, and I read, sitting on an old weighing-machine, close to a window looking on the garden.

When it was quite dark, and the dogs of the neighbouring farm began to howl and a light was seen at the window of our little kitchen, then I went home. Mother

had begun to get supper ready. I climbed three steps of
the attic stairs, sat down without a word and, leaning
my head on the cold rails of the bannisters, watched
Millie light her fire in this narrow kitchen where the
flame of one candle flickered. . . .

But some one has come who has taken from me these
peaceful, childlike delights. Some one has blown out the
candle which lit up for me the gentle motherly face bent
over the evening meal. Some one has extinguished the
lamp around which, at night, we were a happy family,
when Father had fixed the wooden shutters over the
glass doors. And he was Augustin Meaulnes, whom the
other fellows soon called 'Admiral Meaulnes.'

As soon as he became a boarder with us, that is, from
the early days of December, the school was no longer
deserted in the evening after four. Every day then, in
the classroom, despite the cold from the swinging door
and the shouts and clatter of the cleaners with their pails
of water, a score of the big boys, both those from the
countryside and the village, gathered round Meaulnes.
Long discussions followed, never-ending arguments, into
which I was drawn restlessly but with pleasure. Meaulnes
never said anything, but it was because of him that re-
peatedly one chatterbox or another, making of himself
the centre of the group, and taking in turn each of his
noisily approving friends as witness, would relate some
long story of poaching, which the others followed with
gaping mouths and inward laughter.

Sitting on a desk and swinging his legs, Meaulnes was
thoughtful. At exciting moments he used also to laugh,
but softly, as though he reserved his real laughter for
some better story known only to himself. Then, as night
fell and no more light came from the classroom windows
on the throng of boys, Meaulnes used suddenly to get
up, and pushing his way through, call out:

'Come on! Let's go!'

Then all followed him and until pitch dark one could

hear them shouting, towards the heights of the village.

It came about now that I went with them. With
Meaulnes, I went at milking-time to barn doors just outside the village. We entered shops, and the weaver, between two clicks of his loom, used to say out of his
darkness: 'Ha! the schoolboys.'

Generally, at dinner-time, we were to be found near
the Higher Elementary School with Desnoues, the wheelwright, who was also a blacksmith. His shop was an old
inn with big double-leaf doors, always kept open. From
the street you could hear the squeak of the forge bellows,
and you could sometimes make out, by the glow of the
forge fire, in this dark and noisy place, the country folk
who had stopped their cart to have a chat, or a schoolboy like us, his back to a door, a silent onlooker.

And it is there that everything began, about eight days
before Christmas.

Rain had fallen all day; it did not stop till evening.
The day had been deadly tedious. No one went out at
recreation, and all the time M. Seurel could be heard
calling to the form: 'Don't make such a row, boys!'

After the last recreation of the day or, as we called it,
the last 'quarter,' M. Seurel, who for a while had been
walking to and fro lost in thought, suddenly stopped,
banged vigorously on the table with a ruler to put an end
to the confused buzz with which the last hour of a boring
day ends, and, in the attentive silence, asked:

'Who will drive to the station to-morrow with François to fetch Monsieur and Madame Charpentier?'

These were my grandparents; Grandfather Charpentier with his grey woollen burnous; an old man, a retired
gamekeeper wearing a rabbit fur bonnet which he called
his képi. . . . Little boys knew him well. In the morning, to wash himself, he would draw a pail of water and
slosh his face in the manner of old troopers, vaguely
rubbing his small pointed beard. A group of children,
hands behind backs, watched him with respectful curiosity. . . . They also knew Grandma Charpentier, the
small peasant woman and her knitted cap—as Millie
never failed to bring her, at least once, into the infants'
class.

Each year, a few days before Christmas, we were in
the habit of going to the station to meet the 4.2 train
which brought them. To come to us they had crossed
the length of the 'département,' dragging with them
baskets full of chestnuts and other Christmas fare rolled

up in napkins. The moment the two, muffled up, smiling, and rather shy, had crossed the threshold, we shut all doors on them, and a glorious week of happiness began for us all . . .

To drive them from the station I needed a steady fellow with me, one who would not upset us into a ditch, and yet a gay lad, too, because Grandfather Charpentier was pretty free with swear words and Grandma rather talkative.

In answer to M. Seurel's question a dozen voices called out together: 'Admiral Meaulnes! Admiral Meaulnes!' But M. Seurel pretended not to hear.

Then they shouted: 'Fromentin!' Others: 'Jasmin Delouche!'

The youngest, Roy, the boy who rode across the fields on a sow at full gallop, called out in a piercing voice: 'Can I go? Can I go?'

Dutremblay and Moucheboeuf rather shyly put up their hands.

I should have liked it to be Meaulnes. This little drive, in a donkey cart, would have become a more important event. He also longed for it, but remained scornfully silent. All the big boys seated themselves, as he did, on the table, the wrong way round, feet on the bench, as we used to do in times of rest or great rejoicing. Coffin, his overall rolled up round his belt, was hugging the iron pillar which supported the beam of the classroom and, in his excitement, was beginning to climb it.

But M. Seurel damped every one by saying: 'Good! I choose Moucheboeuf.' And each went back to his seat silently.

At four o'clock, in the big icy playground, hollowed into channels by the rain, I found myself alone with Meaulnes. Without speaking, we both stood looking at the shining village drying under the high wind. Soon little Coffin, wrapped in his hooded cloak and holding a

piece of bread in his hand, came out of his home; walking
close to the walls and whistling, he went straight for the
door of the wheelwright. Meaulnes opened the big gate,
hailed the boy, and a moment later the three of us were
settled at the back of the hot red shop, across which
icy gusts of wind swept. Coffin and I sat close to the
forge fire, our muddy feet amongst the white shavings;
Meaulnes, hands in pockets and silent, leaned against
the leaf of the door. From time to time a village woman,
stooping to brave the wind, passed by in the street on
her return from the butcher, and we looked up to see
who she was.

No one spoke. The blacksmith and his assistant—one
blowing the bellows, the other beating the hot iron—
threw big sharp shadows upon the wall. . . . I recall that
evening as one of the great evenings of my youth. I felt
both pleasure and anxiety; I was afraid my companion
would deprive me of the small happiness of driving to
the station, yet, without daring to own it to myself, I
expected some extraordinary scheme from him which
would upset everything.

From time to time the peaceful and regular work of
the forge momentarily paused. The smith let his ham-
mer fall onto the anvil in a series of clear, strong blows.
He held the piece of iron on which he had been working
close to his leather apron and looked at it. Then, raising
his head, he said to us, by way of taking an easy breath:
'Well, my lads! How goes it?'

His man kept his right hand high up on the chain of
the bellows, put his left hand on his hip, looked at us
with a smile.

Then the din of hard work began again.

During one of these pauses, we caught sight of Millie
through the swinging door, as she passed in the high
wind, closely wrapped in her shawl and laden with small
parcels.

The blacksmith asked: 'I suppose Monsieur Charpentier will be coming soon?'

'To-morrow, with Grandmother,' said I. 'I am going to meet the 4.2 train.'

'In Fromentin's cart, eh?'

I replied at once: 'No, in Father Martin's.'

'Ah! then you won't be back in a hurry!'

Both he and his man began to laugh.

His man, to say something, remarked slowly: 'With Fromentin's mare you could have fetched them from Vierzon. There's an hour's wait there. It is fifteen kilometres from here. You could have got there and back afore Martin's donkey's harnessed.'

'Ah!' said the other, 'that mare has got some go in her, and surely Fromentin would gladly lend her.'

The conversation ended there. The forge, once again, became the place of sparks and din where each had his own thoughts.

But when the time had come to leave and I got up to attract Meaulnes' attention, he did not notice me at first. Leaning against the door, his head bent down in deep thought, he seemed absorbed in what had just been said. Seeing him thus lost in thought, looking as though across leagues of fog at these quiet folk at their work, I was reminded suddenly of that picture in 'Robinson Crusoe,' where the young Englishman is seen on the eve of his great adventure 'haunting the shop of a basket-maker.' . . .

And I have often thought of it since.

chapter 4. THE ESCAPE

At two o'clock in the afternoon next day, in the centre
of the freezing country, the form-room stands out clear
as a ship on the ocean. There is no smell of brine or tar
as on a boat, but of herrings fried on the stove and of
the scorched woollens of the boys who, on coming back,
got too close to the fire.

As the end of the year is drawing near, the exercise
books for term examination have been given out. And
while M. Seurel is setting problems on the board silence
prevails, only disturbed by whispered conversations, or
broken into by stifled exclamations and with sentences
of which the first words alone are uttered to frighten
one's neighbour: 'Sir! So and So is . . .'

M. Seurel, writing out the problems, is thinking of
something else. From time to time he turns round and
looks at us in a stern but vacant way. And this covert
disturbance stops entirely for a moment, to begin again
immediately, softly at first like a purr.

I alone keep quiet in the midst of this turmoil. I am
sitting at the extreme end of one of the tables on the
juniors' side and close to the high windows, and I need
only raise myself a little to get a view of the garden, the
stream at the lower end of it, and then the fields.

From time to time I stand on tiptoe and look anxiously towards the farm of the Fair Star. As soon as the
class opened I had noticed that Meaulnes had not come
back after the dinner hour. The boy next him certainly
could not have failed to notice it too. Too busy with
exam work he has not yet said anything. But as soon as
he looks up the news will spread at once, and some one,

as usual, will certainly call out, in a loud voice, the first words of the sentence: 'Sir! Meaulnes . . .'

I know that Meaulnes has gone. To be more exact I suspect him of having run away. As soon as dinner was over he must have jumped over the low wall, taken his course through the fields, and crossed the stream on the old plank for the Fair Star. He must have asked for the mare to go to the station for Monsieur and Madame Charpentier. They are harnessing her this very moment.

The Fair Star, on the other side of the stream, where the hill slopes down, is a large farm hidden from our view in the summer by the oaks and elms in its yard and also by quick-set hedges. It is situated in a little lane which joins the Station Road on one side and on the other an outlying district of the village. The big feudal building is surrounded by high walls, the buttresses of which stand in pools of manure. In the month of June it is buried in leafage, and from the school the rumbling of carts and the shouts of the cowherds alone can be heard at nightfall. But to-day, out of the window and between the stripped trees, I can see the tall grey wall of the farmyard, the entrance gate and then, through gaps in the hedge, a strip of road, white with frost, parallel to the stream and leading to the Station Road.

Nothing moves yet in that clear wintry landscape. Nothing has yet changed.

In the classroom M. Seurel has almost finished writing out the second problem. Generally he set down three. If he only set two to-day . . . He would go back to his desk and notice the absence of Meaulnes. He would send two boys to look for him in the village and they would find him before the mare was harnessed . . .

M. Seurel, once the second problem is on the board, drops his tired arm. Then, to my great relief, he goes to the next line and begins to write again, saying: 'This one is only child's play!'

. . . Two little black streaks showing over the top of
the wall at the Fair Star, certainly the upturned shafts
of a cart, have now disappeared. I feel sure that over
there everything is being made ready for Meaulnes' departure. Soon the head and the fore parts of the mare
emerge between the posts of the gateway, then stop,
while, no doubt, behind the cart, they are fixing a second
seat for the travellers whom Meaulnes proposes to fetch.
At last the complete equipage slowly comes out of the
yard, disappears for a moment behind the hedge, and,
going at the same slow pace, shows itself again on the
strip of white road visible between breaks in the fence.
Then I recognise, in the black figure holding the reins,
one elbow lazily resting on the side of the cart in peasant
fashion, my friend, Augustin Meaulnes.

A moment later everything disappears behind the
hedge. Two men who have remained by the gate, looking at the departing cart, begin to converse with increasing liveliness. One of them at last decides to make a
speaking-trumpet of his hands and to call after Meaulnes
and then to run a few paces along the road in his direction. But then, in the cart, which slowly has reached the
Station Road and can certainly no longer be seen from
the lane, Meaulnes suddenly changes his attitude. Standing up like the driver of a Roman chariot, one foot resting on the front bar and with both hands shaking the
reins, he sets his beast going at a gallop and in a moment
disappears on the other side of the slope. On the road
the man who has been calling begins to run again, and
the other, starting at full speed across the fields, seems
to be coming towards us.

In a few minutes, just as M. Seurel having left the
blackboard is rubbing the chalk off his hands and at the
very moment when three voices call out together from
the back of the classroom: 'Sir! Admiral Meaulnes has
gone!' the man with the blue smock is at the door, which
he suddenly throws wide open and lifting his hat asks

from the doorstep: 'Excuse me, sir, is it you as sent that pupil to ask for the cart to drive to Vierzon to meet your parents? We began to suspect . . .'

'Certainly not!' replies M. Seurel.

And at once all the class is in frightful disorder. The three boys close to the door, whose usual job is to chase away with stones the goats or the pigs which stray in the playground and browse the March Pride, rush out. Following the loud clatter of their hobnailed clogs on the flagstones of the room are heard their muffled and hurried steps crushing the sand of the yard and skidding as they sharply turn by the little gate opening on the road. The other boys have crowded to the garden windows. Some have climbed on the table to see better . . .

But it is too late. Admiral Meaulnes has escaped.

'You will go to the station with Mouchebœuf all the same,' says M. Seurel to me. 'Meaulnes does not know the way to Vierzon. He will lose himself at the Cross-Roads. He will not meet the train at three.'

Millie pokes her head in at the door of the infants' classroom to ask: 'What on earth is the matter?'

In the village street people have begun to form groups. The peasant stands there, hat in hand, obstinate, motionless, like a man demanding justice.

chapter 5. THE CART COMES BACK

When I had brought home my grandparents from the station and after dinner, seated in front of the large hearth, they began to relate in full detail all that had happened to them since the last holidays, I soon realised that I was not listening.

The little gate of the playground was quite near the dining-room door. It used to squeak as it opened. Generally at nightfall, during the long country evenings, I sat secretly waiting for this squeaking of the gate. It was usually followed by the noise of clogs clattering or being wiped outside the door, and sometimes by whispers as of people making some plan before coming in. There was a knock. It was a neighbour, the women teachers . . . anyhow, some one who was coming to cheer us during these long hours.

But that evening I had nothing to hope for from outside, since all those I loved were met together in our house; and yet I continued to be alert to all the noises of the night and to wait for some one to open our door.

Old Grandfather was there, hairy and bushy in appearance like some big Gascon shepherd, his two feet firmly planted as he sat, his stick between his legs, and with the usual slant of his right shoulder when he stooped to tap the ashes from his pipe against his shoe. He was approving with his kind moist eyes what Grandmother was saying about their journey, their neighbours, and the peasants who had not yet paid their rent. But I was no longer with them.

I was imagining the rumbling of a cart which would suddenly stop at our door. Meaulnes would jump from it and walk in as if nothing had happened . . . Or per-

haps he had first gone to take back the mare to the Fair
Star, and I should soon hear his step sounding on the
road, and the gate opening . . .

But nothing happened. Grandfather was gazing fixedly
in front of him and his winking eyelids kept closing over
his eyes as at the approach of sleep. Grandmother awkwardly repeated her last sentence, which no one was listening to.

'Is it about that boy that you are worried?' she said
at last.

As a matter of fact, I had questioned her at the station
to no purpose. She had seen no one at Vierzon who
might have been Admiral Meaulnes. My friend must
have been delayed on the way. His attempt had failed.
During our return journey I had brooded over my disappointment, while Grandmother was chatting with
Mouchebœuf. On the road whitened with frost, small
birds had been fluttering around the hoofs of the trotting
donkey. From time to time above the stillness of the
wintry afternoon had arisen the far-away call of a farm
girl or of a lad hailing a comrade from one clump of firs
to another, and each time that long call over the desolate hills had made me shudder as if it were the voice of
Meaulnes inviting me to follow him from afar . . .

While I was going over all this in my mind, bedtime
came. Already Grandfather had gone into the red room,
the bed-sitting-room so damp and icy cold from having
been closed since last winter. To make him at home the
lace antimacassars of the armchairs had been removed,
the rugs folded up and all the knick-knacks put away.
He had placed his stick on a chair, his thick shoes under
an armchair, he had just put out his candle and we were
standing saying good-night, ready to retire to bed, when
the noise of a cart silenced us.

It almost sounded as if two vehicles slowly followed
each other at a very slow trot. The noise finally came

to a stop under the dining-room window which over-
looked the road, but was never used.

Father had taken up the lamp and, without waiting,
went to open the door which had already been locked.
Then pushing open the gate, he walked to the edge of
the steps and raised his light above his head to see what
was happening.

Two carts had in fact stopped, the horse of one fastened behind the back of the other. A man had jumped
down and was hesitating . . .

'Is this the town hall?' said he, coming near. 'Could
you direct me to M. Fromentin, the farmer at the Fair
Star? I have found his cart and mare without a driver,
going along the lane, close to the road of Saint-Loup-
des-Bois. I was able to read his name and address on the
plate, with my lantern. As it was on my way, I brought
back his trap round here to avoid accidents, but it has
delayed me no end all the same.'

We stood there stupefied. Father approached and lit
up the cart with his lamp.

'There were no traces of a driver,' went on the man.
'Not even a rug. The animal is tired and slightly lame.'

I had got quite at the front and, with the others, I
was looking at this lost vehicle which had come back to
us like wreckage washed ashore by the high tide—the
first and perhaps the last wreckage of Meaulnes' adventure.

'If it's too far to Fromentin's,' said the man, 'I'll
leave the cart with you. I've lost too much time already
and they must be anxious at home.'

Father agreed. In this way we could take back the
trap to the Fair Star that very evening without saying
what had happened. Then we could decide what we
were to tell the village people and to write to Meaulnes'
mother . . . And the man whipped up his horse, refusing
the glass of wine we offered him.

As we were coming in without uttering a word and

Father was leading the cart towards the farm, Grandfather, who had lit his candle again, called out from his
room: 'Has that traveller come back then?'

The women consulted each other's faces by looks for
a moment.

'Yes, he's been to his mother's. Go to sleep. Don't
worry.'

'That's all right. Just what I thought,' said he.

And, reassured, he put out his light and turned over
in bed to sleep.

That was the explanation which we gave to the village
people. As to the mother of the runaway, it was decided
to wait before writing to her. And during three long
days we kept our anxiety to ourselves. I still see my
father coming home from the farm towards eleven, his
moustache damp with the evening mist, talking with
Millie in a very low voice, anxious and angry . . .

chapter 6. SOME ONE KNOCKS AT THE WINDOW

The fourth day was one of the coldest of that winter. From early morning the first comers to the playground kept warm by sliding round the well. They were waiting for the stove to be lit to rush into the classroom.

Behind the front gate several of us waited for the arrival of the boys from the countryside farther off. They came with eyes quite dazed from having crossed hoar-sparkling fields and looked on frozen ponds and coppices from which hares ran . . . Their overalls had a smell of hay and stables which made the air of the classrooms heavy, as they crowded round the red-hot stove. And that morning one of them had brought in a basket a frozen squirrel which he had found on the way. He tried, I remember, to hang up the long stiff animal by its claws to a pillar of the playground shelter . . .

Then the dull class-work of winter began.

A sharp knock on the window made us look up. Upright against the door we saw Admiral Meaulnes shaking off the frost from his overall before he came in, standing there head erect and as if dazzled with rapture!

The two boys of the bench nearest to the door hurried to open it: they had a little confabulation, which we did not hear, just outside, and at last the truant made up his mind to come into the school.

That breath of fresh air coming from the deserted playground, the bits of straw which could be seen clinging to Admiral Meaulnes' clothing, and above all the look he had of a traveller, tired, hungry, but thrilled by wonders, all gave us a strange feeling of pleasure and curiosity.

M. Seurel had come down the two steps of his desk where he had been giving us a dictation, and Meaulnes walked towards him looking aggressive. I recall how handsome he seemed to me then, that big friend of mine, in spite of his battered look and of his eyes reddened by nights spent, most likely, in the open.

He went up to the master's desk and said, in the assured voice of a man who brings news: 'I have come back, sir.'

'So I see,' replied M. Seurel, looking at him with curiosity. . . . 'Go to your seat.'

The boy turned towards us, his back slightly bent, smiling in a mocking way, as do big unruly fellows when punished, and, catching hold of the end of the table with one hand, he let himself drop on his bench.

'You are going to take out a book and read as I tell you,' said the master—all heads were turned then towards Meaulnes—'while the others finish their dictation.'

And the lesson went on as before. From time to time Admiral Meaulnes turned my way, then looked out of the windows from which the white garden was visible, downy and motionless, and the bare fields on which a crow sometimes descended. In the classroom the heat was heavy around the reddened stove. My friend settled himself to read, holding his head in his hands: twice I saw his eyelids close and I thought he was falling asleep.

'I'd like to go to bed, sir,' said he at last, half lifting his arm. 'I've not slept for three nights.'

'Then go!' said M. Seurel, anxious above all to avoid a scene.

We sat up, all of us, pens in the air, and sadly watched him go, his overall rumpled at the back and his shoes earthy.

How slow that morning was in passing! Towards midday we heard the traveller, upstairs in the attic, preparing to come down. At dinner time I found him sitting by the

fire near our puzzled grandparents, and as the clock
struck twelve the boys, big and little, scattered over the
snowclad playground, made off like shadows before the
dining-room door.

Of that dinner I recall only a great silence and a
great distress. Everything was icy; the oilcloth without
a tablecloth, the cold wine in the glasses, the red flagstones under our feet. It had been decided to put no
questions to the truant so as not to rouse him to revolt.
And he availed himself of that truce to say not a word.

At last, dessert ended, and we two were able to make
a dash for the playground. A school playground in the
afternoon, with the snow trampled away by clogs . . .
a playground black all round with drips from the roofs
of the shelters . . . a playground thick with games and
screams! Meaulnes and I pelted along by the school
buildings. At once two or three fellows from the village
left their game and ran up to us with shouts of joy;
hands in pockets, scarves unloosed, and mud squirting
from under their clogs. But my friend burst into the big
classroom, where I followed; he shut the glass door just
in time to stop the rush of the fellows in pursuit. There
was instant uproar loud and clear; glass panes shaken,
clogs stamping on stone; one shove bent the iron bar
holding the two leaves of the door; but Meaulnes had
already turned the little key in the lock, at the risk of
cutting himself on its broken ring.

We used to think it maddening to behave like that.
In summer, fellows who were locked out in this way,
would tear round at full speed into the garden and managed often to climb in at one of the windows, before you
could shut them all. But it was then December and
everything was shut up. For a little while the boys kept
shoving against the door; they yelled insults at us; then,
one by one, they turned tail and went off crestfallen,
doing up their scarves as they went.

Only two boys were in the classroom, which smelt of

chestnuts and sour wine, two sweepers who were shifting
the tables. I went up to the stove to warm myself lazily
till lessons time, while Meaulnes searched the master's
desk and the lockers. He soon found a small atlas which
he studied with eagerness as he stood on the platform,
his elbows on the desk and his head in his hands.

I was just about to go up to him; I should have placed
my hand on his shoulder and, no doubt, we should have
followed together, on the map, the route which he had
taken, when suddenly the door leading to the infants'
room opened with a crash under a violent push, and
Jasmin Delouche, followed by a village boy and three
fellows from the neighbouring countryside, emerged
with a shout of triumph. One of the windows in the
infants' classroom had probably been half shut; they had
pushed it open and jumped through.

Jasmin Delouche, although rather small, was one of
the elder boys of the top form. He was very jealous of
Admiral Meaulnes, though he pretended to be his friend.
Before our boarder's arrival, Jasmin himself had been
cock of the form. He had a pale, rather sallow face, and
pomaded hair. He was the only son of widow Delouche,
the innkeeper, and he played the man, trotting out with
self-conceit what he had heard in the billiard-room and
at the bar.

At his entry Meaulnes looked up frowning and called
out to the boys, as they scrambled to the stove: 'So
one can't have a minute's peace here!'

'If you don't like it, you should have stopped where
you were,' said Jasmin Delouche, without looking up.

I think that Augustin was in that state when temper
comes and gets you so that you cannot control it.

'Now then, you!' he said, a little pale, rising and shutting his book, 'get out of it!'

The other sneered.

'Oh!' he cried, 'because you ran away for three days,
you think you are going to be boss now!' he went on,

dragging in the others. 'A chap like you can't turn us out, I tell you that much!'

But Meaulnes was already on him. A scrap began; a wild scrimmage; sleeves of overalls split and tore at the seams. Martin alone—one of the boys of the neighbourhood who had come with Jasmin—interfered.

'Leave him alone!' he called out, with quivering nostrils, shaking his head like a ram.

With a violent jerk Meaulnes threw him reeling, arms out, to the middle of the room; then gripping Delouche by the neck with one hand and opening the door with the other, he tried to throw him out. Jasmin clung to the tables and dragged his feet, making his hobnailed shoes grate on the flagstones, while Martin, having regained his balance, came back with measured steps, head forward and furious. Meaulnes let go Delouche to collar this idiot, and would soon have found himself in a fix if the door of the living-room had not partly opened. M. Seurel was seen standing there at the door, his back turned towards us, to finish, before he came in, a conversation he was having with some one . . .

At once the battle stopped. Some boys collected round the stove, none too proud of themselves, having, right to the end, avoided taking sides. Meaulnes sat down in his place, his sleeves undone and torn at the gathers.

As for Jasmin, purple in the face, during the few minutes before the ruler rapped for form-work to begin, he could be heard calling out: 'He can't stand anything now. He puts on side. Does he suppose we do not know where he's been!'

'You ass! I don't know myself,' replied Meaulnes, in the immediate silence.

Then, shrugging his shoulders and burying his head in his hands, he began to do his work.

chapter 7. THE SILK WAISTCOAT

Our room was, as I have said, a big attic—half attic,
half room. The other rooms, meant for assistant masters, had windows; no one knows why ours was lighted
only by a skylight. It was impossible to shut the door
fast, as it scraped the floor. When we went up in the
evening, sheltering with one hand the candle which the
draughts of the big house threatened to blow out, every
time we tried to shut this door and every time we had to
give it up. And the whole night long we felt all round
the silence of the three lumber-rooms penetrating our
bedroom.

There we met again, Augustin and I, on the evening
of that same winter day.

I swiftly took off all my clothes and threw them in a
heap on a chair at the foot of my bed, but my companion, without saying a word, began to undress slowly.
I watched him undress from the iron bed in which I
already lay—looking through cretonne hangings adorned
with a wine-stalk pattern. One moment he sat down on
his low curtainless bed; the next he got up and paced to
and fro as he undressed. The candle, which he had placed
on a wicker table, the work of gipsies, threw his moving
and gigantic shadow upon the wall.

Quite unlike me he was folding and arranging his
school clothes in a bitter and distracted way, but with
much care. I still see him drop his heavy belt on a chair,
over the back of which he folded his black overall extremely creased and soiled, then take off a kind of dark
blue tunic which he wore under his overall, and stooping
with his back to me, spread the garment at the foot of
his bed . . . But when he stood up again and turned to

face me, I saw that in place of the brass button uniform waistcoat that should be under the tunic, he was wearing a queer silk waistcoat, cut very open and fastened by a row of small and closely set mother-of-pearl buttons.

It was a garment of fantastic charm, such as must have been worn by the young men who used to dance with our grandmothers, in the days of the dandies.

I distinctly recall, at that moment, the tall peasant boy, bareheaded—for he had carefully placed his cap on his other clothes—his face so young, so gallant, and already so firmly set. He was once more pacing the room when he began to unbutton this mysterious article of a costume which was not his. And it was strange to see him, in shirt-sleeves, with short trousers and muddy shoes, handling this waistcoat of a marquis.

He had no sooner touched it than, starting from his reverie, he turned his face towards me with a look of anxiety. I rather wanted to laugh. He smiled with me and his face brightened.

'What's that? Do tell me,' I said in a low voice, emboldened. 'Where did you get it?'

But his smile vanished at once. Twice, with his heavy hand, he brushed back his closely cropped hair, and suddenly, like a man unable to resist desire, slipped his tunic back over the dainty jabot, buttoned it up tightly, and slipped on his rumpled overall; then he hesitated a moment, looking at me sideways. . . . Finally he sat on the edge of his bed, took off his shoes, which fell noisily onto the floor, stretched himself on the bed, fully dressed like a soldier ready for the fray, and blew out the candle.

About midnight I woke up suddenly. Meaulnes was standing in the middle of the room, his cap on his head, and was looking for something on one of the pegs—a cloak which he threw on his back. . . . The room was very dark. Not even that gleam of light which snow sometimes gives. A black and icy wind was blowing in the garden and over the roof.

I raised myself a little and called to him softly: 'Meaulnes! Are you going away again?' He did not reply. Then, quite beside myself, I said: 'Very well, I shall go with you. You must take me.' And I jumped out of bed.

He came close to me, took hold of my arm, forcing me to sit on the edge of the bed, and said to me: 'I can't take you, François. If I knew my way well, you should come with me. But I must first of all find it on the map, and I can't.'

'Then you can't go either!'

'That's true. It's utterly useless,' he said, discouraged. 'Well, go back to bed. I promise not to go without you.'

And he again began to pace to and fro in the room. I dared say nothing more. He kept walking, stopping and then setting off again more quickly like a man in search of memories which he sorts out, challenges and compares, ponders on, thinks he has discovered, and then the thread breaking the search begins once more. . . .

That was not the only night on which, awakened by the sound of his steps, I found him thus, about one in the morning, treading the attic and lumber-rooms, as do sailors who cannot lose the habit of pacing the deck on night watch and who, in the quiet of their Breton holding, get up and dress of a night, at the regulation hour, to keep a land watch.

Two or three times, during the month of January and the first fortnight of February, I was roused out of my sleep in that way. Admiral Meaulnes was there, on foot, all equipped, his cloak on his back, ready to start, and every time, on the edge of that mysterious country into which he once already had ventured, he stopped, he hesitated. At the moment of lifting the latch of the door to the stairs and of slipping off by the kitchen door, which he could easily have opened without being heard,

he would shrink back once more . . . Then, during the
long midnight hours he paced feverishly the disused
lumber-rooms, lost in thought.

At last one night, towards the fifteenth of February,
he woke me up by gently placing his hand on my shoulder.

The day had been very disturbed. Meaulnes, who had
now entirely dropped out of all the games of his former
comrades, had remained seated at his bench during the
last recreation of the evening, busily sketching out a mysterious plan, following it with his finger and elaborately
measuring it out on the atlas of the Cher. There was an
incessant going and coming between the playground and
the classroom. Clogs kept clattering. Boys chased one
another from table to table, taking benches and platform at a jump. . . . Every one knew that it was not
wise to come near Meaulnes when he was working thus;
yet, as recreation continued past regulation time, two
or three boys from the village advanced towards him for
a joke, without any noise, and looked over his shoulder.
One of them was bold enough to push the others on top
of Meaulnes. . . . The latter hastily closed his atlas,
hid his sheet of paper, and caught hold of the last of
the three boys while the other two managed to escape.

It was that surly Giraudat, who began to whine, tried
to kick, and at last was pushed out of doors by Admiral
Meaulnes, to whom he shouted in a rage: 'You great
coward! No wonder they are all against you and want to
make war on you! . . .' and a lot of insults, to which we
replied without having quite understood what he meant.
I was the one to shout the loudest, because I had sided
with Admiral Meaulnes.

There was now a kind of pact between us. The promise which he had given to take me with him, instead of
saying, like everybody else, that I should not be able to
stand the walking, had bound me to him forever. And

I never ceased thinking of his mysterious journey. I had become convinced that he must have met a girl. She, no doubt, was infinitely more beautiful than Jeanne, who could be seen in the nuns' garden by looking through the keyhole; or Madeleine, the baker's daughter, so pink and so fair; or Jenny, the daughter of the lady of the manor, so handsome, but insane and living in seclusion. It was certainly of a young girl he was thinking at night, like the hero of a novel. And I bravely decided to speak to him about it the first time he wakened me. . . .

After four o'clock, on the evening of that new fight, we were both busy putting away garden tools, pickaxes, and spades which had been used to dig trenches, when we heard shouts on the road. It was a troop of young boys and urchins, formed in fours, marching quickly like a well-drilled squad, led by Delouche, Daniel, Giraudat, and another whom we did not know. They had spotted us and hooted like anything. So all the village was against us, and some fresh soldier stunt, from which we were excluded, was being planned.

Meaulnes, without saying anything, put away in the shed the pickaxe and the spade which he had on his shoulder. But at midnight I felt his hand on my arm, and I woke up with a start.

'Get up,' he said, 'we are going.'

'Do you know the right way to the very end?'

'I know a good part of it. And we shall have to find the rest,' he replied, with clenched teeth.

'Listen, Meaulnes,' I said, sitting up, 'listen to me; there's only one thing to be done!—and that is to look for the bit of the way we don't know in full daylight with the help of your map.'

'But that bit is far away from here.'

'All right, we'll drive there this summer, when the days are longer.'

There was a prolonged silence, which meant that he agreed.

'As we shall try together to find again the girl you love, Meaulnes,' I said at last, 'tell me who she is, talk to me about her.'

He sat down at the foot of my bed. I could see in the darkness his lowered head, his folded arms and his knees. Then he took a deep breath, as some one who has had a weight upon his heart for a long time and who is, at last, going to tell his secret . . .

chapter 8. THE ADVENTURE

My friend did not tell me that night all that had happened to him on the way. And even when he decided to confide everything to me, during days of anguish of which I shall speak later, it remained for a long time the great secret of our youth. But to-day when all is ended, and there remains only dust of so much good and so much evil, I can relate his strange adventure.

At half-past one in the afternoon on the Vierzon road, during that freezing weather, Meaulnes set his beast at a brisk pace, because he knew he was late. At first he thought, with amusement, only of our surprise when, at four o'clock, he brought back Grandfather and Grandmother Charpentier. For certainly, at that moment, he had no other intention.

Little by little, the cold being piercing, he wrapped his legs in a rug, which at first he had refused, but which the folk at the Fair Star had thrown into the cart.

At two o'clock he passed through the village of La Motte. He had never gone through a small hamlet at school-time and was amused to see this one so empty, so asleep. Here and there a curtain was moved revealing the inquisitive face of a housewife.

Leaving La Motte, immediately after the schoolhouse, he hesitated between two roads, but seemed to remember that the left road led to Vierzon. Nobody was there to tell him. He once more put the mare to a trot, though the road became narrower and badly in need of repair. He skirted a fir wood for some time, but at last, meeting a carter, he used his hands as a trumpet to inquire if he really were on the right road for Vierzon. The mare pulled on the reins, without stopping her trot; the man must have failed to understand the inquiry; he called out something with a vague gesture, so Meaulnes chanced it and went on.

Once more there was the vast frozen plain without incident or distraction; only at times a magpie startled by the cart flew off to perch on a stunted elm in the distance. The traveller had wrapped the big rug round his shoulders like a cloak. He must have dozed for a long while with his legs stretched out and one elbow resting on the side of the cart . . .

. . . When Meaulnes recovered his wits, thanks to the cold penetrating the rug, he noticed a change in the countryside. There was no longer the far horizon, no longer that stretch of pale sky in which sight was lost, but little meadows, still green, with high hedges. On both sides water flowed under the ice in the ditches. Everything showed the neighbourhood of a river. And the road between the tall hedges was nothing more than a narrow rutted lane.

A moment before the mare had stopped trotting, Meaulnes tried to whip her up to the same pace again, but she persisted in walking with extreme slowness, and the big schoolboy, leaning forward, his hands resting on the dashboard, noticed that she was lame in one hind leg. He was much troubled and at once jumped out.

'We shall never reach Vierzon in time for the train,' he said half aloud.

And he did not dare to own to himself the thought which upset him most, that perhaps he had lost his way and was no longer on the road to Vierzon.

For a long time he examined the beast's foot and could find no trace of a wound. The mare was frightened and lifted her foot directly Meaulnes tried to touch it, pawing the ground with her heavy clumsy hoof. At last he realised that she had simply got a stone in her shoe. As a boy who was expert in the handling of beasts he sat

on his heels and tried to grasp her right foot with his left
hand and put it between his knees, but he was bothered
by the cart. Twice the mare got away and went on a few
yards. The step struck his head and the wheel hurt his
knee. He would not give in and ended by mastering the
timid beast, but the stone was so embedded that
Meaulnes was obliged to use his peasant's knife before
he could get it out.

When he had finished the job and at last looked up,
rather giddy and dim-eyed, he noticed with horror that
night was falling . . .

Any one else but Meaulnes would immediately have
turned back. That was the only way not to get more
badly lost. But he reflected that he must be very far
from La Motte. Besides, the mare might have taken a
byway while he was asleep. Anyhow, this lane must lead
to some village in time . . .

In addition to all these reasons, the big boy, with his
foot on the step and the mare already pulling on the
reins, ached with exasperation to achieve something and
to get somewhere, in defiance of every obstacle!

He whipped up the mare, who started and set off at a
quick trot. The darkness grew. In the deep-cut lane
there was now only just room for the cart. Sometimes a
dead branch from the hedge caught in the wheel and
broke with a snap. . . . When it was pitch dark
Meaulnes thought suddenly with a pang of our dining-
room at Sainte-Agathe in which, by this time, all of us
ought to be together. Then rage took him; then pride
and the deep joy of having at last run away without
premeditation . . .

Suddenly the mare slowed down as if her foot had stumbled in the dark; Meaulnes saw her head sink and rise twice; then she stopped dead, her nostrils close to the ground, appearing to sniff at something. The trickle of water could be heard by her feet. A stream barred the way. In summer that spot was certainly a ford. But at this time of the year the current was so strong that ice had not formed and it would have been dangerous to push on.

Meaulnes gently pulled on the reins to go back a few yards and stood up in the cart full of perplexity. It was then that he noticed a light between the branches. Only two or three meadows seemed to separate it from the lane . . .

The schoolboy jumped down from the cart and backed the mare, talking to her to quiet her and to stop the frightened tossing of her head.

'Come on, old girl, come on. We shan't go any farther now. We shall soon know where we've got to.'

And pushing open the half-shut gate of a small meadow by the lane, he went through with the trap. His feet sank deep into the soft grass. The cart jolted silently. His head was by the mare's head and he could feel her warmth and her hard breathing . . .

He took her to the far end of the meadow and threw the rug over her back; then thrusting aside the branches of the hedge, he again noticed the light which came from an isolated house.

None the less he had to cross three meadows and jump over a treacherous brook into which he nearly fell with both feet . . . At last, after a final leap from the top of a bank, he found himself in the yard of a rustic farm. A pig was grunting in its sty. At the noise of footsteps on the frozen ground a dog began to bark furiously.

The shutter over the door was open, and the light which Meaulnes had seen came from a wood fire burning on the hearth. There was no other light but that of the fire. In the house, a country woman rose from a chair and came to the door, with no sign of fear. At the same moment the grandfather clock struck half-past seven.

'Excuse me, ma'am,' said the big boy, 'I believe I have trodden on your chrysanthemums.'

She waited, basin in hand, looking at him.

'The fact is,' she said, 'it's that dark in the yard you can't see your way.'

There was a moment's silence, during which Meaulnes stood looking at walls papered with pages out of illustrated papers, as they are in inns, and at the table on which lay a man's hat.

'He's not in, the boss,' he said, sitting down.

'He'll be back in a moment,' she replied, quite at her ease now, 'he's gone to fetch wood.'

'I don't exactly want him,' went on the young fellow, bringing his chair nearer to the fire, 'but out there a few of us—sportsmen, you know—are keeping a lookout. I came to ask if you could spare us a little bread.'

Admiral Meaulnes knew quite well that with country folk, above all in an isolated farm, one must speak with caution, even with diplomacy, and above all never show that one does not belong to the district.

'Bread,' said she, 'we shan't be able to give you much. The baker who always calls on a Tuesday hasn't come to-day . . .'

Augustin, who for a moment had hoped he was near a village, took fright.

'The baker, from where?' he asked.

'Why, of course, the baker from Vieux-Nançay,' replied the woman, astonished.

'How far is it exactly from here to Vieux-Nançay?' went on Meaulnes, very anxious.

'By the road I couldn't tell exactly; but by the short cut it is three leagues off.'

And she began to relate that her daughter was there in service, that she always walked all the way home on the first Sunday of the month, and that her master and mistress . . .

But Meaulnes, completely put out, interrupted her to say: 'Vieux-Nançay, would that be the nearest village from here?'

'No, the nearest is Les Landes, five kilometres off here. But there are no shops and no baker at Landes, only just a small fair each year on Saint Martin's Day.'

Meaulnes had never heard of Les Landes. He saw himself so much lost that he was almost tickled. But the woman, busy at the sink washing her basin, turned round, inquisitive in her turn, and said slowly, looking at him quite straight: 'Don't you, then, belong to these parts? . . .'

At that moment an elderly peasant appeared at the door, carrying an armful of wood, which he threw on the stone floor. The woman explained to him, in a very loud voice, as if he were deaf, what was required by the young man.

'Well! that's easy,' said he simply. 'But come nearer, you're getting no warmth from the fire.'

A moment later both were settled by the hearth: the old man breaking his wood to put on the fire, Meaulnes enjoying a bowl of milk and some bread which had been offered him. Our traveller, delighted at finding himself in that humble dwelling after so many worries, and thinking that an end had come to his strange adventure, was already making plans for bringing friends with him in

the future, to visit these kind people. He did not know
that this was only a halt, and that presently he was to
resume his journey.

He soon asked to be shown the road to La Motte.
And, little by little, coming back to the truth, he related
that he had been cut off, with his cart, from the other
guns and now found himself completely lost.

Then the man and the woman insisted so much on his
putting up at the farm and not starting before broad
daylight, that Meaulnes in the end accepted, and walked
out to fetch his mare and put her up in the stable.

'Mind holes in the path,' said the man.

Meaulnes dared not confess that he had not used 'the
path.' He nearly brought himself to ask if the good fellow could come with him. For a second he hesitated on
the threshold and so great was his indecision that he
almost staggered. But he went out into the gloom of the
yard.

To find where he was he climbed on the bank from which he had jumped.

Slowly and with difficulty, as when he came, he made his way between swamps, through willow hedges, and went to fetch his cart at the farther end of the field where he had left it. The cart was no longer there. Standing still, with throbbing temples, he strained hard to catch all the sounds of the night, sure that he heard, each moment, the jingle of the horse's collar close at hand. Nothing . . . He went all round the meadow; the gate was partly open, partly dilapidated as if a cart wheel had passed over it. The mare must have escaped that way, alone.

Turning back, he walked a little way and caught his feet in the rug which no doubt had slipped from the mare onto the ground. This decided him that the beast had gone off in that direction. He started to run.

Obsessed by the obstinate and insane resolve to overtake the cart, his face on fire, a prey to this panic wish, which resembled fear, he went on running . . . Sometimes he stumbled in a rut. In the utter darkness he ran into hedges when the lane turned, and too tired to stop in time he crashed into brambles, his arms stretched out, his hands torn in the effort to protect his face. Sometimes he stopped and listened and went on again. Once he thought he heard a cart, but it was only a jolting wagon going along a road, in the far distance on the left . . .

Came a time when the knee which he had grazed against the step of the cart hurt so much that he had to stop, his leg quite stiff. Then he realised that unless the mare had run off at a quick gallop, he would long ago have caught her up. He told himself, too, that a cart could not get lost in that way, and that some one would surely find it. At last he retraced his steps, worn out, scarcely able to drag himself along.

After a while he believed that he was again in the neighbourhood of the place he had left, and soon he noticed the light of the house he was looking for. A path opened in the hedge.

'That's the path the old man spoke of,' thought Augustin.

And he entered this passage, glad to have no more hedges and banks to get over. Next moment, the path turning to the left, the light appeared to slip to the right, and Meaulnes reaching a cross-road, in his hurry to regain the poor lodging, without thinking took a path which seemed to lead straight there. But he had hardly walked ten steps along it when the light disappeared, either because the hedge was hiding it, or else because the peasants were tired of waiting and had closed their shutters. Bravely the schoolboy took to the fields and made for the place where the light had just been shining. Then, leaping once more over a hedge, he landed on a new path . . .

Thus, little by little, Admiral Meaulnes' trail was tangled and the thread broke which was connecting him with those he had left.

Discouraged, almost exhausted, in despair he resolved to follow this path right to the end. A hundred yards farther he emerged into a vast grey meadow, where here and there he could distinguish shadows appearing to be juniper trees and a dark shed in a fold of the ground. Meaulnes drew near. It was only a kind of large cattle-pen or forsaken sheepfold. The door yielded with a groan. The light of the moon came through chinks in the wood-work, when the high wind chased the clouds.

Without searching farther, Meaulnes stretched him-self on the damp straw, one elbow on the ground, his head on his hand. Having removed his belt he curled up, knees bent in his overall. He then thought of the mare's rug which he had left in the lane and felt so wretched and so cross with himself that he had a strong desire to cry . . .

So he forced himself to think of something else. Frozen to the bone, he recalled a dream—or rather a vision which he had had when quite a child and of which he had never spoken to any one; one morning, instead of waking up in his room where his trousers and coat were hanging, he had found himself in a long green room with walls like foilage. The light streaming into this place was so sweet that you could simply taste it. Close to the first window a young girl was sewing with her back to him; she seemed to be waiting for him to wake. He had not had strength to creep out of bed into this enchanted dwelling. He had fallen asleep again . . . But next time he swore he would get up. To-morrow morning, perhaps! . . .

At dawn he began to walk again. But his swollen knee
hurt him; he had to stop and sit down every moment,
the pain was so sharp. The place where he was happened to be the most desolate in Sologne. During all the
morning he saw, in the distance, only a farm girl bringing in her flock. In vain he called to her and tried to run;
she disappeared without hearing him.

Nevertheless he went on walking in her direction with
a distressing slowness . . . Not a roof, not a soul. Not
even the cry of a curlew in the reeds of the marshes.
And above this complete solitude shone a December
sun, clear and icy.

It might have been three o'clock in the afternoon
when he noticed at last, above a fir wood, the spire of a
grey turret.

'Some old forsaken manor,' thought he; 'some deserted dovecot!'

And without hurrying he went on his way. At the
corner of the wood, in between two white posts, appeared a drive which Meaulnes entered. He walked up a
few yards and stopped startled, disturbed by inexplicable
feelings. He walked with the same fatigue, the icy wind
cut his lips and took his breath away, and yet a strange
contentment urged him on, a perfect and almost intoxi-
cating peace, the assurance that his goal had been
reached and that he had now nothing but happiness to
expect. In the same way he once used to feel faint with
excitement on the eve of great summer festivals, when
fir trees, whose branches overshadowed his bedroom window, were set up at nightfall along the village streets.

'So much joy,' he said to himself, 'just because

I am coming to this old dovecot full of owls and draughts! . . .'

And angry with himself he stopped, wondering if it would be better to turn back and go on to the next village. He had been thinking thus for a while, with head lowered, when he suddenly noticed that the drive had been swept clean in big regular circles as was usual at his home at festival time. He was really in a lane which looked like the High Street of La Ferté on the morning of Assumption Day! . . . Had he noticed at the bend of the drive a crowd of holiday-makers raising up the dust as in the month of June, he could not have been more surprised.

'Would there be a fête in this lonely spot?' he said to himself.

Advancing as far as the first bend, he heard the sound of approaching voices. He stepped behind some bushy young firs, crouched and listened, holding his breath. They were childish voices. A group of children passed close to him. One of them, probably a little girl, was speaking in a way so wise and so decided that Meaulnes, although he hardly caught the sense of her words, could not help smiling.

'One thing alone worries me,' she was saying, 'that is the question of the horses. No one will ever prevent Daniel riding on the big bay pony.'

'No one will ever prevent me!' replied the mocking voice of a young boy: 'are we not allowed to do just as we please? . . . Even hurting ourselves, if we like . . .'

And the voices grew distant as another group of children approached.

'If the ice thaws,' said a little girl, 'to-morrow morning we shall go boating.'

'But shall we be allowed?' said another.

'You know very well that we are arranging things in our own way.'

'But suppose Frantz was to come back this very evening with his fiancée?'

'Well! he would do as we wish! . . .'

'No doubt a wedding,' thought Augustin. 'But the children lay down the law here! . . . Strange land!'

He wanted to come out of his hiding-place and ask them where he could find something to eat and drink. He stood up and saw the last group going away. There were three little girls with pinafore dresses reaching to their knees. They wore pretty hats with strings. Down the neck of each hung a white feather. One of them, half turning round and slightly leaning towards her friend, was listening to long explanations the other was giving with one finger raised.

'I should frighten them,' thought Meaulnes, looking at his ragged peasant overall and the queer belt of the schoolboys at Sainte-Agathe.

Fearing that the children would meet him on their way back along the drive, he passed on through the firs in the direction of the 'dovecot,' without considering at all what he could ask for there. He was soon stopped at the edge of the wood by a low mossy wall. On the other side, in between the wall and the outhouses of the estate, was a long narrow courtyard as full of carriages as the yard of an inn on the day of a fair. These carriages were of all kinds and shapes: some elegant and small four-seaters with their shafts up in the air; wagonettes; coaches quite out of date with their moulded cornices, and even some old berlins with windows raised.

Meaulnes, hidden behind the firs for fear of being seen, was examining the disorder of the place when he noticed, on the other side of the yard, just above the driver's seat of a tall wagonette, a window in one of the outhouses, half open. Two iron bars, such as are often seen on stable shutters behind old manors, were meant to close this aperture, but time had loosened them.

'I will go in through there,' thought the schoolboy.
'I shall sleep in the hay and leave at daybreak without
having frightened these lovely little girls.'

He climbed over the wall, painfully because of his
wounded knee, and jumping from one carriage to another, from the coachman's box of a wagonette to the
roof of a berlin, he hauled himself up to the window,
which noiselessly opened under his push, like a door.

He found himself, not in a hayloft, but in a big room
with low ceiling, which must have been a bedroom. In
the winter twilight one could make out that the table,
the mantelpiece, and even the armchairs were covered
with tall vases, objects of value, ancient weapons. At
the other end of the room hung curtains to conceal an
alcove.

Meaulnes had closed the window, both because of the
cold and for fear of being seen from outside. He went to
raise the curtains at the back of the room and disclosed
a big low bed covered with old gilded books, lutes with
broken strings, and chandeliers all thrown in a heap. He
pushed all these things to the back of the alcove, then
stretched himself on this couch to rest and to ponder
over the strange adventure which had befallen him.

A deep silence reigned over this domain. Only at intervals the moaning of the high December wind could
be heard.

And Meaulnes, stretched out, began to wonder if in
spite of these strange meetings, in spite of the voices of
the children in the drive, in spite of the carriages huddled together, the place was not simply, as he had
thought at first, an old disused building in the winter
wilderness.

Soon the wind seemed to bring him the sound of
distant music. It was like a memory full of charm and of
regret. He recalled the days when his mother, still young,
used to come in the afternoon, and sit at the drawing-

room piano and he, silently, from behind the door leading to the garden, listened to her until night . . .

'Surely it seems as if some one were playing the piano somewhere?' he thought.

But leaving his question without an answer, worn out with fatigue, he was soon asleep . . .

It was night when he awoke. Chilled with cold he
turned from side to side in his bed, crumpling and rolling his black overall under him. A faint yellow light
bathed the curtains of the alcove.

Sitting up on the bed he pushed his head between the
curtains. Some one had opened the window and had
hung two green Chinese lanterns in the aperture.

But Meaulnes had scarcely time for one look around
before he heard soft footsteps on the landing and whispers. He started back into the alcove and his hobnailed
shoes rang against one of the bronze ornaments which
he had pushed close to the wall.

For an instant he held his breath in anxiety. The footsteps were approaching and two shadows glided into the
room.

'Don't make any noise,' said one.

'Well!' replied the other, 'it's high time he woke up!'

'Got his room ready?'

'Of course, just like the others.'

The wind made the window swing.

'Look,' said the first, 'you didn't even shut the window. The wind has blown out one of the lanterns already.
We shall have to light it again.'

'Bah!' replied the other, suddenly lazy and discouraged, 'what's the good of these illuminations on the countryside, the desert side so to say? There is nobody to see
them!'

'Nobody? But more people will be coming most of
the night. Down there, on the road, in their carriages,
they will be glad to see our lights!'

Meaulnes heard a match struck. The one who had spoken last, and who appeared to be the leader, went on in a drawling voice, like a gravedigger in Shakespeare:

'You are putting up green lanterns in the Wellington room. You would just as soon put red . . . You know no more about it than I do!'

Silence.

'. . . Wellington, he was an American chap? Well! Is green an American colour? You're the travelled comedian, you ought to know that.'

'Oh! Come off it!' replied the 'comedian.' 'Me, travelled? Oh, yes! I have travelled! But I've seen nothing! What can you see in a caravan?'

Meaulnes looked between the curtains with caution.

The manager was a fat bareheaded man, buried in a huge overcoat. He held in his hand a long pole hung with lanterns of many colours, and with his legs crossed he quietly watched his companion work.

As for the comedian, he had the most woeful body imaginable. Thin, tall, and shivering, with squinting greenish eyes, a moustache drooping over a toothless mouth, he called to mind the streaming face of a drowned man stretched on a slab. He was in his shirt-sleeves and his jaws chattered. He displayed in speech and gesture absolute contempt for his own person.

After a moment given to thought—both pitiful and laughable—with arms outstretched, he approached his partner and confided to him:

'Shall I tell you what? . . . I can't understand why they should have fetched rotters like us to help in such a fête! Got that, my lad? . . .'

Disregarding this outburst of emotion, the fat man continued to watch the work with his legs crossed, yawned, quietly sniffed, and then turning his back went away with the pole on his shoulder, saying: 'Come on! It's time to dress for dinner.'

The bohemian[1] followed him, but as he passed in front of the alcove:

---

[1]In French these '*bohémiens*' do not mean gipsies, and are not of gipsy race. Alain-Fournier sometimes calls them '*comédiens*.' They are strolling players such as used to come to my own little native town and pitch their tent on the church square. They travel in caravans at any time during the year and not only for the town fairs, and often give very good shows and plays, going from town to town where there are no theatres. As a child it was thus I saw Musset's *On ne Badine pas avec l'Amour*, Labiche's *Le Voyage de Monsieur Perrichon*, and many of Molière's plays, all acted under canvas, often in the most primitive kind of tent. Molière and his 'illustre Théâtre' were a troupe of that kind.

At the yearly fair these strolling players may often be just a man and his wife, or a small party travelling with a few performing animals. The word *bohémien* is often applied to such actors and showmen with contempt, as in English is the word *gipsy*. Yet again it is used indifferently with *saltimbanque* for real gipsies who travel in caravans and make a trade of wicker chairs, brooms, etc.

But the grand style of *bohémiens*, the strolling actors travelling in caravans, are looked upon as wonderful people surrounded with glamour. They used to fascinate me as a child, and all the town was astir when they came, most people feeling the same fascination. After the play we children would go prowling round their caravans, a land of mystery. Yet, however welcome these people were in our little town—where they brought joy and mirth—one knew that at the back of people's minds was a certain amount of mistrust. One felt that people were purposely over-polite, displaying an exaggerated courtesy, the result of their unconscious distinction between the honest, nice, and gentlemanly *bohémiens* and those who might not be. And indeed one often went to school (as I did) with the other type of *bohémien*: children of sellers of wicker chairs or small peddlers, etc.

From all this it is clear that to translate the word

'Sir Sleeper!' said he, with courtly bows and a clown's diction, 'it's up to you now to wake up and dress like a marquis even though you're only a pot-boy like me, and you will descend to the fancy-dress ball, since that is the good pleasure of these little gentlemen and of these little ladies.'

He added, in the tone of a quack at a fair, with a final bow: 'Our friend Maloyau, of the kitchen department, will present the character of Harlequin and your humble servant that of tall Pierrot . . .'

---

bohémien by *gipsy* is wrong when applied to people not of gipsy race, yet *gipsies* must be used whenever one wants to show contempt or mistrust. Of course the word can never mean here the Bohemian of Bohemian life, of Murger and Montmartre's style; it means these strolling comedians, still a part of French life for people of Alain-Fournier's generation, though now that most little towns boast a theatre these troupes have a tendency to disappear, to be replaced by more modern touring companies.—*Note by Translator*.

chapter 13. THE STRANGE FESTIVAL

As soon as they had disappeared, the schoolboy came
out of his hiding-place. His feet were frozen, his joints
stiff, but he was rested and his knee seemed healed.
'Come down to dinner?' thought he, 'I certainly shall.
I shall simply be a guest whose name every one has forgotten. Besides, I am not an intruder here. It is quite
clear that M. Maloyau and his companion were expecting me . . .'

Coming out of the absolute darkness of the alcove,
he managed to see fairly well about the room, by the
light of the green lantern.

The bohemian had 'decorated' it. Cloaks had been
hung from curtain hooks. On a heavy dressing-table,
with its broken marble top, was displayed all that was
necessary to transform into a beau any lad who might
have spent the previous night in a forsaken sheepfold.
A matchbox lay on the mantelpiece by the side of a tall
candlestick. But they had neglected to polish the floor;
and Meaulnes was aware of sand and rubbish under his
shoes. Again he had the impression of being in a house
which had been disused for a long time. Going towards
the fireplace he nearly stumbled over a pile of cardboard
boxes large and small: he reached out an arm, lit the
candle, then lifted the lids of the boxes and stooped
down to look.

He found young men's costumes of days long gone by,
frock coats with high velvet collars, dainty waistcoats cut
very open, interminable white cravats, and patent-leather
shoes dating from the beginning of the century. He
dared not touch a thing even with his finger-tips; but
shivering as he cleaned himself, he put one of the long

cloaks over his schoolboy overall and raised its pleated collar; he changed his hobnailed shoes for elegant pumps and prepared to go downstairs bareheaded.

He reached the bottom of a wooden staircase in a dark corner of the yard, without meeting any one. The icy night air blew on his face and raised one side of his cloak.

He took a few steps and thanks to the faint clearness of the sky he was at once able to get an idea of his surroundings. He was in a little yard formed by outhouse buildings. Everything appeared old and ruined. Gaps yawned at the bottom of the staircase, for the doors had long since been removed; nor had the panes been replaced in the windows, which made black holes in the walls. Yet all these buildings had a mysterious holiday aspect. A coloured reflection hovered about in the low rooms, where also lanterns must have been lit looking on the countryside. The ground had been swept, invading weeds pulled up. Meaulnes, listening, thought he heard something like a song, like children and young girls' voices down there towards the shadowy buildings where the wind shook the branches in front of the pink, green, and blue opening of the windows.

There he was, in his long cloak, like a hunter, stooping to listen, when an extraordinary little fellow came out of a neighbouring building any one would have thought deserted.

This little fellow wore a top hat very much curved in, which shone in the night as if made of silver, a frock coat with its collar reaching his hair, a low-cut waistcoat, and peg-top trousers . . . This dandy, who might have been fifteen, was walking on tiptoe as though lifted up by the elastic straps of his trousers, but very swiftly.

He greeted Meaulnes as they met without stopping, automatically bowing low, and disappeared in the darkness in the direction of the central building, farm, castle,

or abbey, the turret of which had guided the schoolboy
early in the afternoon.

After a moment's hesitation, our hero followed in the
wake of the strange little personage. They crossed a wide
open space, half garden, half yard, passed in between
clumps of bushes, went around a fenced fish-pond, then
a well, and found themselves at last at the entrance of
the central building.

A heavy wooden door, rounded at the top and studded
with nails like a church door, was half open. The dandy
hurried in; Meaulnes followed him and from his first
steps in the corridor, he found himself, without seeing
any one, in the midst of laughter, songs, shouts, and
chases.

A passage ran across the end of the corridor. Meaulnes
was hesitating whether to push on to the end or open
one of the doors behind which he could hear voices,
when he saw two little girls, at the end, chasing each
other. He ran to see them and catch them up, moving
noiselessly in his pumps. A sound of opening doors, two
faces of fifteen which the freshness of the evening and
the chase had made quite rosy under their poke bonnets,
and everything disappeared in a sudden glare of light.

For an instant they twirled round in fun, their wide
light skirts rose and bellied up; one could see the lace
of their long quaint drawers; then, after this pirouette,
they bounced into the room together and shut the door
again.

Meaulnes remained for a moment dazed and staggering in this dark corridor. He now feared to be discovered.
His clumsy and hesitating gait might lead him to be
mistaken for a thief. He deliberately retraced his steps
towards the front door, when again he heard a sound
of steps and children's voices at the end of the corridor.
Two little boys were talking as they approached.

'Will dinner be ready soon?' Meaulnes asked them
with assurance.

'Come with us,' replied the bigger of the two, 'we'll take you in.'

And with that ease and need of friendliness which children have before a great party, they each took hold of one of Meaulnes' hands. Most likely they were two little peasant boys. They had been dressed in their best clothes: short knickers above the knees, which showed their thick woollen stockings and their heavy boots, a small blue velvet jacket, a cap of the same colour, and a white necktie.

'Do *you* know her?' asked one of the children.

'Me,' said the smaller one, who had a round head and naïve eyes; 'Mummy says that she had a black dress and a round collar and that she looked like a pretty Pierrot.'

'Whom do you mean?' asked Meaulnes.

'Why! Frantz's fiancée, whom he has gone to fetch . . .'

Before Meaulnes could say anything, the three of them reached the door of a large room where a big fire was burning. For table, boards had been placed on trestles; while tablecloths had been spread and people of all kinds were dining with ceremony.

(continuation)

It was a meal spread in a great room with a low ceiling, like those offered on the eve of a country wedding to relatives who had come from a distance.

The two children had let go the schoolboy's hands and had rushed into an adjoining room from whence could be heard childish voices and the clatter of spoons on plates. Meaulnes climbed over a bench boldly and calmly and found himself seated beside two old peasant women. He at once began to eat with fierce appetite; and only after a while did he raise his head to look at other guests and listen.

Little, as a matter of fact, was being said. These folk seemed but slightly acquainted. They must have come, some from far off in the country, others from distant towns. Scattered about along the tables were some old men with side whiskers and others clean-shaven, who might have been old sailors. Dining near them other old men looked very much like the first: the same tanned faces, the same sharp eyes under bushy eyebrows, the same narrow ties like shoestrings. But it was easy to see that these had never voyaged farther than the other end of the parish, and if they had been tossed and beaten by winds and storms it had occurred on that rough yet un-dangerous voyage in cutting the furrow to the field end and guiding back the plough. Few women were to be seen; only some old peasants with round faces as wrin-kled as apples under their goffered caps.

With every one of these guests Meaulnes felt confi-dent and at ease. Later he came to explain that feeling by saying: If you have ever done something unpardonable you sometimes think, in the midst of much bitterness: 'Yet there are people in the world who would forgive me.' You imagine old people, indulgent grandparents, who are, beforehand, certain that all you do is well done. Undoubtedly the guests in the hall had been chosen from good folk of that kind; the rest were young people and children.

Meanwhile, two old women were chatting close to Meaulnes.

'Even if all is for the best,' said the elder in a very shrill comical voice which she vainly tried to soften, 'the lovers will not be here before three o'clock to-morrow.'

'Be quiet! or you'll make me angry,' replied the other in the most peaceful manner.

She was wearing over her forehead a knitted hood.

'Let's work it out!' replied the first, undisturbed. 'An hour and a half by train from Bourges to Vierzon and seven leagues by coach from Vierzon here . . .'

The talk went on. Meaulnes lost not a word. This friendly squabble helped to clear matters up a little. Frantz de Galais, the son of the house—who was a student or a sailor or perhaps a cadet in the Navy, one could not be sure—had gone to Bourges to fetch a young girl and marry her: strange to say, this boy, who must be very young and very fantastic, arranged everything in his own way at the manor. He had wanted the house where his fiancée was to live to look like a festive palace. And to welcome the young girl he had himself invited these children and these kind-hearted old people. Such were the points which the discussion of the two women elucidated. They left everything else in mystery and always came back to the question of the lovers' return. The one insisted on to-morrow morning, the other on to-morrow afternoon.

'Poor old Moinelle, you always are so stupid,' said the younger quietly.

'Poor Adèle, you're always so obstinate. I haven't seen you for four years and you haven't changed an atom,' replied the other with a shrug of her shoulders, but in the most peaceful voice.

And thus they had it out together, without the least bad feeling.

Meaulnes joined in with the hope of learning more: 'Is she as pretty as people say, Frantz's sweetheart?'

They looked at him bewildered. No one but Frantz had seen the girl. Coming home from Toulon one evening, he had found her wandering in great distress in one of the gardens of Bourges which are called Les Marais. Her father, a weaver, had turned her out of the house. She was very pretty and Frantz had decided at once to marry her. It was a strange story, but had not his father M. de Galais and his sister Yvonne always allowed him to do as he liked!

Meaulnes was cautiously going to put other questions when a charming couple appeared at the doorway; a girl of sixteen wearing a velvet bodice and a skirt with deep flounces, a young fellow in peg-top trousers and a frock coat with a high collar. They crossed the room dancing a *pas de deux*; others followed, then again others rushed through screaming and chased by a tall ghastly Pierrot in dangling sleeves, who wore a black cap and smiled from a toothless mouth. He was running in big clumsy strides, as if each step preceded a jump, and he flapped his long empty sleeves. The girls were a little frightened of him, the young men shook him by the hand, and he appeared to be the delight of the children, who chased him with shrieks and laughter. As he passed he looked at Meaulnes with his glassy eyes, and the schoolboy thought he recognised, now completely clean-shaven, the companion of M. Maloyau, the bohemian who a little while before was hanging up the lanterns.

The meal ended. Every one rose.

In the corridors round games and country dances began. A band played a minuet somewhere. Meaulnes,
with his head half hidden by the collar of his cloak, as
by a ruff, felt himself a different person. He, too, caught
the fun of it all and began to chase the tall Pierrot
through the corridors, now like the wings of a theatre
where the play had overflowed from the stage, in every
direction. He thus found himself part of a gay crowd in
extravagant fancy dress. Sometimes he opened a door
and was in a room with a magic lantern. Children
clapped loudly. Sometimes, in a corner of the room de-
voted to dancing, he talked with some dandy and tried
hastily to find out the sort of dress to be worn on the days
following.

Rather troubled at last by all this gaiety offered him,
and every moment fearing lest his partly open cloak
would reveal his schoolboy overall, he sought refuge for
a while in the quietest and darkest part of the dwelling.
No other sound could be heard there but the muffled
music of a piano.

He entered another door and found himself in a
dining-room lit by a hanging lamp. There also fun was
on, but fun for the children. Some of these, seated on
hassocks, were busy turning over the pages of albums
open on their knees; others, squatting on the floor in
front of a chair, were gravely engaged in displaying pictures on the seat; others, again, near the fire said nothing
and did nothing but listen to the hum of the fête audible
throughout the great house.

One door of this dining-room was wide open. In the
next room could be heard the piano being played.
Meaulnes, inquisitively, put his head in. It was a sort
of drawing-room parlour; a woman or a young girl, with
a brown cloak thrown over her shoulders and her back
turned, was very softly playing tunes of round games
and nursery rhymes. Close to her, on the sofa, six or

seven little boys and girls sat in a row as in a picture,
good as children are when it grows late, and listened.
Only now and again one of them, using his wrist as prop,
lifted himself up, slid down to the ground, and passed
into the dining-room: then one of those who had finished
looking at the pictures came to take his place.

After the ball where everything was charming but
feverish and mad, where he had himself so madly chased
the tall Pierrot, Meaulnes found that he had dropped
into the most peaceful happiness on earth.

Noiselessly, while the girl played on, he went back to
sit in the dining-room, and opening one of the big red
books scattered on the table, he absent-mindedly began
to read.

Almost at once one of the little boys crouched on the
floor came up to him, and catching hold of his arm,
climbed on his knee to look over; another settled on the
other side. Then began a dream like his old dream. His
mind could dwell on the fancy that he was married and
in his own home during a beautiful evening and that this
lovely unknown person playing the piano, close to him,
was his wife.

Next morning Meaulnes was one of the first to be ready. He put on, as he had been told, a simple black old-fashioned suit; a tight-waisted jacket with sleeves puffed out at the shoulders, a double-breasted waistcoat, trousers so wide at the bottom that they hid his dainty shoes, and a top hat.

The courtyard was deserted when he came down. He took a few steps and felt projected into a day of spring. It proved, indeed, to be the most lovely morning of that winter, sunny as in the first days of April. The frost was giving way and the damp grass shone as with dewdrops. In the trees many small birds were singing, and from time to time a warm breeze touched his face as he walked.

He behaved as guests do who wake before their host. He went out into the courtyard, thinking that, at any moment, a friendly and gay voice would call from behind him: 'Up already, Augustin?'

But he walked alone for a long time in the garden and in the courtyard. Over there, in the main building, nothing stirred, either in the windows or in the turret. Yet the two wings of the heavy-studded door were already open. And at one of the top windows a ray of sunshine shone as in summer in the early morning.

Meaulnes for the first time saw the grounds of the manor in broad daylight. Remains of a wall separated the unkept garden from the courtyard, where quite recently sand had been spread and smoothed over with the rake. At the end of the annex where his room was stood stables built in quaint disorder, which multiplied corners thick with ramping bushes and Virginia creeper.

The fir woods, which hid the manor from all the flat
country around, encroached onto the very grounds—except towards the east where could be seen blue hills
covered with rocks and yet more firs.

For one moment, in the garden, Meaulnes leaned over
the shaky fence enclosing the fish-pond; near the edges
there remained a little thin ice in folds like froth . . . He
saw himself reflected in the water, as if bending over the
sky in his romantic student's costume. And he fancied
it was another Meaulnes; no longer the schoolboy who
had run away in a peasant's cart, but a charming youth
of romance from the pages of some handsome prize-
book . . .

He hurried towards the main building, for he was
hungry. A peasant woman was laying the table in the
large hall where he had dined the previous evening. As
soon as Meaulnes sat down in front of one of the bowls
set in a line on the cloth, she poured him some coffee
and said: 'You are the first down, sir?'

He did not wish to answer lest he should suddenly be
recognized as a stranger. He only asked at what time
the boat would leave for the morning excursion which
had been announced.

'Not for half an hour, sir. No one has come down
yet,' was the reply.

So he continued to wander in search of the landing-
stage, all around this long castle-like house, built with
unequal wings in the style of a church. When he turned
round the south wing, he suddenly saw the reeds which,
as far as the eyes could reach, formed the landscape.
The water of the lakes, on that side, bathed the foot of
the walls, and in front of several doors little wooden
balconies overhung the rippling wavelets.

The youth, idly, rambled at leisure along a shore
sandy as a towing-path. He peered through the dusty
panes of large doors into dilapidated or forsaken rooms
and sheds encumbered with wheelbarrows, rusted tools,

and broken flower pots, when, suddenly, at the other end of the building, he heard footsteps crunching the sand.

Two women were approaching, one very old and bent, the other a young girl, fair and slender, whose charming dress, after all the fancy costumes of the previous evening, at first appeared strange to Meaulnes.

They stopped a moment to look at the view, while Meaulnes said to himself, with an astonishment which he later viewed as vulgar: 'That girl must be what is called eccentric—perhaps an actress who has been asked for the fête.'

Meanwhile, the two women passed close to him, and Meaulnes, motionless, watched the girl. Often, in after days, when falling asleep, after having tried in vain to recall the beautiful elusive face, rows of young women, not unlike this one, would pass before him in his dream. One had a hat like hers, another her slightly drooping head; this one her clear gaze, this other her small waist and yet another her blue eyes; but none of these women was ever the tall young girl.

Meaulnes had time to notice under the mass of fair hair a face, rather short but with features outlined with almost painful delicacy. And when she had passed, he observed that she wore what was certainly the most simple and sensible of dresses.

In some perplexity he was asking himself if he should accompany them, when the girl, turning imperceptibly towards him, said to her companion: 'Surely the boat will soon be here, now? . . .'

And Meaulnes followed them. The old lady, shaky and worn with age, never ceased chatting and laughing. The girl answered her gently. And when they walked down to the landing-stage she once again had that innocent grave look which seemed to say: 'Who are you? What are you doing here? I don't know you. And yet it seems to me that I do know you.'

Other guests were now scattered amongst the trees, waiting. Three pleasure boats came to the shore, ready to take the holiday-makers on board. One by one, as the women, who seemed to be the lady of the manor and her daughter, passed by, the young men bowed low and the girls curtsied. Strange morning! Strange pleasure party! It was cold, in spite of the winter sun, and the women were twisting round their necks those feather boas which were then fashionable.

The old lady remained on shore and, without knowing how, Meaulnes found himself in the same boat as the young lady of the manor. He leaned at the side of the deck, one hand holding on his hat in the high wind, and he was able to watch at his ease the girl who sat in shelter. She watched him, too. She answered her friends, smiled, and then gently let her blue eyes rest on him, biting her lip a little.

There was deep silence on the near banks. The boat glided on with a quiet sound of engine and water. It was easy to imagine one was in the heart of summer. They were going to land, so it seemed, in the beautiful garden of some country house. There, the girl would walk about under a white sunshade. Until evening the moan of doves would be heard. . . . But suddenly an icy blast came to remind the guests at this strange fête that it was December.

They landed in front of a fir wood. On the landing-stage, the passengers had to wait a moment huddled, one against the other, while one of the boatmen unlocked the gate. With what joy, in after days, Meaulnes recalled the one minute when, on the shore of the lake, he had felt, close to his own, the girl's face, since lost! He had gazed at that profile, so pure, until his eyes had nearly filled with tears. And he remembered having seen, like a delicate secret she had confided to him, a little powder on her cheek . . .

On land everything happened as in a dream. While the children ran about with shouts of joy, while groups formed and scattered through the woods, Meaulnes entered a path where ten paces ahead of him the girl was walking.

He was close to her without having had time to think. 'You are lovely,' he said simply.

But she hurried on and without replying turned off along another path. Other people were playing and running about the avenues, each wandering where the fancy took him. The young man sharply reproached himself with what he called his thick-headedness, his grossness, his stupidity. He rambled on aimlessly, convinced that he would never again set eye on this gracious being, when suddenly he saw her approaching and forced to pass close to him in the narrow path. With two bare hands, she pushed the folds of her long cloak out of the way. She wore black shoes cut very open. Her ankles were so slender that at times they appeared to bend and you feared they might break.

This time, the young man took off his hat and said, very softly: 'Will you forgive me?'

'I forgive you,' she said gravely. 'But I must go back to the children, as they are the masters to-day. Goodbye.'

Augustin begged her to stay a moment longer. He spoke to her awkwardly, but in a voice so agitated and so disturbed, that she walked more slowly and listened to him.

'I do not even know who you are,' she said at last.

She spoke in an even tone, dwelling on each word in the same way, but saying the last one more softly . . . Then she regained her steady look, still biting her lips a little, and her blue eyes looked into the distance.

'I do not know your name either,' replied Meaulnes.

They were following a lane no longer under the cover of the woods, and some way off the guests could be seen crowding around an isolated house in the open country.

'Here is "Frantz's House," ' said the girl. 'I must leave
you . . .'

She hesitated, looked at him a moment, and smiling
said: 'My name? . . . I am Mademoiselle Yvonne de
Galais . . .'

And she hurried away.

'Frantz's House' was then uninhabited. But Meaulnes
found it invaded, up to the attics, by the crowd of guests.
He had scarcely leisure, however, to examine the spot
where he now stood: they all hastened to eat a cold
lunch which had been brought in the boats and which
was hardly seasonable, but most likely the children had
decided on it; then they set off again.

Meaulnes came close to Mademoiselle de Galais as
soon as he saw her leave the house, and in answer to
what she had said previously: 'The name I had given
you was much nicer,' he said.

'How is that? What was the name?' she replied, always with the same seriousness.

But he was afraid of having said something silly, and
he did not answer.

'Well, my own name is Augustin Meaulnes,' he went
on, 'and I am a student.'

'Oh! you are studying?' she said.

And they spoke a moment longer. They spoke slowly
with happiness—with friendship. Then the girl's attitude changed. Less haughty and less serious, she now
also seemed more uneasy. She seemed to be dreading
what Augustin might say and was troubled beforehand.

She was close to him, trembling like a swallow alighted
for a moment on the ground and already quivering with
the longing to resume its flight.

'What is the good? What is the good?' she replied
gently to the plans which Meaulnes proposed.

But then at last he dared to ask her permission to come back one day to this delightful manor.

'I will wait for you,' she replied simply.

They came in sight of the landing-stage.

She stopped suddenly and said thoughtfully: 'We are two children, we have behaved foolishly. We mustn't get into the same boat this time. Good-bye; do not follow me.'

For an instant Meaulnes remained dumbfounded, watching her go away. Then he continued his walk. And the girl in the distance, stopped at the moment of disappearing in the crowd of guests, and turning, for the first time, took a long look at him. Was that a last farewell? Was it to forbid him to follow her? Or had she perhaps something else to tell him? . . .

As soon as they returned to the manor the pony-race started in a big meadow that sloped down at the back of the farm. It was the last item of the fête. According to the arrangements the fiancés were to arrive for it and Frantz was to manage it all.

Yet they had to begin without him. The boys in their jockey suits and the little girls as horsewomen led in some frisky ponies decked with ribbons as well as very old docile horses, amid shouts, children's laughter, betting, and prolonged sounding of the bell. One could have fancied one's self on the green and newly mown turf of a miniature race-course.

Meaulnes spotted Daniel and the little girls with feathers in their hats whose voices he had heard the day before in the drive near the wood. . . . The other part of the show was lost on him, so great was his anxiety to find, among the crowd, the charming hat trimmed with roses and the long brown cloak. But Mademoiselle de Galais never appeared. He was still looking for her when a full peal of the bell and joyful hurrahs announced that the race was over. A little girl mounted on an old white

mare had won the prize. She proudly passed by on her
mount, the feather of her hat fluttering in the wind.

Then suddenly all was still. The games were ended
and Frantz had not come back. There was a moment
of hesitation; people consulted uneasily. At last, in
groups, the guest went back to the house to await in
silence and anxiety the home-coming of the engaged
couple.

The race had ended too soon. It was half-past four and
still daylight when Meaulnes found himself again in his
room, his head full of the events of this extraordinary
day. He sat down idly at the table, waiting for the dinner
and the fête which would follow.

The great wind which had blown on the first evening
blew again. It could be heard roaring like a torrent or
passing by with the insistent hiss of a waterfall. Every
now and then the damper in the grate shook.

For the first time Meaulnes felt the little pang that
gets you at the close of too lovely a day. It occurred to
him to light a fire, but he tried vainly to raise the rusted
damper. Then he began to tidy the room; he hung up
his handsome clothes on the pegs, arranged the disor-
dered chairs in a row along the walls, as if he were anxious
to make preparations for a long stay.

Remembering, however, that he ought to be ready to
leave at a moment's notice, he carefully folded his overall and his other school things like travelling clothes on
the back of a chair and put his hobnailed shoes, still
thick with mud, under the chair.

Then he sat down again and, feeling calmer, inspected
his dwelling-room now set in order.

From time to time a drop of rain left a streak on the
window which looked on the stable-yard and the fir wood.
At peace since he had tidied his room, the big boy felt
perfectly happy. There he was, mysterious, a stranger in
the midst of this unknown world, in the room he had
chosen. What he had found surpassed all his hopes. And
it was enough now for his joy to recall, in the high wind,
the face of that girl who turned towards him . . .

Night had fallen during this reverie, and he had not
given a thought even to lighting the tall candles. A gust
of wind banged the door of the dressing-room adjoining
his, which also looked on the stable-yard. Meaulnes was
about to close it when he noticed, in that room, a faint
light as of a candle burning on the table. He put his
head through the half-open door. Some one had got in
there, by the window, no doubt, and was walking up
and down with silent tread. So far as one could see it
was a very young man with a long travelling cloak on
his shoulders. Bareheaded, this young man paced up
and down without a stop, like one distracted by some
unbearable grief. From the window, which he had left
wide open, the wind made his cloak flutter, and each
time he passed close to the light a glint of brass buttons
on his handsome frock coat caught the eye.

He was whistling between his teeth a kind of chanty
such as sailors and prostitutes sing, to keep up their
spirits in the pot-houses of seaports.

He stopped for an instant in the midst of his troubled
walk, leaned over the table, searched in a box, took out
several sheets of paper . . . By the light of the candle
Meaulnes saw in profile very fine and very aquiline features, clean-shaven, under a thick head of hair which was
parted on one side. He had stopped whistling. He was
very pale; his lips were half open, and he seemed short of
breath as if he had received a violent blow on the heart.

Meaulnes wondered whether it would be wise to retire
or to go in and put a hand on his shoulder like a friend
and talk to him. But the other raised his head and saw
him. He looked at him for a moment; then, without surprise, came up and said, steadying his voice:

'I do not know you, sir, but I am pleased to see you.
As you are here it is to you I will explain . . . Listen! . . .'

He appeared completely broken. After he had said
'Listen,' he caught hold of Meaulnes by his coat lapel,

as though to fix his attention. Then he turned his head
towards the window, as if to collect his thoughts, blinked
—and Meaulnes realized that he badly wanted to cry.

But suddenly he swallowed back this childlike grief
and, still gazing at the window, he went on in an altered
voice:

'Well! listen; it's all ended; the fête is ended. You
can go down and tell them. I've come back alone. My
fiancée will not come. Scruples, fear, lack of faith . . .
besides, sir, I must explain to you . . .'

But he could not go on. His face screwed up. He explained nothing. He suddenly turned away and went, in
the dim light, to open and then close drawers full of
clothes and books.

'I am going to get ready to go away again,' he said.
'Let no one disturb me.'

He placed various things on the table, a dressing-case,
a revolver . . .

And Meaulnes walked out, full of dismay, not daring
to say a word or to shake hands.

Downstairs everybody seemed to have guessed something already. Nearly all the girls had changed dresses.
In the main building dinner had started, but people ate
in haste, anyhow, as at the moment of starting on a
journey.

There was a constant going to and fro from this large
kitchen hall to the bedrooms and stables. Those who
had done eating formed groups and said 'Good-bye' to
each other.

'What's happening?' asked Meaulnes of a peasant boy
who was making haste to finish his meal, a felt hat on
his head and a table napkin tucked into his waistcoat:

'We are leaving,' he said. 'It's been decided very suddenly. At five o'clock we found ourselves quite alone, all
the guests together. We had waited as long as we possibly
could. Too late for the lovers to turn up. Somebody said,
"Let's go" . . . And everybody made ready to leave.'

Meaulnes made no reply. He did not mind going now. Had he not reached the end of his adventure? . . . Had he not this once obtained all that he wished for? Scarcely had he had time even quietly to go over in his mind the beautiful conversation of the morning. At the moment the only thing was to go. And soon he would come back—without trickery this time . . .

'If you like to come with us,' went on his companion, who was a boy of his own age, 'look sharp and get ready; we are going to harness up at once.'

Meaulnes hurried out, leaving his meal unfinished and omitting to tell the guests what he knew. The park, the garden, and the yard were now plunged in total darkness. There were no lanterns that evening at the windows. But as this dinner was, after all, not unlike the meal at the conclusion of a wedding, the less considerate of the guests, who had perhaps been drinking, began to sing. As he went off, Meaulnes heard their cabaret songs fill the air of the park which for two days had held so much grace and so much wonder. And it proved the beginning of confusion and chaos. He passed close to the fish-pond into which he had looked, that very morning, at his own reflection. How everything seemed changed already . . . with this song, sung in chorus, which reached him in snatches:

> *Where have you come from, little wanton?*
> > *Your cap is in two*
> > *Your hair all askew* . . .

And this one, too:

> > *My shoes are red* . . .
> > *Good-bye, my lover* . . .
> > *My shoes are red* . . .
> > *Good-bye forever!*

As he reached the foot of the stairs leading to his isolated lodging, some one came down and bumped into

him in the dark, saying: 'Good-bye, sir!'—and wrapping
himself in his cloak as if it were very cold, disappeared.
It was Frantz de Galais.

The candle which Frantz had left in his room was
still burning. Nothing had been touched. Only, written
on a conspicuous sheet of note-paper, were these words:
'My fiancée has disappeared, letting me know that
she cannot be my wife; that she was a dressmaker and
not a princess. I do not know what will become of me.
I am going away. I no longer wish to live. May Yvonne
forgive me for not saying good-bye to her, but she could
not do anything for me . . .'
It was the end of the candle, the flame of which gut-
tered, flickered a moment and went out. Meaulnes returned to his own room and shut the door. In spite of
the darkness he made out all the things which he had
tidied, in full daylight and in full happiness, a few hours
before. Garment after garment, all intact, he found again
his old wretched suit, from his hobnailed shoes to his
clumsy belt with the brass buckle. He undressed and
dressed again swiftly, but distraught, placing his bor-
rowed clothes on a chair, putting on the wrong waistcoat . . .
Under the windows, in the stable-yard, the bustle of
departure had begun. Pulling, shouting, and pushing,
each one wanted to get his vehicle out of the confused
crowd in which it was hemmed. From time to time a
man would climb on the driver's seat of a trap or on the
hood of a big covered cart and search about with his
light. The reflection of the lantern came in at the window; for a brief moment the room around Meaulnes,
once familiar and where everything had been so friendly,
breathed again, lived again . . . And thus it was that,
carefully closing the door, he left this mysterious place
which no doubt he was never again to see.

Already, night as it was, a string of vehicles wound slowly towards the gate at the entrance of the wood. A man, in a goatskin, holding a lantern, led the first horse of the procession.

Meaulnes was anxious to find some one to give him a lift. He was anxious to go away. Deep within him he dreaded finding himself suddenly alone at the manor and his trick discovered.

When he arrived in front of the main building, he found the drivers assigning their occupants to the last carriages. The travellers were made to stand while the seats were brought forward or pushed backward, and the girls, swathed in shawls, got up clumsily, the rugs slipping to their feet, and one could distinguish the anxious faces of those whose heads were lowered towards the carriage lights.

One of these drivers Meaulnes recognised as the young peasant who had offered to see him home a while ago.

'May I get in?' he called out.

'Where are you going, my lad?' replied the other, not recognising him.

'Sainte-Agathe way.'

'Then you should ask Maritain for a seat.'

And the big schoolboy started in search of this unknown Maritain amongst the guests who were late in leaving. The man was pointed out to him amongst the convivial spirits in the kitchen.

'He's a slacker,' they told him; 'he'll be here till three in the morning.'

Meaulnes thought for a moment of the poor worried

girl who, in the midst of her grief and anxiety, would
hear the songs of these tipplers filling the place far into
the night. In which room was she? Where was her window amongst these mysterious buildings? But there was
no point in stopping. He must go. Once back at Sainte-
Agathe everything would become clearer; he would no
longer be a runaway schoolboy; he would once more be
able to dream of the young mistress of the manor.

One by one the vehicles left; the wheels grated on the
sand of the drive. One could see them turn to disappear
in the night with their loads of muffled-up women and
children wrapped in shawls and already dropping asleep.
One more big covered cart; then passed a wagonette in
which women were huddled shoulder to shoulder, and
Meaulnes was left standing bewildered on the steps of
the house. Soon, only an old berlin, driven by a peasant
in a smock, would be left.

'You can get in,' he replied to Augustin's inquiries.
'We are going your way.'

With some difficulty Meaulnes opened the door of the
rickety old vehicle, while the panes rattled and the
hinges creaked. On the seat, in a corner of the carriage
two quite small children, a boy and a girl, were asleep.
The noise and the cold woke them. They stretched,
looked vaguely about them shivering, nestled back in
their corner and dropped off to sleep again.

Now the old carriage set off. Meaulnes closed the
door more gently, and carefully settled in the other corner; then, hungrily, he tried to make out, through the
window, the place he was about to leave and the road by
which he had come: he guessed, in spite of the darkness,
that the carriage was crossing the courtyard and the
garden, passing in front of the stairway leading to his
room, going through the gate and leaving the manor
grounds to enter the woods. The trunks of the old fir
trees could be distinguished moving by the window.

'Perhaps we shall meet Frantz de Galais,' Meaulnes
said to himself with beating heart.

Suddenly, the carriage swerved in the narrow lane to
avoid collision with an obstacle. From its heavy appearance, as far as one could tell in the night, it was a caravan, almost in the middle of the road, which had stopped
there during these last days in proximity to the fête.

Having passed that obstacle, the horses started again
at a trot, and Meaulnes was beginning to tire of looking
out of the window in a vain effort to pierce through the
surrounding darkness, when suddenly, in the depths of
the woods, there was a flash of light followed by a report.
The horses set off at full gallop and Meaulnes could not
make out, at first, whether the peasant who drove was
attempting to hold them back or on the contrary urging
them on. He wanted to open the door. As the handle was
on the outside, he tried without success to lower the window; he shook it . . . The children waking up in a fright
huddled against each other without saying a word. And
while he shook the window, his face close to the glass,
a bend in the road enabled him to see a white figure running. It was the tall Pierrot of the fête, the bohemian in
his fancy costume, but haggard and distracted and carrying in his arms a human body clasped closely to him.
Then all disappeared.

In the carriage, tearing on at full gallop in the night,
the children were once more asleep. No one to whom
to speak of the mysterious happenings of the past two
days. After reviewing at length all he had seen and heard,
the young man, himself tired, his heart heavy, dropped
off to sleep like a sad child . . .

. . . It was scarcely dawn when the carriage stopped
on the road and Meaulnes was awakened by some one
knocking at the window. With some difficulty the driver
opened the door and shouted, while the icy wind froze
the schoolboy to the bone:

'You get out here! It's almost daylight. We are going to take the short cut. You're quite near Sainte-Agathe.'

Half asleep, Meaulnes obeyed, felt about in the darkest corner of the carriage for his cap which had rolled under the feet of the sleeping children; then he got out, stooping.

'Well, good-bye,' said the man, climbing back to his seat; 'you've only got six kilometres to do. Look, there is the milestone by the roadside.'

Meaulnes, still heavy with sleep, dragged himself up to the milestone and sat down with his arms folded and his head bent forward as though to fall asleep again.

'No, no!' called out the coachman; 'you mustn't think of sleeping there. It's too cold. Come on, up you get, walk a bit . . .'

Staggering like a drunken man, the big boy with his hands in his pockets and his shoulders hunched up, went slowly along the road to Sainte-Agathe, while the old berlin, the last trace of the mysterious festival, quitted the highroad and jolted silently off over the grass track. Now only the hat of the driver could be seen, dancing above the hedges . . .

Part II

chapter 1.   THE GREAT GAME

Wind and cold, rain or snow, the impossibility of making any long expedition prevented Meaulnes and me
from mentioning again the Lost Land before the end of
the winter. There was nothing worth beginning during
these short February days—these Thursdays[1] broken up
by squalls which invariably ended, about five, in a dismal
freezing downpour.

Nothing recalled Meaulnes' adventure except the
strange fact that since the afternoon of his return we no
longer had friends. At recreation time the same games
were got up as before, but Jasmin never spoke to Admiral Meaulnes. In the evenings, as soon as the classroom was swept, the playground became deserted, as in
the days when I was alone, and I now watched my friend
strolling to and fro from the garden to the shed and
from the playground to the dining-room.

On Thursday mornings each of us settled at the master's desk in one of the two classrooms to read Rousseau
and Paul Louis Courrier whom we had dug out of the

_____
[1]Thursday is, everywhere in France, a school holiday.

cupboards from amongst English textbooks and copy-
books of carefully transcribed music. In the afternoon
some caller or other often caused us to leave the house
and return to the school. . . . Sometimes we used to
hear some of the senior boys stop for a moment, as if by
chance, in front of the big gate, bang against it during
some unintelligible military games, and then go away.
. . . This melancholy life went on until the end of February. I was beginning to think that Meaulnes had forgotten everything when an adventure, stranger than the
others, came to prove to me that I had been mistaken
and that a violent storm was brewing under the dreary
surface of this winter life.

It happened to be a Thursday evening towards the
end of the month, that the first news of the mysterious
manor, the first ripple of that adventure of which we
never spoke, reached us. We were all snug for the evening. My grandparents having left, there remained only
Millie and my father, who had not the least idea of the
secret quarrel by which the form was split into two clans.

At eight o'clock Millie, who had opened the door to
shake out the crumbs after the meal, exclaimed: 'Ah!'
in a voice so clear that we all came near to look. On the
doorstep there was a layer of snow . . . As it was very
dark, I walked a few steps into the playground to see if
the layer was thick. I felt light flakes touch my face,
to melt at once. I was quickly made to come in, and
Millie, feeling chilly, hastened to shut the door.

At nine o'clock we prepared to go to bed; Mother was
already holding the lamp in her hand when we quite
distinctly heard two violent bangs hammered with great
fury against the big gate at the other end of the playground. Millie put down the lamp on the table and we
all stood there alert, listening.

No one dreamed of going to see what was the matter.
Before getting halfway across the playground the lamp
would have been out and the glass broken. There was

a short silence and Father was beginning, 'It must have been . . .' when right under the dining-room window looking on the Station Road, as I have said before, sounded a shrill prolonged whistle which must have been heard as far as the church. And immediately behind the window, scarcely softened by the glass, and coming from people who seemed to have hoisted themselves up to the window-sill, burst loud shouts of: 'Fetch him along! Fetch him along!'

At the other end of the building other loud shouts responded. These people must have gone through Father Martin's field and climbed on the low wall separating the field from the playground.

Then cries of 'Fetch him along,' shouted on every side by eight or ten unknown persons disguising their voices, burst out from the roof of the larder which they could only reach by climbing over a heap of faggots leaning against the outside wall; from a little wall which ran from the shed to the big gate and on which being rounded you could sit comfortably astride; from the railed wall along the Station Road, quite easy to climb . . . Finally a number of stragglers came up from the garden behind, making the same din, but shouting: 'Let 'em have it!'

And we heard the sound of their yells echoing in the empty classrooms where they had opened the windows.

Meaulnes and I knew so well all the corners and corridors of the big building that we could clearly see, as on a plan, the positions from which the unknown people were launching their attack.

To tell the truth, it was only just at first that we were frightened. The shrill whistle had made the four of us think of tramps and gipsies breaking in. As a matter of fact, for the last fortnight, a tall rogue and a youngster with his head bandaged up had been about in the square behind the church. There were strange workmen, too, at the wheelwright's and the blacksmith's.

But as soon as we heard the cries of the assailants we were convinced that we had to do with people—probably youngsters—from the village. Absolute little scalawags—you could spot them by their piercing voices —were among the crowd who stormed our house as they would board a ship.

'Well, I never . . .' exclaimed my father.

And Millie asked in a faint voice: 'What on earth does it all mean?'

Suddenly the voices near the big gate and the adjoining wall stopped, then those near the window. Two blasts of a whistle came from behind the French window. The cries of those hanging on the larder roof and of those attacking from the garden grew fainter and fainter, then ceased; we heard along the dining-room wall the scuttering steps of the whole gang in hasty retreat, getting lost in the snow.

Some one obviously was disturbing them. At an hour when all slept, they thought they could easily storm a house isolated at the far end of the village. But here was some one upsetting their plan of campaign.

We had scarcely time to recover—for the attack had been sudden as a well-planned boarding of a ship—and prepared to sally out, when we heard a voice we knew call out at the same gate:

'Monsieur Seurel! Monsieur Seurel!'

It was M. Pasquier, the butcher. The fat little man scraped his clogs on the doorstep, shook his short smock powdered with snow, and came in. He put on the knowing and startled air of one who has surprised the secret of a mystery.

'I was in my yard which faces the Cross-Roads. I was going to lock up the goats' shed. Suddenly, standing there in the snow, what d'ye think I saw? Two tall lads as looked posted like sentries or on the watch for something. They were standing by the cross. I went towards them, just two steps. —Lord! there be these lads starting off at full speed towards here. I didn't wait: not me. I picked up my lantern and I said: I be off to tell M. Seurel of this . . .'

And once more he begins his story. 'I was in my yard at the back of my place . . .' So we offer him a drink, which he accepts, and we ask him details which he cannot give.

He had seen nothing on reaching our house. All the bands, warned by the two sentries whom he had disturbed, had at once vanished. As for knowing who the rascals could be . . .

'Gipsies, quite likely,' he suggested. 'For a month they've been about in the square waiting for fine weather to give us a play, and must have been hatching some mischief.'

This did not help us much, and we all stood there very puzzled while the man sipped his drink and once more started his story, when Meaulnes, who so far had listened attentively, took the butcher's lantern from the floor and exclaimed: 'We must go and see!'

He opened the door and we followed him, M. Seurel, M. Pasquier, and myself.

Millie, quite herself again after the attackers' departure, and, like all orderly and careful people, very uninquisitive by nature, said: 'Well, go if you like, but close the door and take the key. As for me, I am going to bed; I'll leave the lamp burning.'

We went out over the snow in absolute silence.
Meaulnes walked ahead, raying out the light from his
storm lamp, like a fan. We had scarcely set foot outside
the big gate when two figures in hoods sprang up like
startled partridges from behind the town weighing-
machine. Either to cheek us, or from pleasure at the
game they were up to there, or from nervousness and
fear of being caught, they spoke a few words and laughed
as they ran away.

Meaulnes dropped his lantern in the snow, calling
out:

'Follow me, François! . . .'

And leaving behind the two elderly men who could
not stand the pace, we rushed in pursuit of the two
shadows, who, after skirting the lower part of the village
by the Old Plank Road, deliberately went back towards
the church. They ran steadily, without hurrying, and we
kept up with them easily. They crossed Church Street,
where all was asleep and silent, and passed into a maze
of by-streets and blind alleys at the back of the church-
yard.

This was the quarter of the journeymen, sempstresses,
and weavers known as 'The Nookery.' We did not know
it well and we had never been there at night. The place
was deserted in the daytime: the journeymen being
away, the weavers working indoors; and during this night
of absolute silence it appeared even more forsaken, more
asleep than other parts of the village. So there was no
possible chance of any one unexpectedly coming to lend
us a hand.

I knew only one way amongst these small houses, scattered about at random like cardboard boxes, and that was the one leading to the dressmaker known as the 'Dumb Girl.' You had to go down a rather steep slope paved here and there; then, taking two or three turns amongst weavers' back yards and empty stables, you came to a wide blind alley closed up by a farmyard long since deserted. I used to visit the Dumb Girl with my mother, and while they talked on silently with flashing fingers and grunts common to people with her affliction, I could look out from the window at the high wall of the farm—the last house on that side of the village—and the closed gate of a disused yard destitute of straw, where nothing ever passed by . . .

That is exactly the way the two unknown persons took. At each turning we feared to lose them, but, to my surprise, we always reached the corner of the next alley before they had left it. I say to my surprise, because this could not possibly have been done, so short were these alleys, had they not slowed down whenever we were out of sight.

At last, without hesitating, they took the street leading to the Dumb Girl's, and I called out to Meaulnes: 'We've got them. It is a blind alley!'

The truth is, they had got us . . . They had led us exactly where they wanted. When they reached the wall, they resolutely turned on us, and one of them let out that shrill whistle which we had already heard twice during the evening.

At once a dozen fellows came out of the abandoned farmyard where they had apparently been posted to await us. They had pulled their hoods over their heads and hidden their faces in their scarves.

We knew beforehand who they were, but we had decided not to tell M. Seurel, as our affairs were not his concern. There were Delouche, Denis, Giraudat, and all the others. We recognised each one during the skirmish by his way of fighting and by snatches of talk. But one

worrying thing remained and seemed almost to frighten
Meaulnes: some one was with them whom we did not
know and who seemed to be their leader . . .

He never touched Meaulnes: he watched the work
of his men, who, being dragged in the snow and their
clothes torn, had all they could do to tackle the great
breathless chap. A couple of them had gone for me, and
had had a job to put me out, as I fought like a demon.
I was on the ground, knees bent, sitting on my heels;
they twisted my arms behind my back, and I watched
it all with intense curiosity mingled with terror.

Meaulnes shook off four top-form boys by twisting
violently round on himself and throwing them headlong
into the snow . . . And the Unknown, standing very
straight, followed the fight with interest, but perfect
calm, saying now and again in a clear voice: 'Go on . . .
Courage . . . Once more . . . Go on, my boys . . .'

Obviously he was in command . . . Where had he
sprung from? Where and how had he trained them for
the fight? This remained a mystery to us. His face, like
the others', was hidden in a scarf, but when Meaulnes
shook off his adversaries and advanced towards him, the
gesture the Unknown made to see clearly and face the
position, exposed some white linen with which his head
was swathed as in a bandage.

At this moment I cried out to Meaulnes: 'Look out
behind! There's another.'

He had scarcely turned round when a lanky fellow,
springing from the gate at Meaulnes' back, cleverly
twisted a scarf around my friend's neck and threw him
backward. At once the four boys who had fallen in the
snow came back to the fray to pin Meaulnes down, ty-
ing his arms with a cord, his legs with a scarf, while the
young man with the bandaged head searched his
pockets . . .

The late comer, the thrower of the lasso, had lit a
small candle which he protected with his hand, and at

each find of some new piece of paper the leader went to this light to examine what it contained. He, at last, unfolded the kind of map covered with inscriptions at which Meaulnes had worked since his return, and exclaimed with glee: 'This time we've got it! There's the plan! That's the guide! We are going to see if this gentleman has really been where I imagine.'

His accomplice blew out the candle. Each one picked up his cap or his belt. And all disappeared as silently as they had come, leaving me free to hasten to release my friend.

'He won't go far with that plan,' said Meaulnes, rising on his feet.

And we went off slowly, as he walked rather lame. In Church Street we came upon M. Seurel and M. Pasquier.

'You didn't see anything, I bet!' they said . . . 'Neither did we.'

Thanks to the pitch darkness they noticed nothing queer. The butcher left us and M. Seurel went in quickly and then to bed.

But once upstairs in our room, by the light of the lamp which Millie had left us, we both remained a long time mending our overalls and quietly discussing all that had happened, like two brothers in arms on the evening of a lost battle . . .

Waking up next morning was painful. At half-past eight, just as M. Seurel was giving the signal to enter school, we arrived, quite out of breath, to line up. As we were late, we crept in wherever we could, though generally, during M. Seurel's inspection, Admiral Meaulnes headed the long row of boys who stood elbow to elbow, loaded with lesson-books and pencil-boxes.

It surprised me to see the silent alacrity which every one displayed to make room for us in the middle of the column; and while M. Seurel delayed opening school by a few seconds to inspect Meaulnes, I inquisitively looked around to right and left to see the faces of our enemies of the previous day.

The first one I noticed was that same fellow who had been in my mind ever since, but who was the very last person I expected to see here. He was in Meaulnes' usual place, at the head, one foot on the stone step, one shoulder and the corner of the satchel he carried on his back, resting against the doorpost. His fine face, very pale and slightly freckled, was turned towards us with a sort of disdainful and amused interest. The top of his head and one side of his face were bandaged in white linen. I recognised the leader of the gang, the young bohemian who had robbed us on the preceding night.

But we were now entering the classroom and each one took his seat. The new pupil sat close to the pillar, on the left of the long bench where Meaulnes occupied the first seat on the right. Giraudat, Delouche, and the three other first-bench boys sat quite close to each other to make room for him, as if this had been arranged beforehand . . .

The winter often brought us in this way casual pupils, lads in apprenticeship, sons of bargees held up by the ice on the canal, or of pedlars delayed by the snow. They remained at school from two days to a month, rarely more . . . Objects of great interest at first, they were soon unheeded and quickly forgotten in the crowd of ordinary pupils.

But this one was not to be forgotten so soon. I still remember that strange fellow and the queer treasures he used to bring, in the satchel strapped on his back. First there were 'sight-seeing' penholders which he took out to write his dictation with. Through a peephole in the handle, by shutting one eye you could see the church of Lourdes or some unknown building, dim and magnified. He chose one, and the others passed from hand to hand. Then came a Chinese pencil-box, full of compasses and exciting implements which travelled along the bench on the left, being silently and furtively thrust on from hand to hand under the desks, so that M. Seurel might not see.

Then came round some perfectly new books, the titles of which I had often read with longing on the covers of the few books in our library: 'The Blackbirds on the Heath,' 'The Seagull's Rock,' 'My Friend Benedict.' . . . Some of the boys, resting a story-book on their knees, used one hand to turn over the pages of these volumes procured no one knew how, probably by theft, and with the other hand wrote their dictation. Others played with compasses inside their lockers. Others, while M. Seurel's back was turned and he dictated walking from desk to window, quickly closed one eye and applied the other to the greenish hollow view of Notre Dame of Paris. And the unknown pupil, pen in air and his refined profile outlined against the grey pillar, winked his eyes, happy at all the furtive play which had started around him.

Little by little, however, the class became anxious:

the objects which were passed round had one by one
come to Meaulnes' hands, but absent-mindedly and
without looking at them, he carelessly placed them by
his side. They soon mounted up to an angular and di-
versely coloured heap such as may be seen at the feet
of the woman symbolising Science in allegorical pictures.
M. Seurel would inevitably discover this unusual display and notice the game. Then he would remember
to inquire into the events of the night. The presence of
the bohemian would facilitate his task.

Soon, indeed, he stopped, surprised, in front of Admiral Meaulnes.

'To whom does all this belong?' he asked, pointing to
'all this' with the back of the book folded over his fore-
finger.

'I don't know,' replied Meaulnes surlily and without
raising his head.

But the unknown pupil intervened. 'They are mine,'
he said.

And at once he added, with a young aristocrat's ease
and freedom of manner which the old schoolmaster
could not resist: 'But I place them at your disposal, sir,
if you wish to look at them.'

Then, in a few seconds, without any noise, as if not to
disturb the new atmosphere just created, the whole class
gathered inquisitively around the master whose head,
half bald, half curly, bowed over the treasures, while the
pale youth, serenely triumphant in the middle of the
group, gave all necessary explanations. Meanwhile,
seated silently at his desk and completely forsaken, Admiral Meaulnes had opened his rough notebook and
with brow knitted was absorbed in a difficult problem . . .

The 'last quarter' found us thus occupied. The dictation was not finished and disorder reigned in the class-

room. To tell the truth, it had been recreation all the morning.

So, at half-past ten, when the dark and muddy playground became invaded by the pupils, a new leader was soon observed to be running the games.

Of all the new plays which the bohemian introduced amongst us that morning, I remember only the most violent: a sort of tournament where the bigger boys were horses with the younger ones hoisted on their shoulders.[1]

Divided into two camps at either end of the playground, they charged each other, seeking to upset the enemy by the force of the shock, and the cavaliers using scarves as lassos or their outstretched arms as spears, tried to unhorse their opponents. Sometimes the charge was dodged, and the cavalier, losing his balance, was sent sprawling in the mud under his mount. Some fellows, half dismounted, were kept up by the horse gripping their legs; they scrambled up again and charged into the fray. The slim cavalier with the bandaged head, mounted on Delage, who had lanky limbs, red hair, and flapping ears, urged on the two rival troops and steered his mount adroitly, shouting with laughter. At first Augustin, in a bad temper, watched from the classroom step as this play started. And I was waiting by his side, uncertain.

'He's a clever rascal,' he said between his teeth, his hands in his pockets. 'To come here the very next morning, that was the only way to avoid suspicion. And M. Seurel got taken in!'

---

[1]Nowhere but in France would this game be played by boys over twelve or thirteen. This is another detail so typically French that it may mislead the reader as to the ages of these boys. As will be seen in a subsequent chapter, Delouche is now seventeen and Meaulnes eighteen. Such games, until recently, took in French school life the place of football and were apt to be played with the same violence.

He remained there a long while, his cropped head bare, fuming at the comedian who would bring to some harm these lads of whom, not so long ago, he, Meaulnes, was the captain. And I, peaceful youngster as I was, entirely agreed with him.

Everywhere on the playground, in the absence of M. Seurel, the fight went on: the smaller boys had now climbed on each other's backs; they were running and tumbling about even before they received the enemy's charge. . . . Soon, in the middle of the playground, there remained only one savage whirling group out of which emerged, now and again, the white bandage of the new leader.

Then Admiral Meaulnes could no longer keep back. Lowering his head and placing his hands on his thighs, he called out: 'Now for it, François!'

Surprised at this sudden decision, I none the less jumped upon his shoulders without a moment's hesitation, and in a second we were in the thick of the fray, while most of the combatants, scared, fled away shouting: 'There's Meaulnes! There's Admiral Meaulnes!'

He began to turn sharply round among those who remained, saying to me: 'Reach out your arms: collar 'em as I did last night.'

And I, intoxicated by the fray and certain of victory, gripped the youngsters as they went by; they struggled a little on the big boys' shoulders, then toppled off into the mud. In less than no time only the newcomer on Delage remained unthrown; but the latter, not too keen to stand up to Augustin, pulled himself up with a violent jerk of the hips and forced the white rider to dismount . . .

Thus dismounted, the young fellow, with one hand on his mount's shoulder as a captain holds his horse's bridle, looked at Admiral Meaulnes with some astonishment and immense admiration.

'Good work!' he said.

But at that very moment the bell rang, dispersing the pupils who had crowded round us in expectation of a queer scene. And Meaulnes, vexed at not having thrown his enemy, turned upon his heels saying with some temper: 'Next time you're in for it!'

Up to noon the class went on as at the end of the term, full of comic incidents and chat, the centre of which was the pupil-comedian.

He explained that, being held up by the cold on the square and not even dreaming of arranging evening shows to which no one would come, they had decided he should go to school to amuse himself during the daytime, while his companion looked after the tropical birds and the performing goat. Then he related their wanderings in the neighbourhood, when the rain pelts on the wretched tin roof of the caravan and you have to get out on steep hills and put your shoulder to the wheel. The pupils at the back of the room left their bench to come nearer and listen. The less romantic took that chance of warming themselves at the stove. But soon curiosity got the better of them, and they also drew near the chatting throng to listen, keeping one hand on the top of the stove not to lose their place by it.

'And what do you live on?' asked M. Seurel, who had followed the proceedings with the rather childish curiosity of a schoolmaster and was asking a lot of questions.

The youth hesitated a moment as if he had never bothered about that detail.

'Well,' he replied, 'on what we earned last autumn, I suppose. It's Booby who keeps the accounts.'

No one asked him who Booby was. But I thought of the tall rascal who, on the previous evening, had treacherously attacked Meaulnes from behind and thrown him.

During the afternoon the same distractions occurred
again; all through every class disorder persisted and the
same trickery. The bohemian produced other exciting
things: shells, games, songs, and even a little monkey
who stealthily scratched inside his satchel. . . . At every moment M. Seurel was obliged to interrupt work to
inspect something the clever rogue had pulled out of
his bag. . . . Four o'clock came and Meaulnes was the
only one to have finished his problems.

No one was in a hurry to leave. It seemed as if, between school hours and recreation, there no longer existed that sharp distinction which renders school life as
simple and as regular as the succession of night and
day. We even forgot to tell M. Seurel, as we usually did
about four o'clock, the names of the two boys who had
to stay to sweep the room. Yet we had never before failed
to do so, as it was a way of announcing the end of school
and hastening it.

As luck would have it, that day it was Meaulnes'
turn; and that very morning, while talking with him, I
had warned the bohemian that newcomers as a matter
of course were always appointed second sweeper on the
day of their arrival.

Meaulnes came back to the classroom as soon as he
had fetched his bread for the usual four o'clock snack.
But we had to wait a long time for the bohemian; he
arrived at last, running, just as night was falling . . .

'Stop in the form-room,' my friend had said to me,
'and while I hold him, you must bag that plan he stole.'

So I sat down on a small table, close to the window, and read by the last glimmer of daylight, while I saw them both silently shifting the school benches—Admiral Meaulnes glum and cross, his black overall well buttoned up at the back and tightly belted at the waist; the other delicate and nervous, his head bandaged up like a wounded soldier. He wore an old jacket which showed tears I had not noticed during the day. Full of a sort of savage zeal, he lifted and pushed the desks in feverish haste, smiling a little. You would have said he was playing some queer game, the secret of which escaped us.

Thus they reached the darkest corner of the room, to move the last desk.

At that spot Meaulnes could have knocked down his adversary at one blow and no one outside could have seen or heard anything through the window. I could not understand why he missed such a chance. The other fellow, back at the door, could at any moment escape, pretending the work was finished, and we should never see him again. The map and all the information which Meaulnes had taken such a time to discover, to unravel and piece together, would be lost for us . . .

At any moment I was expecting a signal from my friend, a gesture warning me of the start of the fight, but the big schoolboy did not stir. Now and again, however, he fixed strange questioning eyes on the bohemian's bandage which, in the falling light, appeared profusely stained with black spots.

The last desk was moved without anything happening.

But at the moment when both were going up the classroom about to end their job by sweeping the threshold, Meaulnes lowered his head, and without looking at our enemy said in a low voice: 'Your bandage is red with blood and your clothes are torn.'

The other looked at him a moment, not surprised at what he said, but deeply moved at hearing him say it.

'A little while ago, on the square,' he replied, 'they
tried to take your plan away from me. When they heard
that I wanted to come back here to sweep, they understood that I was going to make peace with you and they
all went for me. But still, I did save it,' he added proudly,
holding forth to Meaulnes the precious folded paper.

Meaulnes slowly turned towards me.

'You hear?' he said. 'He's just been fighting and getting hurt on our account, while we were laying a trap
for him!'

He spoke rather formally, but then, throwing aside all
ceremony, unusual with the boys at Sainte-Agathe:
'You are a good chap,' he said, and held out his hand.

The comedian took hold of it and for a second remained speechless, very much moved, words failing him
. . . But soon, keenly interested, he went on:

'And so you laid a trap for me! What a lark! I'd
guessed it and I was thinking: Won't they be surprised,
when they get back their plan to see that I've completed
it . . .'

'Completed it?'

'Hold hard! Not entirely . . .'

Leaving off this flippant manner, he added gravely
and slowly, coming nearer to us:

'Meaulnes, it's time to tell you: I, too, have been
where you went. I was present at that extraordinary
fête. It occurred to me, when the other boys told me
about your mysterious adventure, that it concerned the
old forsaken manor. To make sure of it I stole your map.
But, like you, I don't know the name of the manor; I
couldn't go back to it; I don't know the whole of the
way to it from here.'

With what eagerness, with what intense curiosity,
with what friendliness we drew close to him! Greedily
Meaulnes put questions to him . . . It seemed to us both
that we could, by ardent pressure, make our new friend
say even what he pretended not to know.

'You'll see, you'll see!' replied the young fellow, rather disturbed and embarrassed. 'I've put on the plan a few indications you hadn't got . . . That's all I could do.'

Then, seeing us full of admiration and enthusiasm: 'Oh!' said he sadly but proudly, 'I'd better warn you: I'm not like other chaps. Three months ago I tried to blow my brains out, and that accounts for this bandage on my forehead like a soldier of 1870 . . .'

'And this evening, as you fought, the wound reopened,' said Meaulnes with friendliness.

But, taking no notice, the other went on in a voice slightly emphatic: 'I wanted to die. And as I didn't manage it, I shall go on living, but only for fun, like a child, like a gipsy. I've left everything behind. I have neither father, sister, home, nor sweetheart . . . Nothing left, only playfellows!'

'And these playfellows have already betrayed you,' I said.

'Yes!' he replied, with animation. 'That's because of that fellow Delouche. He guessed that I was going to side with you. He demoralised my men, whom I had so well in hand. Look at the boarding of this house last night; wasn't it well managed? Didn't it come off well? Never, since I was a child, have I organised anything so successfully . . .'

He was for a moment lost in thought; then he added, so as to leave us no illusions about himself: 'The reason I came to you both this evening is that—I was sure of it this morning—there is more fun to be got with you than with the whole gang of the others. That Delouche above all is hateful to me. Why play the man at seventeen? Nothing sickens me more . . . Do you think we can catch him out again?'

'Of course,' said Meaulnes. 'But are you stopping with us long?'

'I don't know, I'd love to. I am terribly lonely. I've only Booby.'

His excitement, his gaiety suddenly vanished. For a moment he fell into the same despair in which no doubt, one day, the idea of killing himself had overcome him. 'Be my friends,' he said suddenly. 'Look: I know your secret and I've kept it from everybody. I can put you back on the track you have lost . . .'

And he added, almost solemnly: 'Be my friends in readiness for the day when I shall be again within a hairbreadth of hell, as I have already been . . . Give me your word that you will come to me if ever you hear me call—when I shall call like this—(he uttered a queer call: Hou-ou!) . . . You, Meaulnes swear to it first.'

And we swore to it because, as we were only children, all that was serious and solemn beyond reason strangely attracted us.

'In exchange,' he said, 'this is all I can tell you now: I'll tell you the house in Paris where the young lady of the manor usually goes to spend the holidays: Easter and Whitsun, the month of June and sometimes part of the winter.'

At that moment, from the big gate, an unknown voice called many times in the darkness. We guessed it was Booby, the bohemian, who dared not or did not know how to cross the playground. His insistent, anxious voice was calling, sometimes very loud, sometimes almost in whispers: 'Hou-ou! Hou-ou!'

'Tell it! Tell it quick!' called out Meaulnes to the young bohemian who had started up and was readjusting his clothes to go.

The young fellow rapidly gave us an address in Paris, which we repeated in whispers. Then, running out into the night to join his companion at the gate, he left us in a state of inexpressible agitation.

That night, about three o'clock, the innkeeper widow
Delouche, who lived in the middle of the village, got up
to light her fire. Her brother-in-law Dumas, who lived
with her, had to start at four, and the sad-looking woman,
whose right hand bore the shrivelled scar of an old burn,
was hurrying to make coffee in the dark kitchen. It was
cold. She threw an old shawl over her night camisole,
then holding a lighted candle in one hand and with her
scarred hand raising her apron to shelter the flame, she
crossed the yard littered with empty bottles and pack-
ing-cases, and opened the door of the shed, which was
also used as a chicken-run, to get her kindling . . . But
she had hardly pushed the door ajar, when some one
sprang from the darkness, extinguished the candle with
a blow of his cap, and with the same blow knocked over
the good woman, then took to his heels while the terrified cocks and hens set up an infernal row.

The man was carrying away in a sack—as widow
Delouche realised a moment later when she regained her
balance—a dozen of her finest chickens.

At the cries of his sister-in-law, Dumas ran up. He
discovered that the scamp, to get in, must have opened
the gate of the small yard with a skeleton key, and that
he had escaped by the same way, without shutting it
again. At once, being accustomed to poachers and
thieves, Dumas lighted his cart-lamp and carrying it in
one hand with his loaded gun in the other, proceeded
to follow the track of the thief, a very faint trail—the
fellow most likely wore sand-shoes—which led to the
Station Road, then disappeared at the gate of a meadow.
Obliged to leave his search at this, he looked up, stopped

. . . and heard in the distance, on the same road, the noise of a cart going at full gallop, evidently running off . . .

For his part, Jasmin Delouche, the widow's son, had also got up, and hastening to throw his hooded cloak on his shoulders, had gone out in his slippers to inspect the village. Everything was asleep, everywhere reigned darkness and the deep silence which precede the first glimmer of dawn. Reaching the Cross-Roads he heard in the distance—as his uncle had—only the noise of a cart with the horse apparently at full gallop. The wily and cowardly boy then said to himself, as he later repeated it to us with that unbearable thick pronunciation peculiar to Montluçon: 'They've gone towards the station, but who knows if I mayn't catch others, red-handed, the other side of the village!'

And he walked back towards the church in the silence of the night.

On the square, a light shone in the gipsies' caravan. Somebody must be ill. He was going to draw near and ask what had happened when a silent shadow, a shadow walking in sand-shoes, emerged from the Nookery and heeding nothing else rushed at full speed towards the steps of the van.

Jasmin, who had recognised the gait of Booby, came forth suddenly into the patch of light and asked in a low voice: 'Well! What's the matter?'

Haggard, dishevelled, toothless, the fellow stopped, looked at Delouche with a wretched grin caused by fear and lack of breath and replied in a jerky voice: 'It is my friend who's ill. . . . He had a fight last night and his wound's reopened . . . I've just been to fetch the nurse.'

As a matter of fact, about the middle of the village, as Jasmin Delouche, sorely puzzled, was going home to bed, he met a Sister of Mercy who was hurrying.

In the morning several inhabitants of Sainte-Agathe

appeared on their doorsteps with heavy eyes tired by a
sleepless night. There was a general cry of indignation
which spread through the village like a trail of gun-
powder.

At Giraudat's, a cart had stopped about 2 A.M. and
had been loaded with parcels which fell in softly. There
were only two women in the house and they had not
dared to move. At daybreak they had realised, on opening the yard gate, that the parcels in question were
rabbits and poultry. Millie, during the first recreation,
found several burnt matches outside the wash-house
door. We came to the conclusion that the thieves did
not know our house and had not been able to break in
. . . At Perreux's, at Boujardon's, and at Clément's it
was at first supposed that pigs even had been stolen,
but these were found during the morning busily up-
rooting greens in several gardens. The whole herd had
seized the chance of the opened gate to take a little
nocturnal outing . . . Nearly everywhere poultry had
been carried away, but that was all. Madame Pignot,
the baker-woman, who did not rear chickens, complained
loudly during all that day, that her washing-board and a
pound of rinsing blue had been stolen from her, but the
deed was never proved and never entered in the records
of the case . . .

This agitation, these fears, this gossip lasted the whole
morning. In class, Jasmin related his night adventure.

'Ah! they're clever beggars,' he said. 'But if Uncle had
met one of them, he says he'd 'ave shot him like a
rabbit!'

And he added, looking at us: 'What luck it is he
didn't meet Booby; he'd sure enough have fired. They
all be one gang, he says, and Dessaigne said the same.

Yet no one thought about disturbing our new friends.
It was only the next day in the evening that Jasmin re-
marked to his uncle that Booby and their thief both
wore sand-shoes. Then they agreed that this fact was

worth mentioning to the police. So they decided, in great secrecy, to go, when they had a moment, to the chief town of the district and inform the head constable.

During the following days the young bohemian, still ill with his wound, did not appear. Every evening we went prowling on the church square merely to watch his lamp behind the caravan's red curtain. Feverish with anxiety we stood there, not daring to draw near this humble abode which seemed to us the magic portal of the Land to which we had lost the way.

chapter 6

A QUARREL BEHIND THE
SCENES

The numerous disturbances and troubles of these last
days prevented us from noticing that March had come
and that the wind had softened. But one morning, three
days after our adventure, as I went down into the playground, I suddenly realised that it was spring. A breeze,
delicious as cool water, blew over the wall; the silent rain
of the night had moistened the leaves of the peonies;
a rich pervasive smell rose from the freshly turned soil
in the garden, and in the tree close to the window, I
heard a bird which was trying to learn music . . .

Meaulnes, during the first recreation, spoke of attempting to find at once the way which the bohemian
boy had outlined. With difficulty I persuaded him to
wait until we had, once more, seen our friend, until the
weather was really fine . . . and the plum trees in bloom
at Sainte-Agathe. We talked leaning against the low wall
of the narrow lane, hands in pockets, bareheaded, while
the wind sometimes made us shiver with cold, and at
other times, with warm puffs, awoke some deep urge
within us. Ah! friend, brother, fellow-traveller, how convinced we both were that happiness was close, and that
we had only to set out to reach it! . . .

At half-past twelve, during dinner, we heard the rolling of a drum at the Cross-Roads. In the twinkling of an
eye, we were all at the small gate, napkins in hand. . . .
It was Booby announcing for that evening at eight
o'clock, 'in view of the fine weather,' a great performance on the church square. At all events, 'to run no risks
in case of rain,' a tent would be erected. Then followed

a long programme of attractions which the wind prevented us from catching except such words as 'dumb
show . . . songs . . . riding displays . . .' the whole
thing punctuated by renewed rolling of the drum.

During the evening meal the big drum announced
the show and thundered under our windows, making the
panes rattle. Soon after people of the village passed by,
with a buzz of talk, going in small groups towards the
church. And there we were both of us, forced to remain
at the table, though burning with impatience!

At last, about nine, we heàrd a scraping of shoes and
stifled laughter at the small gate: the women teachers
had come to fetch us. In the pitch darkness, our little
party made its way towards the show. We could see
from afar, the church wall brightly lit up, as if by a big
fire. Two naphtha flares swung in the wind at the door
of the tent . . .

Inside, benches were arranged in tiers as at a circus.
M. Seurel, the women teachers, Meaulnes and myself
took our places on the lowest of these. I recall the place,
which must have been rather small, as a real circus, with
its wide dark stretches of rising seats, where could be
seen Madame Pignot, the baker-woman; Fernande, from
the grocer shop; the girls from the village; the appren-
tices from the forges; ladies, urchins, country folks, and
every sort of people.

The show was more than half through. In the arena, a
small goat was performing, standing obediently on four
glasses, then on two, then on one alone. Booby was gently
directing her with little taps from a switch, but all the
while looking at us in a worried way, his mouth gaping,
his eyes dead.

Seated on a stool, near two other flares, and at the
place where the arena was connected with the caravan,
was a fellow with bandaged head, wearing elegant black
tights, whom we recognised as the leading man and our
friend.

Scarcely were we seated when a pony, fully harnessed, pranced onto the track. He was several times led around the arena by the wounded comedian, and invariably stopped in front of one of us when asked to find the most charming person or the bravest in the audience, but always pointed to Madame Pignot when he had to spot who told the greatest lies, or was the most avaricious or 'the most in love' . . . And all round the lady, there were shrieks of laughter, screams and cackling, as when a flock of geese is chased by a spaniel! . . .

At the interval, the leading man came to have a chat with M. Seurel, who could not have felt more proud had a Talma or a Léotard spoken to him; as for us, we listened with eager interest to what the comedian was saying: first about his wound—now closed up; then regarding this show—rehearsed during the long days of winter; then concerning their departure—which was not to be before the end of the month, for they meant to give other variety shows up to then.

The performance was to finish up with an elaborate dumb show.

Towards the end of the interval, our friend left us, and to reach the caravan's steps was obliged to go through a group of people who had invaded the arena, in the midst of which we suddenly noticed Jasmin Delouche. The women and the girls got out of the way. The black costume, the strange but gallant figure of the wounded man, had won their hearts. As for Jasmin, who appeared to be coming back from a long journey and was talking in a low but animated voice to Madame Pignot, he would evidently have found the local costume with the low collar, the bow of silken cord, and the elephant-like trousers, more to his taste . . . Both thumbs raised to the lapel of his jacket, he stood in a very affected and uneasy attitude. Out of spite, as the bohemian went by, he said aloud to Madame Pignot a few words I did not catch, but which were certainly an

offensive remark, an insult meant for our friend. It must
have been a serious and unexpected threat, for the young
fellow could not help turning round and looking at the
other, who, to carry it through, grinned and poked his
neighbours in the ribs as if to bring them onto his side
. . . All this happened in a few seconds. I was perhaps
the only one on our bench to notice it.

The leading man joined his companion behind the
curtain which hid the door of the caravan. All went
back to their seats, thinking that the second part of the
show would soon begin, and great silence ensued. Then,
from behind the curtain, while the last whispered conversations were fading away, rose the noise of a quarrel.
We could not hear what was being said, but we recognised the two voices as those of the tall man and the
young fellow—the first explaining and justifying; the
other scolding with both indignation and sadness.

'But you wretch!' the latter was saying; 'why didn't
you tell me? . . .'

And we heard nothing further, though every one was
listening. Then, suddenly, all was quiet. The dispute
went on in whispers; and urchins at the top rows began
to call out: 'Curtain! Curtain!' and stamped their feet.

At last, peering in slowly between the curtains, a face
emerged, furrowed by wrinkles, expanding in a grin both
of mirth and distress, and bespeckled with black
patches; there followed the figure of a lanky Pierrot made
of three badly jointed parts, screwed up by some awful
colic, who, with excess of caution and fear, advanced on
tiptoes, his hands entangled in long dangling sleeves
which swept the track.

I could not to-day reconstruct the plot of his dumb
show. I remember only that, as soon as he entered the
arena, in spite of vain and hopeless efforts to keep his
feet, he fell. It was useless getting up again; he could
not help it; he fell. He never ceased falling. He entangled himself in between four chairs all at once. He
dragged after him, in his fall, a huge table which had
been brought into the arena. At last he managed to meas-
ure his length beyond the barrier, at the very feet of the
spectators. Two handy men, enticed with much trouble
out of the audience, then dragged him by the feet and
after tremendous efforts stood him up. And at each fall
he uttered a little scream, each time different, a little
unbearable scream, in which distress and satisfaction
had an equal share. At the climax, perched on a scaffold-
ing of chairs, he dropped in a very long slow fall, and his
piercing, melancholy hoot of triumph lasted as long as
the fall and was mingled with shrieks of fear from the
women.

During the second part of his show, though I do not
know why, I recall 'poor wobby Pierrot' producing a lit-

tle sawdust doll from his sleeves and acting with her a
long tragi-comical scene. He ended it all by emptying
the sawdust of her body out of her mouth. Then, with
little pitiful cries, he filled her with porridge, and at the
moment when all were attentive and the gaping spectators had their eyes fixed on Pierrot's daughter, bursting
and sticky—suddenly catching hold of her by one arm,
he hurled her flying across the audience at the face of
Jasmin Delouche whose ear she messed before she
landed on Madame Pignot's bosom, just under that
lady's chin. The baker-woman shrieked so loud, drew herself back so sharply, and all her neighbours imitated her
so well that the bench broke and the baker-woman,
Fernande, sad widow Delouche, and twenty others tumbled down, legs in the air, amidst laughter, shrieks, and
clapping, while the tall clown, who had fallen on his
face, got up to bow and say:

'Now, Ladies and Gentlemen, we beg to thank you
for your kind attention!'

But at that very moment and in the midst of the uproar, Admiral Meaulnes, who had kept silent since the
beginning of the dumb show, and seemed every moment
more absorbed, hastily got up and clinging to my arm, as
if unable to contain himself, said aloud to me: 'Look at
the bohemian! Look! Now, I recognise him.'

Even before looking, as if all the while, subcon-
sciously, this thought had been dormant in me, only
awaiting the moment to dawn, I too had guessed! Standing by one of the naphtha flares, at the door of the
caravan, the young unknown actor had taken off his
bandage and thrown a cloak over his shoulders. One
could see by the smoking flare, as once by candlelight in
the room at the manor, the clean-shaven features, very
fine and aquiline. Pale, his lips half open, he was hastily
turning over the leaves of a small red album, most likely
a pocket atlas. Except for a scar cutting across his temple
and disappearing under the mass of hair, it was, just as

Admiral Meaulnes had minutely described him to me, the fiancé from the unknown manor.

It was evident that he had taken off his bandage to be recognised by us. But scarcely had Meaulnes made his gesture and uttered his cry than the young man went into the caravan after giving us a knowing look and smiling with vague sadness, as he usually smiled. 'And the other!' said Meaulnes with excitement; 'how was it I didn't recognise him straightaway! He is the Pierrot of the fête, out there . . .'

And he walked down the tiers to go towards him. But already Booby had cut off all access to the track and, one by one, was putting out the four flares; we were obliged to follow the crowd, which in the dim light, and through the narrow channels of the parallel benches, streamed slowly out while we stamped about with impatience.

When at last Admiral Meaulnes was outside, he hastened to the caravan, rushed up the steps, and knocked at the door, but all was already secured for the night. Already, no doubt, in the van with the curtains as well as in the one reserved for the pony, the goat, and the performing birds, every one was tucked up and falling asleep.

chapter 8. THE POLICE

We were obliged to join again the throng of people
who were going through the dark streets towards the
Higher Elementary School. But now we understood
everything. The tall white shadow which Meaulnes had
seen hurrying amongst the trees, on the last evening of
the fête, was Booby, who, having rescued the disconso-
late financé, was running away with him. The latter had
accepted this wild life, full of risks, games, and adventures. It had seemed to him like starting his childhood
over again . . .

Frantz de Galais had, so far, hidden his name from us
and pretended not to know the way to the manor, for
fear of being forced to go back home; but why had he,
this evening, suddenly wished to reveal himself, letting
us guess the whole truth? . . .

No end of plans went through Admiral Meaulnes'
head while the crowd slowly dispersed across the village.
He decided that early next day, which was a Thursday,
he would go to see Frantz, and together they would start
for that place! What a lovely journey on the dewy road!
Frantz would explain everything; all would be put right,
and the glorious adventure would begin again from
where it left off . . .

As for me, that night, I walked with an indescribable
elation of heart. Everything contributed to my joy,
from the paltry pleasure of awaiting the Thursday holiday to the great discovery we had just made and the fine
piece of luck befalling us. And I remember that, with
sudden generosity of heart, I went up to the ugliest of
the notary's daughters, to whom I was often forced to

offer my arm, and spontaneously held my hand out to
her.

Bitter memories! Great hopes crushed!

The next day at eight o'clock, as we both emerged on
the church square, our shoes well polished, the buckles
of our belts shining bright, and our caps brand-new,
Meaulnes, who so far had repressed a smile whenever he
looked at me, gave a shout and rushed towards the
empty square . . . At the place where the tent and the
vans had stood were only a broken jug and some rags.
The gipsies had gone! . . .

A light wind was blowing which felt icy to us. It
seemed as if at every step we were about to stumble and
fall on the hard stony ground of the square. Meaulnes,
enraged, twice made as if he would rush off, first along
the road to Vieux-Nançay, then along the road to Saint-
Loup-des-Bois. One hand over his eyes, he scanned the
neighbourhood hoping our people had only just started.
But what could be done? The tracks of a dozen vehicles
were all mixed up on the square and then effaced on the
hard road. We were stuck there, powerless.

And as we were coming back across the village where
the life of a Thursday morning was beginning, four
mounted policemen, warned the evening before by
Delouche, arrived at a gallop on the square and scattered in the by-streets to block all issues, exactly as a
patrol of dragoons sent to reconnoitre a village . . . But
it was too late. Booby, the chicken-snatcher, had escaped
with his companion. The policemen found nobody,
neither Booby himself nor the fellows who had loaded
the carts with the birds he had strangled. Warned in
time by the incautious remark of Jasmin, Frantz must
have suddenly understood what trade kept his companion and himself alive when the cash-box was empty;
full of shame and anger, he had at once mapped out the
route and decided to make off before the police came.
But, no longer fearing to be taken back to his father, he

had shown himself to us without a bandage before he disappeared.

One thing alone remained a puzzle: how could Booby both rob the poultry-yards and at once fetch the nun for his feverish friend? But did not that sum up the whole story of the poor devil? Thief and tramp on the one hand, a kind-hearted chap on the other . . .

chapter 9. IN SEARCH OF THE LOST TRAIL

The sun was breaking through the morning mist on our return: housewives were shaking carpets or chatting in front of their doors: the loveliest spring morning my memory can recall was beginning in the fields and woods round the village.

All the big boys of the top form had been told to come about eight that Thursday morning to prepare, some for Matriculation, others for the Entrance Examination to Training College. When we arrived together—Meaulnes so full of regret and uneasiness that he could not keep still, myself very depressed—the school was empty . . . A ray of bright sunlight was glinting on the dust of a worm-eaten bench and the peeling varnish of the globe.

How could we stop there in front of a book, to brood over our disappointment, when everything was calling us out-of-doors: birds chasing one another in the branches close to the windows, the other boys gone off to the woods and the fields, and above all our burning wish to try at once the incomplete route on the map approved by the bohemian—our last card, the one key left which might open the lock? . . . It was more than we could stand! Meaulnes kept walking up and down, going to the windows to look at the garden, then back again for a look towards the village, as if he was expecting some one who certainly would not come.

'I've a notion,' he said to me at last—'I've a notion that it mayn't be as far as we think . . . Frantz struck off my plan a good bit of the road I had marked. That may mean the mare went a long way round while I was asleep . . .'

I sat idle and discouraged on the edge of a big table,

one foot on the ground, the other swinging, and I re-marked in a dejected way: 'Yes, but coming back, in the berlin, your journey lasted all night.'

'We left at midnight,' he replied quickly. 'They put me down at four in the morning, six kilometres west of Sainte-Agathe, whereas I'd gone by the east Station Road. So we must knock off these six kilometres from the distance between Sainte-Agathe and the Lost Land. I feel almost sure that from the wood on the Commons to what we're after, it can't be more than eight kilo-metres.'

'They're precisely the eight kilometres missing on your map.'

'That's true. And getting out of the wood means at least six kilometres from here; but a good walker can do it in a morning.'

Moucheboeuf came in at that moment. He had an irritating way of appearing to be a good pupil, not by working better than others, but by showing off on occa-sions like this.

'I knew,' he said proudly, 'I should find only you two. The others have gone to the Commons wood, under Jasmin Delouche: he knows the nests.'

And to show off his goodness, he began to relate what they had said to rag the Matric form, M. Seurel, and ourselves while planning this expedition.

'If they've gone to the wood, I shall most likely come across them,' said Meaulnes, 'as I'm going that way too. I'll be back about half-past twelve.'

Moucheboeuf was aghast.

'Aren't you coming?' said Augustin to me, stopping a moment on the step of the partly open door—and thus brought into the room a whiff of air softened by the sun, a medley of twittering, calling, and chirping, the sound of a pail on the curb of a well and the cracking of a whip in the far distance.

'No,' I replied, although the temptation was strong,

'I can't because of M. Seurel. But hurry up, I'll be on the itch to know.'

He made a vague gesture and went off quickly, full of hope.

When M. Seurel came in about ten, he had discarded his black alpaca jacket, having put on a fisherman's coat with big buttoned pockets, a straw hat, and short leather leggings to hold in his trousers. I believe he was hardly surprised at finding no one. He paid no heed to Mouchebœuf, who told him three times that the boys had said: 'Well, if he wants us, let him come and find us!'

He just said: 'Put away your things, take your caps, it's our turn to get even with them, then . . . Can you walk as far as that, François?'

I assured him I could and we started.

It was agreed that Mouchebœuf would guide M. Seurel and be his decoy-bird . . . That is to say that, knowing the thickets where the nest-hunters had gone, he would call aloud, from time to time: 'Holla! Hoa! Giraudat! Delouche! Where are you? Got any? . . . Made any finds? . . .'

As for me, to my great delight, I was told to follow the outskirts of the wood on the east side, in case the runaways should try to escape that way.

It so happened that, on the plan as altered by the bohemian, which I had many times studied with Meaulnes, a line seemed to indicate a path, a beaten track, starting from that side in the direction of the manor. What if I should discover it this morning! I began to feel certain that before midday I should find myself on the road to the Lost Land . . .

What a marvellous walk! . . . As soon as we had passed the glacis and gone round the mill, I left my two companions: M. Seurel looking as if he was off to the wars (I believe he had an old pistol in his pocket) and that traitor Mouchebœuf.

I took a cross-road and soon came to the edge of the wood—being alone in the open country for the first time in my life, and feeling like a patrol which has lost its corporal.

Here I am, I imagine, close to that mysterious happiness of which Meaulnes, one day, had a glimpse. The whole morning is mine to explore the edge of the wood —the most deliciously cool and secreted part of the district—while my big brother, too, is off on the search. It is like the old bed of a brook. I make my way under the low branches of trees unknown to me by name, but which must be alders. I have just jumped a hurdle at the end of the path, and I am under a roof of leaves in this wide grass track, treading down nettles and crushing tall valerians.

Sometimes, for a few steps, my foot rests on a stretch of fine sand. And in the silence I hear a bird—I imagine it to be a nightingale, but most likely this is wrong, as nightingales only sing at night—a bird who persists in repeating the same phrase: the voice of the morning, a loving word under the shade of the trees, a charming invitation to a walk amongst the alders. Invisible, obstinate, he seems to follow me under the leaves.

For the first time I, too, am on the road of adventure. I am no longer hunting for shells of bygone streams, under M. Seurel's guidance, nor orchids unknown to the schoolmaster, nor even, as often before, for the deep and dried-up spring in Father Martin's field, with a grating so well hidden by weeds and grass that to rediscover it gave us each time greater trouble. . . . I am searching for something far more mysterious. It is the path told of in books, the ancient obstructed path, the path to which the weary prince could find no entrance. It is found at last at the most forlorn hour of the morning, when you have long since forgotten that eleven or twelve is about

to strike. . . . And suddenly, as one thrusts aside bushes
and brier, with a movement of hesitating hands unevenly
raised level to the face, it appears in sight as a long
shadowy avenue, the outlet of which is a small round
patch of light.

But while I hope thus and am enraptured, I unexpectedly come out into a clearing, which is simply a
meadow. Without giving it a thought, I have reached
the other side of the Commons, which I had always imagined a very long way off. And there, on my right, in between stacks of logs, and astir with life in the shade,
stands the forester's house. Two pairs of stockings are
drying on the window-sill. In previous years, whenever
we had reached the entrance of the wood, we used to
point to a patch of light at the end of a long, dark avenue
and say: 'That house out there, that's the forester's cottage, Baladier's.' But we had never pushed on as far as
that. We had often heard people say, as if referring to
some extraordinary venture, 'He's been as far as the
forester's cottage! . . .'

This time, I have been as far as Baladier's cottage,
and I found nothing.

I was just beginning to feel my tired legs and the heat,
which I had not so far noticed; I was fearing the return
journey all by myself, when close at hand I heard the
voice of M. Seurel's decoy-bird, Mouchebœuf, then
other voices calling me . . .

I saw a group of six big lads, amongst whom Mouchebœuf the traitor was the only one triumphant. There
were Giraudat, Auberger, Delage, and others. . . .
Thanks to the decoy, they had been caught, some up a
mulberry tree that stood solitary in the clearing, others
in the act of robbing a woodpecker's nest. That fool of a
Giraudat, with his swollen eyes and greasy overall, had
hidden the little ones against his stomach, in between
his shirt and his skin. Two of their companions had run

off at M. Seurel's approach: probably Delouche and the
little Coffin. At first they had answered Mouchebœuf
by jokes on his name, which the echoes of the wood repeated, and he, believing he had caught them, had replied stupidly in a temper: 'You'd better come down
from there, you know! M. Seurel's here . . .'

Then the noise had stopped at once. There had been
a silent flight across the wood. As they knew it thor-
oughly, it was useless to think of catching them. On the
other hand, no one knew what had become of Admiral
Meaulnes. His voice had not been heard, and we had to
give up looking for him.

It was past midday when we slowly started back towards Sainte-Agathe, with drooping heads, tired and
muddy. On coming out of the wood, where we scraped
and stamped the mud from our shoes on the dry road,
the sun began to strike fiercely down. Already it was
no longer the fresh and bright morning of spring. The
noises of the afternoon had started. Now and again, a
cock set up a melancholy crowing in the deserted farms
by the roadside. At the descent of the glacis we stopped
a moment to chat with some farmhands back at their
work after lunch. They were resting with their elbows
on the stile, and M. Seurel was saying to them: 'Ah! the
rascals! Here, look at Giraudat. He's put the brood inside his shirt. They've done in there what they liked.
It's *all* right! . . .'

It seemed to me the men were laughing at my disaster,
too. They laughed and shook their heads, but did not
altogether blame the youngsters, whom they knew well.
They even confided to us, while M. Seurel was starting
off again at the head of our party: 'There was another
chap as went by. That tall fellow, you know . . . On the
way back he must've met the cart from the Barns and
been given a lift. He was put down here, at the entrance
of the lane to the Barns, covered with mud and ragged.
We told him as we'd seen you go by, this morning, but

that you were not back yet. He slowly set off for Sainte-Agathe.'

In fact Admiral Meaulnes was waiting for us, seated on a pier of the glacis bridge and looking worn out with fatigue. He said, in answer to M. Seurel's questions, that he also had gone to look for the truants. But to the question I put to him in whispers, he shook his head and only said with disappointment: 'No! Nothing! Nothing at all like it!'

After lunch, he sat at one of the big tables in the class-room—stuffy, dark, and empty amidst the glorious countryside—and burying his head in his arms, fell into a long sleep, sullen and heavy. Towards evening he wrote a letter to his mother, after having been a long time lost in thought, and as if coming to an important decision. And that is all I can remember of that melancholy ending to a great day of defeat.

We had reckoned too soon on the coming of spring. On Monday evening we decided to do our home work immediately after four as in the summer, and to get a better light, we dragged two big tables into the playground. But the sky became suddenly cloudy; a drop of rain fell on an exercise-book; we hastened to go in. And we silently watched, out of the large windows of the big classroom now so dark, the flight of the clouds in the grey sky.

Then Meaulnes, who was at the window with us, one hand on the handle, could not refrain from saying, as if he were angry to feel so much regret rise up in him: 'Ah! the clouds rolled along better than this when I was on the road, in the Fair Star cart.'

'On what road?' asked Jasmin.

But Meaulnes made no reply.

'As for me,' I said, to create a diversion, 'I should have loved travelling that way in a carriage, with the rain pouring down, sheltered under a big umbrella.'

'And reading all the while during the journey, as if you were indoors,' added another.

'It was not raining and I had no longing to read,' replied Meaulnes. 'I thought only of looking at the countryside.'

But when in his turn Giraudat asked him of what country he spoke, Meaulnes again kept silent. And Jasmin said: 'I know . . . Always that famous adventure! . . .'

He had said these words in conciliatory and important tones, as if he was himself a little in the secret. It was trouble lost; his advances met with no response; and as night was falling, every one raced off through the cold downpour, his overall wrapped over his head.

The rain continued until the following Thursday. And that Thursday was even gloomier than the last. The whole countryside was bathed in a sort of icy mist as in the worst days of winter.

Millie, led astray by the beautiful sun of the week before, had had the washing done, but there could be no question of hanging it out to dry on the garden hedges, nor even on lines in the lumber-rooms, as the air was so damp and cold.

Discussing the matter with M. Seurel, she conceived the idea, as it was Thursday, of spreading the washing in the classrooms and of heating the stove red-hot. Meals were to be cooked on the stove to dispense with fires in the kitchen and in the dining-room, and we were to spend the day in the top-form classroom.

At first—I was so young!—I regarded this novelty as a treat. A dreary treat! . . . All the heat of the stove was taken by the washing; it was extremely cold. In the playground a fine wintry rain fell softly and endlessly. Yet it was there that at nine o'clock in the morning, bored to death, I discovered Admiral Meaulnes. Through the bars of the tall gate against which we silently rested our heads, we looked towards the top of the village and watched a funeral procession which had come from remote parts of the country and had stopped at the Cross-Roads. The coffin, brought on an ox wagon, was lowered and placed on a flagstone at the foot of the tall cross where the butcher, one night, had noticed the bohemian's sentries! Where was he now, the young captain who could so well fake the boarding of a ship? . . . The vicar and the choir boys, as was the custom, walked up to the coffin and their mournful chants reached us. This, as we knew, would be the only sight the whole day, which would pass like muddy water along the gutter.

'And now,' said Meaulnes suddenly, 'I am going to

pack. I must tell you, Seurel: I wrote to my mother last
Thursday asking her to let me complete my studies in
Paris. I am leaving to-day.'

He continued looking towards the village, his hands
against the bars, level with his face. No use asking if
his mother, who was rich and indulged all his whims,
had allowed this one. No use either to ask why he suddenly wanted to go to Paris! . . .

But certainly there was regret in him, and fear at
leaving this dear land of Sainte-Agathe from which he
had set out on his adventure. As for me, a heavy distress rose in my heart which I had not felt at first.

'Easter is coming!' he said with a sigh, by way of
explanation.

'As soon as you find her, out there, you will write,
won't you?' I asked.

'Of course, that's agreed. Aren't you my friend and
my brother? . . .'

And he placed his hand on my shoulder.

Little by little I understood that all was at an end,
now that he wanted to complete his studies in Paris;
never again should I have my big brother with me!

Our one hope of coming together again was that house
in Paris where the trail of our forlorn adventure might
be rediscovered . . . But with Meaulnes himself so sad,
what a poor hope was that for me!

My parents were told the news: M. Seurel showed
great surprise, but soon yielded to Augustin's reasons;
Millie, the good housewife, was most upset at the idea
that Meaulnes' mother would see our house in a state
of unusual untidiness . . . The trunk, alas! was soon
packed. We sought out his Sunday shoes from under
the stairs; a few underclothes from the cupboard; then
his papers and schoolbooks—all that a boy of eighteen
possesses in the world.

Mme. Meaulnes arrived at midday with her carriage.
She lunched with Augustin at the Café Daniel and took

him away with hardly a word of explanation, as soon as the horse had been fed and harnessed. We said good-bye to them on the threshold; and the carriage disappeared at the turning of the Cross-Roads.

Millie rubbed her shoes in front of the door and went back into the cold dining-room, to tidy what had been disarranged. As for me, I found myself obliged, the first time for months, to face alone a long Thursday evening —with the clear feeling that the old carriage had borne away my youth forever.

chapter 11. I BETRAY HIM

What was I to do!

The weather was clearing a little. It seemed as if the
sun would come through. Occasionally a door banged
in the big house. Then silence returned once more. From
time to time my father crossed the playground to fetch
a scuttle of coal to feed the stove. I saw the white washing hanging on the lines, and I had no wish to go back
to the sad room, changed to a drying-room, in order to
face my last task of the year, the preparation for the
Training College Entrance Exam, which, however, ought
to have been my only thought.

A queer thing: a feeling akin to freedom was blended
with the boredom which tortured me. Meaulnes gone,
the whole adventure ended in failure, I seemed at any
rate free from that strange longing, that mysterious pre-
occupation which kept me from behaving like every one
else. Meaulnes gone, I was no longer the fellow-adven-
turer, no longer the brother on the trail; I became a boy
again like other village boys. And this was easy, for I had
only to follow my natural inclination.

The youngest of the brothers Roy passed along the
muddy street; he was swinging at the end of a string,
then flinging into the air three horse-chestnuts which
fell into the playground. I was at such a loose end that
three or four times I quite liked throwing back the chestnuts to him over the wall.

Suddenly I saw him give up this childish game and
run towards a cart which was coming along the Old
Plank Road. To climb in at the back of the cart without
it stopping was quickly done. I recognised Delouche's
horse and cart. Jasmin was driving and the big Bou-

jardon was standing up in it. They were coming back
from the meadow.

'Come with us, François!' called out Jasmin, who must
already have known that Meaulnes had gone.

And indeed, without a word to a soul, I clambered up
into the jolting cart and stood like the others with my
back against the tall uprights. It took us to the house
of the widow Delouche.

We are now in the back parlour of the good woman
who keeps what is both an inn and a grocer's shop. A
white ray of sunlight glints in at the low window, onto
the tin boxes and a barrel of vinegar. Big Boujardon sits
down on the window-sill, and the huge fellow munches
Savoy biscuits, facing us with a fat smile. The biscuit
tin, opened on a barrel within reach, is half empty. The
young Roy screams with delight. There is a kind of in-
timacy of the wrong sort between us. Jasmin and Boujardon are to be my friends, now, I see. The course of
my life has suddenly changed. It seems to me that
Meaulnes has been gone a very long time and that his
adventure is an old sad story, but finished.

Young Roy has discovered on a shelf a half-empty
bottle of liqueur. Delouche offers us each a drink, but,
as there is only one glass, we all drink out of it. They
help me first, with slight condescension, as if I were not
one of themselves, not a sportsman, not a peasant. This
rather annoys me. And when Meaulnes is spoken of I
become anxious to show that I know his story and to
tell some of it, just to scatter my annoyance and regain
my composure. In what way could this hurt him since
all his adventures here are now finished? . . .

Am I telling this story badly? It does not produce the
effect which I was expecting.

My companions, like good country folk whom nothing
surprises, remain unimpressed by such trifles.

'Only a wedding! What!' says Boujardon. 'Delouche has seen one at Preveranges which was still more peculiar.'

The mansion? Oh, there would be in the neighbourhood people who'd heard of it, right enough.

The girl? Meaulnes would marry her when once he had served his year as a soldier. 'He should have spoken to us about it,' adds one of them, 'and shown us his plan, instead of confiding in a gipsy!'

I am caught in failure: here is my chance to quicken their curiosity: I decide to explain who this gipsy was, where he came from; his strange fate . . . Boujardon and Delouche do not care to listen.

'That fellow's done it all. It's him who made Meaulnes unsociable. Meaulnes who used to be such a jolly chap! It's him who started that silly nonsense about boarding ships and night attacks, making us into a kind of school brigade . . .'

'You know,' said Jasmin, looking at Boujardon and shaking his head in repeated nods, 'it was a jolly good job I reported him to the police. That chap did a lot of mischief in these parts and would have done more! . . .'

And I almost agree with them. The whole affair would have taken a different turn if we had not come to look upon it as so mysterious and tragic. The influence of that Frantz spoiled everything . . .

But suddenly, while I am absorbed in these thoughts, a noise is heard in the shop. Jasmin Delouche quickly hides the bottle of liqueur behind a barrel; the fat Boujardon climbs down from his window, places his foot on an empty and dusty bottle which rolls away, and twice he nearly topples over. Young Roy, half choking with laughter, pushes us all from behind to hurry us out.

Without quite understanding what is happening, I run away with them; we cross the yard and by means of a ladder we climb into a hayloft. I hear the voice of a woman calling us good-for-nothings.

'I should never have thought she would be back so soon,' says Jasmin in a whisper.

Only then do I understand that we were there for no good, but to steal biscuits and liqueur. I am as much disappointed as that wrecked mariner who, fancying he was talking with a man, suddenly found himself conversing with a monkey. I think only of leaving the loft, these adventures displease me so much. Besides, night is falling . . . My companions make me go by back ways, then across two gardens, and round a pond, until I find myself back in a muddy wet street in which the lights of the Café Daniel are reflected.

I am not proud of the way I have spent my evening. I soon find myself at the Cross-Roads. Suddenly, against my will, at the bend of the road, I seem to see, once more, the clean-cut face of a brother smiling at me; a last waving of the hand and the carriage disappearing . . .

A cold wind, getting into my overall, makes it flap, a wind similar to those of that memorable winter so tragic and so fine. Already everything appears to me less easy. In the big classroom, where my parents await me for dinner, sudden draughts mingle with the feeble heat of the stove. I shiver, while I am being reproached for my afternoon of idle roaming. Though the very thing that might help me would be to resume my old regular life, I am even deprived, that evening, of the consolation of sitting at my usual place at dinner. The table has not been laid; we all eat off our knees, each settling where best he can in the dark classroom. I eat in silence the thin cake which has been cooked on the top of the stove and which, intended as a reward for a Thursday of diligent work, has been left to burn on the red-hot rings.

In the evening, alone in my room, I hasten to bed to stifle the remorse which I feel surging up from the depths of my grief. But twice I awoke during the night,

fancying at first that I heard the creaking of the bed in
which Meaulnes used to turn over, all of a heap, and the
second time listening for the light steps of the hunter
upon the watch, in the dim distance of the lumber-
rooms . . .

chapter 12.   THE THREE LETTERS FROM
MEAULNES

In all my life I have received only three letters from
Meaulnes. They are still at home in a chest of drawers.
Each time I read them again, I feel the same sadness as
of old.

The first arrived two days after he had left.

My DEAR FRANÇOIS,

To-day, as soon as I got to Paris, I went in front of
the house mentioned. I saw nothing. There was no one
there. No one will ever be there.

The building mentioned by Frantz is a private house
one storey high. Mademoiselle de Galais' room must be
on the first floor. The top windows are the most hidden
by the trees, but one sees them quite well from the pavement, as one walks by. All the curtains have been drawn
and it would be mad to hope that, one day, Yvonne de
Galais' face would appear from behind the drawn curtains.

The house stands on a boulevard. . . . It was raining
a little on trees already green. You could hear the sharp
clanging of the tramcars always going by.

I walked up and down, underneath the windows, for
nearly two hours. I went in for a drink at a bar close by,
so as not to be taken for a burglar up to some mischief.
Then I returned to my hopeless watch.

Night came. Windows lit up nearly everywhere, but
not in that house. There is certainly no one there. And
yet Easter is approaching.

Just as I was about to leave, a girl or a young woman

—I don't know which—came and sat on one of the rain-soaked benches. She was dressed in black with a small white collar. When I left, she was still there, not having stirred in spite of the cold of the evening, and waiting, goodness knows for what or for whom. You see, Paris is full of fools like me.

AUGUSTIN

Time passed. I waited in vain for a word from Meaulnes all Easter Monday and the following days—days so calm after the Easter fever that just to wait for summer seemed the only thing to be done. June brought examinations and a terrible heat, a suffocating haze hovering over the countryside, without a breath of wind to dispel it. Night afforded no coolness and consequently no respite from this torture. It was during this unbearable month of June that I received the second letter from Admiral Meaulnes.

June, 189. .

MY DEAR CHAP,

This time all hope is gone. I have known it since yesterday evening. My grief, which I hardly felt at first, has been increasing ever since.

Every evening I went and sat on that bench, watching, pondering, hoping in spite of all.

Yesterday, after dinner, the night was dark and stifling. People were talking on the pavement, under the trees. Above the dark leaves—toned to green by the lights —flats were lit up on the second and third storeys. Here and there, summer had forced a window to be thrown wide open. . . . The lamp could be seen standing alight on the table, scarcely changing the sultry obscurity of June; you could see almost to the other end of the room. . . . Ah! if the dark window of Yvonne de Galais had suddenly lit up as the others, I believe I should have found courage to go up the stairs, to knock and enter . . .

The girl of whom I spoke to you was still waiting there, like me. I came to think that she might know the house, and I asked her.

'I know,' she said, 'that at one time, in this house, a girl and her brother used to come for the holidays. But I learned that the brother had run away from his parents' country-house and was never found again, and that the girl had married. That explains why the house is shut up.'

I walked off. Ten steps farther, I stumbled against the curb of the pavement and nearly fell. During the night—it was last night—when the women and the children left off their noise in the back yards, and I might have gone to sleep, I began to hear the cabs rolling by in the street. They passed only now and then. But no sooner had one gone by than, in spite of myself, I waited for the next: the horse's bell, his hoofs clinking on the asphalt . . . And it went on repeating: empty town, your poor love gone, eternal night, summer, fever . . .

Seurel, dear man, I am in great distress.

AUGUSTIN

Few confidences in these letters, whatever you may think! Meaulnes did not tell me either why he had remained silent so long, or what he now intended to do. I had the impression that he was breaking with me, his adventure over, as he was breaking with his past. It was no good my writing to him; I received no reply. Only a word of congratulation when I passed my preliminary Matriculation. In September I heard through a school friend that he had been for his holidays to his mother's at La Ferté d'Angillon. But, that year, invited by my Uncle Florentin, we had spent the holidays at Vieux-Nançay. And Meaulnes went back to Paris without my having a chance to see him.

I received the last of the three letters I ever received from Meaulnes, on my return to school, at the end of November, while I was working with melancholy zeal for my final Matriculation,[1] hoping in the following year to secure a teacher's post without going through Bourges Training College.

'I still go under that window,' he wrote. 'I still wait, not that there is any hope: just sheer madness. At the end of these cold autumn Sundays, about the time when night comes, I cannot decide to go home and close the shutters of my room without returning to stand there in the chilly street.

'I am like the mad woman of Sainte-Agathe who would go to her front door every minute and look towards the station, one hand raised above her eyes, to see if her dead son were coming home.

'Seated on a bench, shivering and wretched, I take pleasure in imagining that some one is going to take me gently by the arm. . . . I should turn round. It would be she. "I am a little late," she would simply say. And all suffering and all madness vanish away. We enter our home. Her furs are cold, her veil damp; she brings in with her a flavour of the outside mist; and as she draws near the fire, I see the flaxen fairness of her hair and the soft outlines of her beautiful face bent towards the flame . . .

'Alas! the pane remains white, with the curtain drawn across it. And should the girl from the Lost Land draw it aside, I have no longer anything to tell her.

'Our adventure is at an end. Winter, this year, is as dead as the grave. Perhaps when we die, perhaps death

---

[1] No accurate translation can be found for these examinations, as every country has its own system. The French system is complicated and it is unnecessary to give here elaborate explanations.

alone will give us the key, the sequence and the end of
this adventure that failed.

'Seurel, the other day, I asked you to think of me.
Now, on the contrary, it is better to forget me. It would
be better to forget everything.

.   .   .   .

'A. M.'

And this new winter proved as dead as the preceding
one had been alive with mysterious life: the church
square without gipsies; the playground which the boys
deserted on the stroke of four . . . the classroom where
I studied alone and without pleasure. . . . In February,
for the first time that winter, snow fell, definitely burying the tale of our adventures, blurring every trail, blot-
ting out the last traces. And I tried, as Meaulnes had
asked me in his letter, to forget everything.

Part III

chapter 1. BATHING

The bad lads of the countryside thought it a lark to smoke cigarettes, to put sugar and water on their hair to make it curl, to kiss girls from the Continuation School in the street, and to call out from behind a hedge, 'Poke-bonnet,' to rag a passing nun. At twenty, however, bad lads of that kind can very well improve and become often most sensible fellows. The problem is graver when the bad lad's appearance is wizened and old, when his mind is occupied with low tales of the women roundabout, when he is always making stupid remarks about Gilberte Poquelin for the other boys to laugh. But even so there is still room for hope . . .

That was the case with Jasmin Delouche. He continued, I do not know why, but certainly from no wish to pass exams, to study with the top form when every one would rather he gave it up. Between whiles, too, he learned the plasterer's trade with his Uncle Dumas. And soon this Jasmin Delouche and Boujardon and a softish fellow called Denis, son of the deputy mayor, were the only big boys with whom I cared to associate, because they belonged to 'Meaulnes' time.'

Besides, Delouche was genuinely keen to be my friend. To tell the truth, though he had been Admiral Meaulnes' enemy, he wanted to be the Admiral Meaulnes of the school: at any rate, he regretted perhaps not having been his lieutenant. Less thick than Boujardon, he had felt I believe, what an extraordinary event Meaulnes had been in our life. And I often heard him repeat: 'Ah! that's what he used to say, Admiral Meaulnes . . .' or again, 'Just as Admiral Meaulnes would've said . . .'

This old-looking fellow, besides being more of a man than we were, got hold of ripping things which gave him a pull over us: a mongrel with long white hair who answered to the irritating name of Bécali and fetched stones thrown ever so far, without being much good for anything else; a second-hand bicycle which Jasmin let us ride sometimes in the evening after school, but on which he preferred to exercise the village girls; last but not least, a white donkey, quite blind, which could be harnessed to any vehicle.

It was Dumas' donkey, but, in the summer, it was lent to Jasmin whenever we went bathing in the Cher. His mother, at such times, always gave him a bottle of lemonade which we placed under the driver's seat, amongst the stiff, dry bathing-drawers. And we set out, eight to ten big boys from the top form, going with M. Seurel, some on foot, others hoisted in the donkey cart which we left behind at Deep Waters Farm, where the path along the Cher became like a ravine.

I have good reason to remember in all its minute details one outing of this kind, when Jasmin's donkey took to the Cher the slips, luggage, lemonade, and M. Seurel, while we followed on foot. It was during the month of August. We had just finished examinations. We were care-free, and the whole summer, all happiness, seemed to belong to us; so, early that fine Thursday afternoon,

we marched along the road singing, not knowing what
we sang or why we sang it.

On the way, only one shadow fell on this innocent
picture. We noticed Gilberte Poquelin ahead of us. She
walked alluringly, in a rather short skirt and high-heeled
shoes; she had the sweet yet bold air of a girl who was
nearly a woman. She left the road for a by-lane, no doubt
on her way to fetch milk. Little Coffin at once proposed
to Jasmin to follow her.

'It wouldn't be the first time I'd kissed her either . . .'
said the other. And he began to relate several risky
stories concerning her and her girl friends, while, by
way of bragging, our little troop took to the lane and
left M. Seurel on the road forging ahead in the donkey
cart. Once in the lane, however, our band began to scatter. Even Delouche, in our presence, did not appear
over-anxious to approach the girl who hurried on, and he
did not come nearer than fifty yards. There was a display of cock-crowing and hen-clucking, a few enticing
little bursts of whistling; then we walked back the way
we had come, feeling uncomfortable and thwarted.
Back on the road, we had to run, under the blazing sun,
too. We no longer sang.

We undressed and dressed again in the parched wil-
low-ground bordering the Cher. The willows sheltered
us from onlookers, but not from the sun. Our feet were
on sand and dry mud; our one thought was for the bottle of widow Delouche's lemonade being kept cool in the
pool at Deep Waters, a pool hollowed out in the very
bank of the Cher.

There were always pale-greenish weeds to be found at
the bottom, and two or three creatures which looked
like woodlice; but the water was so clear, so transparent,
that fishermen never hesitated to kneel and drink at it,
one hand placed on either bank.

Alas! it happened that day as it always did . . . Once
we were dressed and, squatting on our heels in a circle,

were ready to share the cool lemonade out of two tum-
blers, after inviting M. Seurel to take his share, there
came to each of us scarcely more than a little froth
which grated on the throat and only aggravated one's
thirst. So finally, as his turn came, each of us went to
the pool we had at first despised and slowly lowered his
face to the level of the clear water. But we were not all
used to these peasant's ways. Several of us, myself included, never managed to quench our thirst: some because they did not like water; others because their throats
contracted at the fear of swallowing a woodlouse; others
again, deceived by the transparency of the still water and
unable to estimate the exact distance to its surface,
pushed half of their faces in with their lips and drew
in through the nose stinging water which seemed quite
hot; others for all these reasons put together . . . What
did it matter! It always seemed to us, there on the
parched banks of the Cher, that the whole fresh beauty
of nature was enclosed in that spot. And even now, whenever I hear the word pool anywhere, it is of that one pool
I lovingly think.

We came back at dusk with the same care-free spirit
as when we went. The Deep Waters' track, leading up
to the road, was a brook in the winter, but in the summer a ravine unfit for traffic, obstructed by holes and
big roots and leading uphill between tall rows of shady
trees. Some of the bathers went that way, just for fun.
But with M. Seurel, Jasmin, and several other boys, we
followed an easy sandy path running parallel to the first
and bordering a neighbouring farm. We could hear the
others talk and laugh close to us, down below, hidden
from sight in the shady path, while Delouche told his
mannish tales . . . At the top of the tall row of trees,
evening insects were droning and could be seen against
the clear sky, as they moved around the lacework of the
leaves. Sometimes, one suddenly tumbled down, its hum
fizzling out all at once. . . . A beautiful quiet summer

evening! . . . A peaceful homecoming, void of hope,
but also of longing, after an ordinary little country outing. . . . Once again, without realising it, Jasmin came
to disturb this peacefulness. . . .

Just as we reached the top of the hill, at the place
where two huge ancient stones stand—they are rumoured
to be the remains of a fortress—he began to speak of
the estates he had visited, above all of one half forsaken
in the neighbourhood of Vieux-Nançay: the Sand Pit
Manor. With his Allier accent, which shows affectation
in rounding off some words and in shortening others, he
related having seen, some years previously, in the tum-
ble-down chapel of the old manor, a tombstone on which
were carved the words:

HERE LIES SIR GALOIS, KNIGHT,

FAITHFUL TO HIS GOD, HIS KING AND HIS LOVE.

'Well! I never!' said M. Seurel, slightly shrugging his
shoulders, ill at ease at the turn the conversation had
taken, yet anxious nevertheless to let us talk like men.

Then Jasmin went on describing the manor house as
if he had spent his life there.

On their way home from Vieux-Nançay, he and
Dumas had more than once been puzzled by the old
grey tower which could be seen above the firs. There, in
the middle of the woods, you came to a maze of decrepit
buildings which you could visit when the owners were
away. One of the keepers of the place, to whom they
had given a lift, had once taken them to the mysterious
manor. But since then everything had been razed to the
ground; there only remained, people said, the farm and
a small country-house. The occupiers were still the same:
an old naval officer, in reduced circumstances, and his
daughter.

He went on talking . . . talking. . . . I listened attentively, feeling, without being aware of it, that all this
concerned facts well known to me, when suddenly, in

the simple way extraordinary things do happen, Jasmin
turned to me and touched me on the arm as if struck by
an idea which had never occurred to him.

'My goodness, now I come to think of it,' he said, 'it
must have been there Meaulnes—you know, Admiral
Meaulnes?—went.

'Of course,' he went on, for I did not answer him,
'and I remember that the keeper used to speak of the
son of the place, a queer fellow who had very weird
ideas. . .'

I no longer listened to him, convinced as I was from
the first that he had guessed right and that in front of
me, far from Meaulnes, far from all hope, there had just
opened out, as clear and easy as a familiar road, a path
to the manor without a name.

Just as far as I had been an unhappy child, dreamy and retiring, so I now became resolute and as we say at home 'determined,' when I felt that upon me depended the outcome of this high adventure.

From that evening, I believe, my knee definitely ceased to hurt me.

Vieux-Nançay was the parish to which the Sand Pit estate belonged and where all M. Seurel's relatives lived, and in particular my Uncle Florentin, a tradesman with whom we often spent the end of September. Free as I was from examinations, I did not want to wait, and was granted permission to go at once to my uncle. But I decided to say nothing to Meaulnes as long as I could not be certain of having good news to impart. For, indeed, what was the good of drawing him out of his despair, to plunge him back into it, perhaps more deeply, afterwards?

Vieux-Nançay was for many years my favourite place in the world, the place that meant holidays, where we only went on rare occasions, when a carriage could be hired to take us. There had formerly been some disagreement with the branch of the family living there, and no doubt this explains why one had each time to beg Millie so hard to get her to come. But I cared little about these squabbles! . . . No sooner was I there than I became lost in the crowd of uncles and cousins, boys and girls, and enjoyed a life crammed with jolly doings.

We used to live with Uncle Florentin and Aunt Julie. They had a boy of my age, Cousin Firmin, and eight daughters, the two eldest of whom, Marie-Louise and Charlotte, might have been seventeen and fifteen. They

kept a large shop in front of the church, at the entrance
to this small town in Sologne—a sort of general store,
the shopping centre for all the neighbouring gentry and
sportsmen living in lonely places in the remote country,
often thirty kilometres from any station.

This shop, with its grocery and drapery counters, had
numerous windows looking on the road and a glass door
opening on the church square. But a strange thing,
though quite ordinary in this poor district, the floor of
the shop was of trodden earth.

At the back of the premises were six rooms, each
stocked with a different kind of goods: the room with
hats, the room with garden tools, the room with lamps
. . . goodness knows what! When, as a child, I used to
go through this maze of a store, it seemed as if my eyes
would never exhaust all its marvels. And even at that
time I still thought that there could be no real holidays
in any other place.

The family lived in the big kitchen, the door of which
opened on the shop, and in this kitchen, at the end of
September, huge fires were blazing by the side of which
the gamekeepers and poachers who sold game to Florentin often came for a drink quite early in the morning,
while the little girls, who were already up, went all over
the place, making much noise, or smoothed one another's
hair with 'some nice-smelling stuff.' On the walls some
old photographs, yellowish groups of schoolboys, de-
picted my father—after one had taken some time to recognise him in his uniform—amidst his Training College
friends . . .

The mornings were always spent there; or in the yard
where Florentin grew dahlias and reared guinea-fowls;
here, seated on soap chests, you set about roasting coffee,
or unpacking crates filled with all kinds of carefully
wrapped things, the name of which we did not always
know . . .

All day long the shop was invaded by peasants or by

the coachmen of the neighbouring gentry. Carts, coming from far out in the country and dripping with the
September fog, would pull up and stop in front of the
glass door. And from the kitchen we listened to the peas-
ant-women's talk, curious to hear all their stories . . .

But in the evening, after eight o'clock, when we went
out with lanterns to take hay to the horses whose reeking
skins filled the stables with steam, the whole of the shop
belonged to us!

Marie-Louise, the eldest of my cousins, though one of
the smallest, was still in the shop, folding and putting
away rolls of cloth and coaxing us to come and cheer her
up. So Firmin and I with all the girls burst into the huge
shop, under the overhead porcelain lamps, and coffee-
grinders were set turning and acrobatic stunts performed
on the counters; sometimes Firmin brought out from
the attics some old trombone covered with verdigris, for
the trodden earth floor was good to dance on . . .

I still blush at the idea that, at any moment in those
previous years, Mlle. de Galais might have come in and
caught us at these childish games. . . . But it was just
before nightfall, one evening of that month of August,
while I was quietly talking with Marie-Louise and
Firmin, that I saw her for the first time . . .

The very first evening of my arrival at Vieux-Nançay
I had questioned my Uncle Florentin concerning the
Sand Pit estate.

'It is no longer an estate,' he told me. 'Everything
has been sold, and the buyers, sportsmen, have pulled
down the old buildings to enlarge their shoot; the great
courtyard is by now just a waste land of heather and
broom. The former owners have only kept a one-storey
shack and the farm. You'll often have a chance of seeing
Mademoiselle de Galais here; it's she does all the shopping, coming sometimes on horseback, sometimes driv-

ing, but always the same old horse, old Bélisaire . . .
It's a funny turn-out!'

I was so upset that I no longer knew what question
to ask so as to learn more.

'But surely they were rich?'

'Yes. M. de Galais used to give parties to amuse his
son, a strange boy, full of queer ideas. To give him a
good time, the father always thought of some grand new
thing. They had girls come from Paris . . . fellows from
Paris and elsewhere . . .

'The Sand Pit was all falling to ruins, Mme. de Galais
was near her end, they were still trying to amuse him,
putting up with all his whims. 'Twas last winter—no,
the winter before, they gave their biggest fancy-dress
fête. Half of their guests were from Paris, others were
country folk. They had bought or hired any amount of
marvellous fancy costumes, games, horses, boats. Always
to amuse Frantz de Galais. It was said that he was about
to marry, and that it was his betrothal party. But he was
much too young. And it was all broken off suddenly; he
ran away and he's never been seen since. . . . After the
lady's death, Mademoiselle de Galais was suddenly left
alone with her father, the old sea captain.'

'Isn't she married?' I asked at last.

'No,' he said, 'I've heard nothing of it. Might you
be a suitor?'

Very much put out, I confessed to him, as briefly
and as discreetly as possible, that my best friend,
Augustin Meaulnes, would perhaps be one.

'Ah!' said Florentin, smiling, 'if he's not particular as
to money, it is a good match. . . . Should I say a word
about it to M. de Galais? He still comes here sometimes
to get small shot for game. I always give him a taste of
my old brandy.'

But I begged him to do nothing of the sort, to wait.
And on my part, I delayed to inform Meaulnes. Such
an accumulation of lucky circumstances made me feel

rather anxious. And this anxiety forced me not to inform Meaulnes of anything before I had at least seen the girl.

I had not long to wait. The next day, a little before dinner, night began to fall, and with it came a fresh mist, more like September than August. Firmin and I, guessing the shop would be empty of customers at the moment, had come to talk to Marie-Louise and Charlotte. I had confided to them the secret which had brought me to Vieux-Nançay earlier than usual. Elbows on the counter or seated with both hands stretched out flat on the polished wood, we were telling one another all we knew about the mysterious girl—and that was precious little—when a noise of wheels made us turn round.

'There she is, that's her,' they whispered.

A few seconds later the queer equipage stopped in front of the glass door. An old farm carriage with rounded panels and small moulded cornices, the like of which I had never seen before in that district; an old white horse which always seemed to want to graze along the road, so low did he bend his head as he walked; and on the box—I say it in all simplicity of heart, but knowing well what I say—the most beautiful girl the world may ever have held.

I never saw so much grace combined with so much gravity. Her costume gave her so slender a waist that she seemed fragile. A long brown cloak, which she took off as she came in, was thrown on her shoulders. She was the gravest of girls, the frailest of women. A mass of fair hair weighed on her forehead and over her face which was delicate in outline and delicate in moulding. On her pure complexion summer had placed two freckles. . . . I detected only one defect in so much beauty: in moments of sadness, discouragement, or simply deep thought, this pure face was slightly dappled with red, as happens to people suffering from some serious and unsuspected complaint. Then one's admiration on looking at her was replaced by a kind of pity, the more heart-rending because the more surprising.

At least this is what I seemed to discover as she slowly got down from the carriage, and Marie-Louise, with complete ease, at last introduced me and encouraged me to speak.

They offered her a polished chair, and she sat down, her back resting against the counter, while we remained standing. She appeared to know the shop well and to be fond of it. Aunt Julie, being at once informed, came in, and talked quietly, with her hands crossed over her stomach and her peasant shopkeeper's white cap nodding gently. And thus the moment when conversation would begin on my part—which I rather dreaded—was postponed . . .

It came very simply.

'And so,' said Mademoiselle de Galais, 'you will soon be a teacher?'

Aunt Julie was then lighting over our heads the porcelain lamp which gave dim light to the shop; I saw the girl's sweet childlike face, her candid blue eyes, and was all the more surprised at her clear and serious voice. Whenever she stopped talking, her gaze settled away from the listener, not moving while she awaited the answer, and she slightly bit her lip.

'I should also be teaching,' she said, 'if only M. de Galais would let me! I would teach little boys, like your mother . . .'

And she smiled, showing me thus that my cousins had spoken to her of me.

'You see,' she went on, 'the village people are always very polite and kind and obliging to me. And I am very fond of them. But then, what credit can there be in my loving them? . . . While, with a school teacher, they are apt to be rather cross and critical, don't you think? There are endless tales of lost pencils, exercise-books too dear, and of children who do not learn. . . . Well, I would fight it out with them and they would like me nevertheless. It would be far more difficult . . .'

And, without a smile, she dropped back into her thoughtful and childlike attitude, with her motionless blue gaze.

We were, the three of us, embarrassed by that ease in speaking of delicate things, of what is secret and subtle, and only comes off well in books. There was a moment's silence; and slowly a long discussion began . . .

But with a sort of regret and of animosity against I know not what essence of mystery in her life, the girl went on:

'And then I would teach the boys to be wise with a wisdom I know. I would not put into their hearts any longing to go about the world, as you will most likely do, M. Seurel, when you are an assistant master. I would teach them to find the happiness which is quite close to them, though it does not appear so . . .'

Marie-Louise and Firmin were as much confused as I was. We stood there, not saying a word. She felt our embarrassment, stopped, and bit her lip, and lowered her head, then she smiled as if she was making fun of us.

'For instance,' she said, 'there is perhaps some big silly boy who is looking for me at the other end of the world, while I am here, in Madame Florentin's shop, under this lamp, and my old horse is waiting at the door. If the young man did see me, he most likely would not believe his eyes? . . .'

To see her smile, daring seized me, and I felt that it was time to say, while I also laughed: 'And it may be that I know him, that big silly boy?'

She quickly looked up at me.

At that moment there was a ring at the shop door; two country women entered carrying baskets.

'Come in the "dining-room," you will be in peace,' said my aunt, as she pushed open the kitchen door.

And, as Mademoiselle de Galais was refusing and

wanted to go at once, my aunt added: 'M. de Galais is there, chatting with Florentin by the fire.'

There was always, even in the month of August, the habitual fir-faggot crackling and blazing in the big kitchen. There also a porcelain lamp was lit and an old man with a kind, wrinkled face entirely shaven—the type of man nearly always silent like one burdened with age and memories—was seated close to Florentin in front of two glasses of brandy.

Florentin greeted me.

'François!' he called out in his strong huckster's voice, as if there was a river between us or many acres of land, 'I have just arranged an afternoon's outing on the banks of the Cher for next Thursday. Those who like can shoot game, others can fish, or dance, or bathe! . . . Mademoiselle, you will come on horseback; that's agreed with M. de Galais. I've arranged everything . . .

'And François!' he added, as if he had only just thought of it, 'you might bring your friend, Monsieur Meaulnes . . . It's Meaulnes he is called, isn't it?'

Mlle. de Galais had stood up, suddenly growing very pale. And at that precise moment, it came back to my mind that one day, at the mysterious manor, by the side of the lake, Meaulnes had told her his name . . .

When she held out her hand to me at the moment of leaving, there was between us, more clearly than if we had spoken many words, a secret understanding which death alone was to break, and a friendship more moving than a great passion.

. . . At four o'clock next morning, Firmin knocked at the door of the little room which I occupied in the guinea-fowls' yard. It was still night and I had great trouble in finding my belongings on the table, amongst the brass candlesticks and the brand-new statuettes of saints which had been chosen out of the shop to decorate my dwelling on the day before my arrival. In the yard, I heard Firmin pumping up my bicycle tyres, and in the

kitchen Aunt Julie using the bellows to make up the fire.
The sun was hardly risen when I left. But my day was
to be long: I was first going to lunch at Sainte-Agathe
to explain my prolonged absence, then, continuing my
way, I meant, before the evening, to reach La Ferté
d'Angillon and the home of my friend Augustin
Meaulnes.

chapter 3. THE GHOST

I had never been for a really long ride on a bicycle. This was my first. But for a long time Jasmin had been secretly teaching me how to ride in spite of my bad knee. A bicycle is fairly good fun for any ordinary fellow: what should it not mean to a poor chap like me, who, only a short time back, dragged his leg wretchedly along, sweating after a mile or two? To sweep down hills and plunge into the valley hollows; to cover as on wings the far stretches of the road ahead and to find them in bloom at your approach; to pass through a village in a moment, and to take it all with you in one glance . . . in dreams only, till then, had I known such a delightful, such an easy way of getting about. I tackled even the hills with zest. For I must own, it was the road leading to Meaulnes' village I was thus eating up . . .

'A little before you reach the place,' Meaulnes had once said to me, describing his village, 'you see a great wheel with arms which the wind turns . . .' He did not know what it was used for, or perhaps pretended not to know to arouse my curiosity the more.

It was only when this August day was drawing to its close that I noticed, turning to the wind in a huge meadow, the big wheel which must have served to bring up water to a small farm near by. The first dwellings could be seen behind poplars in the meadow. Gradually, as I made my way along the curve where the road turns to follow the brook, the view expanded and opened out. . . . On reaching the bridge, I discovered at last the village High Street.

In the meadow, cows were grazing, hidden by the reeds, and I heard their bells while, having dismounted from my bicycle, and my hands on the handlebar, I surveyed the country into which I was bringing tidings of such gravity. Houses with approaches over a small wooden bridge were lined up by the side of a ditch which ran down the street and looked like fishing boats at anchor on a peaceful evening with their sails clewed up. It was the time of day when a fire is being lighted in every kitchen.

Then it was that fear, and a kind of vague reluctance at coming to disturb so much peace, began to sap my courage. To increase my sudden weakness, I recalled that my Aunt Moinel lived there, on the small square of La Ferté d'Angillon.

She was one of my great-aunts. All her children were dead, but I had known Ernest well, the youngest of all, a tall boy who was to be a teacher. My great-uncle Moinel, the old registry clerk, had soon followed him, and my aunt had remained alone in her queer little house, with the rugs all of patchwork, the tables full of paper cocks, hens, and cats, and the walls decked with old diplomas, portraits of the dear defunct, and lockets containing dead hair.

With all her griefs and mourning, Aunt Moinel was the soul of oddness and good temper. When once I had found the little square where her house stood, I called her loudly through the half-open door, and from the other end of her three rooms leading out of each other, I heard her utter a shrill little cry: 'Well! Good Heavens!'

She spilled her coffee into the fire—how could she be making coffee at this time of day?—and she appeared . . . shoulders well thrown back, and on her head, something which might have been either hat, bonnet, or hood, perched high up over a huge bumpy forehead, suggesting a cross between a Mongol and a Hottentot: and she laughed with little jerks, showing what remained of her small teeth.

But while I kissed her, she clumsily and hastily took hold of the hand which was behind my back. With an air of great mystery—perfectly out of place, as we were quite alone—she squeezed into my palm a small coin which I dared not look at, but guessed to be a franc. Then, as I made a pretence at asking explanations and thanking her, she gave me a poke in the ribs, exclaiming loudly: 'Oh! go on! As if I didn't know all about it!'

She had always been poor, always borrowing, always spending.

'I have always been stupid, always unfortunate,' she would say without bitterness, in her high-pitched voice.

Feeling sure that I worried over pennies as she did, the dear woman had not waited for me to take breath before pressing into my hand her scanty savings of the day. And, in later days, too, this was always how she welcomed me.

Dinner was as strange as the greeting—both melancholy and queer at the same time. She always had a candle within reach of her hand: sometimes she carried it off and left me in the dark: sometimes she put it on the little table which was littered with chipped and cracked dishes and vases.

'The Prussians,' she said, 'broke the handles off this one in 1870, as they couldn't take it away.'

It was only then I remembered, on seeing once again this tall vase with its tragic history, that we had once dined and slept there in former days. Father was taking me to the Yonne to see a specialist who was to cure my knee. We had had to take a fast train which started before daybreak. . . . That melancholy dinner now came back to my mind, and all the stories related by the old clerk as he rested his elbows on the table before his rose-coloured drink.

And I was reminded also of my fears. . . . After dinner, sitting by the fire, my aunt had taken Father aside to tell him ghost stories: 'I turn round . . . Ah! my dear

Louis, what do I see? A little grey woman . . .' Her head was known to be packed with terrifying nonsense of this kind.

And this very evening when dinner was over and, tired out with my bicycle ride, I had gone to bed in one of Uncle Moinel's check nightshirts, she came and sat at the foot of my bed and began to talk in the shrillest, most mysterious voice.

'Poor François, I must tell you something I've not told a soul.'

I thought: 'Now I'm in for it. Here's for another night of terror, like ten years ago! . . .'

And I listened. She nodded her head, looking straight in front of her as if she were relating the story to herself:

'I was coming back from a party with Moinel. It was the first wedding we'd been to together since poor Ernest's death; and I met my sister Adèle there, whom I'd not seen for four years. An old friend of Moinel, a very rich man, had invited us to his son's wedding at his place, the Sand Pit. We'd hired a carriage. That had cost us a good bit of money. We were making our way along the road about seven in the morning, in the middle of winter. The sun was just rising. There was no one about. But what do you think I saw all at once, right in front of us, there on the road? A little fellow posted there, a small young man, as handsome as the day, not moving, but looking at us coming. As we got nearer, we could make out his pretty face—so white and so pretty that it gave one a turn! . . .

'I clung to Moinel's arm; I was shaking like a leaf; I thought it was God himself! . . . I said to Moinel: "Look! A ghost!"

'He replied in whispers, quite furious: "Well! I saw it. You'd better shut up, you old chatterbox . . ."

'He didn't know what to do, when suddenly the horse stopped. . . . At close quarters, it showed a pale face, a forehead covered with beads of sweat, a dirty tammy

and long trousers. We heard its sweet voice saying: "I
am not a man, I am a girl. I ran away, and I am tired
out. Could you take me in your carriage, please, kind
people?"

'At once we got her in. No sooner was she seated than
she fainted. And guess who that was we'd come across?
It was Frantz de Galais' sweetheart, the young man at
the Sand Pit, where we'd been invited to the wedding!'

'But there could've been no wedding,' I said, 'as the
fiancée had run off!'

'Well, of course not,' she went on, looking at me quite
dejectedly. 'There'd been no wedding, on account of
that poor silly girl having got into her head a thousand
mad notions that she explained to us. She was one of
the daughters of a poor weaver. She firmly believed that
so much happiness was impossible; that the young fellow was too young for her; that all the marvels he'd told
her about were imagination; so when at last Frantz came
to fetch her, Valentine took fright. He used to walk with
her in the garden of the Archbishop's Palace at Bourges,
not minding the cold or the wind. The young fellow—
out of delicacy, of course, and because he loved the
younger sister—was full of attention to the elder. So, my
silly girl must needs get notions. She said she wanted
to go home and fetch a shawl; but once there, to make
sure no one would come after her, she put on man's
clothes and set off on foot along the road to Paris. Her
young man got a letter from her in which she said she
was off to Paris to join a fellow she was in love with. But
that wasn't true . . .

' "I'm happier in my sacrifice," she said to me, "than
if I were his wife." Yes, poor idiot, but as a matter of
fact he had never thought for a second of marrying the
sister; he blew out his brains; his blood was seen in the
wood, but his body was never found.'

'And what did you do with that wretched girl?'

'First of all we brought her round with a drop of

brandy. Then we gave her something to eat, and we no
sooner got home than she fell asleep by the fire. She
stayed with us a good bit of the winter. All day long,
while it was light, she stitched, making dresses, trim-
ming hats, or else she cleaned the house in a sort of rage.
She it was who stuck back that wall-paper you see there.
But in the evening, at nightfall, when her work was done,
she would always find some excuse for going into the
yard, or into the garden, or just outside the front door,
even when it was cold enough to freeze one to death.
And there she would be found weeping fit to break her
heart.

' "Well, what's the matter now? Tell us!"

' "Nothing, Madame Moinel!"

'And she would go in.

'The neighbours used to say: "What a pretty little
servant you've found, Madame Moinel!"

'In spite of all we could say, when March came she
made up her mind to go on to Paris; I gave her some old
dresses which she altered, Moinel paid for her ticket at
the station and gave her a little money. She's not forgotten us; she's now doing dressmaking in Paris, close to
Notre-Dame; she still writes at times to ask if we know
anything about the Sand Pit. Once and for all, to free
her of these thoughts, I replied that the estate had been
sold, the buildings pulled down, the young man gone
forever, and the girl married. All this is true, I should
think. Since then, dear Valentine has written far less
often . . .'

It was not a ghost story Aunt Moinel was relating in
her thin piercing voice, so well fitted for such stories.
Yet I was feeling utterly wretched. For we had sworn
to Frantz, the bohemian, always to help him as brothers,
and now the chance had come . . .

But was it the moment to spoil the joy I was to bring
to Meaulnes the next morning, by telling him what I
had just learned? What would be the good of putting

him on such an impossible job? True, we had the address of the girl; but where could we find the bohemian
who was always on the move? . . . Better let mad people alone, I thought. Delouche and Boujardon were quite
right. How much harm this romantic Frantz had done
us! And I resolved to say nothing until I had witnessed
the marriage of Augustin Meaulnes with Mademoiselle
de Galais.

After making this decision, a painful feeling of ill
omen persisted in my mind—a stupid feeling which I
quickly brushed aside.

The candle was almost out; a mosquito hummed; but
Aunt Moinel, with her elbows on her knees and her head
on one side under the velvet bonnet which she never
took off except when she went to bed, began her story
over again. . . . From time to time she sharply raised
her head to observe what my feelings were or perhaps to
see if I was still awake. At last, cunningly, with my head
on the pillow, I closed my eyes pretending to be doz-
ing. . .

'There! You are asleep . . .' she said in a deeper voice
and slightly disappointed.

I took pity on her and I protested: 'Oh, no, Auntie,
I assure you . . .'

'Oh! but you are,' she said; 'besides, I quite understand that all this can hardly interest you. I am talking
of people you've never known . . .'

And this time, like a coward, I made no reply.

chapter 4. GREAT NEWS

Next morning, when I reached the High Street, it was such fine holiday weather, it was so still, and so many peaceful and familiar sounds rose from all over the village, that the happy confidence of a bearer of good news came back to me.

Augustin and his mother lived in the old schoolhouse. On the death of his father—retired long before this and enriched by a legacy—Meaulnes had pressed his mother to buy the school in which the old schoolmaster had taught for twenty years and where he himself had learned to read. Not that it was a pleasant house to look at: it was a big square building like a little town hall, which indeed it had once been; the ground-floor windows opened on the street and were so high that no one ever looked in through them; and the yard at the back, where no tree grew and a high shelter blocked any view of the countryside, was certainly the most denuded and the most forlorn of all the forsaken playgrounds I have ever seen.

In the odd-shaped hall on which four doors opened, I found Meaulnes' mother bringing back from the garden a huge bundle of clothes which she must have put to dry at a very early hour of this long holiday morning. Her grey hair was carelessly twisted up; wisps of it fell across her face; her regular features, under her old-fashioned cap, looked tired and her eyes heavy, as if after a sleepless night, and she kept her head lowered sadly in a dreamy way.

But suddenly she saw me, and recognising me she smiled.

'You come just in time,' she said. 'Look! I was bringing in the clothes I'd put out to dry for Augustin's journey. I've spent the night looking over his accounts and getting his things together. The train leaves at five, but we shall manage to get everything ready.'

You would have said—for she showed such assurance —that she had herself taken this decision. Yet it is likely she did not even know where Meaulnes intended to go.

'Upstairs,' she said, 'you will find him busy writing in the town hall.'

I climbed up the stairs, opened the door on the right, over which the words 'Town Hall' still remained on a board, and found myself in a big room with four windows—two opening on the village, two on the country; the walls were decorated with faded portraits of the Presidents Grévy and Carnot. The chairs of the town councillors still stood in front of a table with a green baize cover, on a long platform which filled the back of the room. And there, seated in the centre of the room in the mayor's old armchair, was Meaulnes, busy writing, dipping his pen in an old-fashioned inkstand shaped like a heart. This place, which seemed meant for some well-to-do villager, was the room where Meaulnes liked to retire during the holidays, whenever he was not roaming about the country . . .

As soon as he had recognised me, he got up, but not with the eagerness I had pictured in my mind.

'Seurel!' he merely said in astonishment.

He was still the same tall youth, with marked bony features and closely cropped hair. An untrimmed moustache was beginning to droop over his lips. Always the same loyal look . . . But something like a veil of mist covered the ardour of the past, though every now and then his old passion dispelled it.

He appeared very upset to see me. At one bound I was on the platform. But, strange to say, he did not even think of holding out his hand. He turned towards me, both hands behind his back, and seeming very ill at ease. And already, looking at me without seeing me, he was absorbed in what he was going to say to me. Slow to break into speech, then and always, like men who live alone—hunters and adventurers—he had come to a decision without bothering about the words required to explain it. And only now that I was in front of him did he begin painfully to seek the necessary words.

However, I gaily related to him how I had come, where I had spent the night, and that I was very surprised to see Madame Meaulnes preparing for her son's departure.

'Ah! so she's told you? . . .' he asked.

'Yes. You're not going far, I hope?'

'Yes, very far.'

Out of countenance for a moment, I no longer dared to say anything and did not know where to begin with my message, for I felt that presently, by a mere word, I was going to wipe out this decision which I did not understand.

But he himself spoke at last like some one who wishes to justify himself.

'Seurel,' he said, 'you know what the strange adventure of Sainte-Agathe meant to me. It was all I lived and hoped for. With that hope lost, what was to become of me? . . . How could I live like other people?

'Well, I tried to live out there in Paris, when I saw that all was finished and that it was scarcely worth while even looking for the Lost Land. . . . But how could a man, who had once leapt at one bound into Paradise, get used to living like everybody else? What means happiness for others appeared to me absurd. And the day when I sincerely and deliberately decided to behave as others do, I piled up remorse for a long time to come . . .'

I sat on one of the platform chairs with my eyes on the ground and listened without looking at him; I could not tell what to think of these obscure explanations.

'Come on, Meaulnes,' I said, 'explain yourself more clearly! Why this long journey? Have you made a mistake you must make amends for? a promise you must keep?'

'That's just it,' he replied. 'You remember that promise I made to Frantz? . . .'

'Ah!' I said relieved, 'is that all?'

'That's all. But perhaps also a fault to make good. Both things at once . . .'

There followed a moment of silence during which I decided to begin speaking and prepared my words . . .

'There's only one explanation, so I've come to believe,' he said again. 'Of course, I would have liked, once more, to see Mademoiselle de Galais, simply to see her once more . . . But I am convinced, now, that when I discovered the nameless manor, I was at the height of what stands for perfection and pure motive in any one's heart, a height I shall never reach again. In death alone, as I once wrote to you, I may hope to find again the beauty of that day . . .'

He changed his tone only to begin again with strange animation, while he came nearer to me.

'But listen, Seurel! This new intrigue and this long journey, this mistake I made and must make amends for, it is all, in a way, my old adventure still going on . . .'

A pause, during which he painfully tried to grasp once more the events of the past. I had missed the previous opportunity. For nothing on earth would I let this chance slip; and this time I spoke—too hastily, for later I bitterly regretted not having waited for his confession.

So I uttered the sentence which I had prepared for the previous occasion, and which no longer seemed to work. I said, without a gesture, and scarcely raising my head: 'But what if I came to tell you that all hope is not lost?'

He looked at me; then, suddenly taking his eyes away, blushed as I have never seen any one blush: a rush of blood which must have beat hard against his temples . . .

'What do you mean?' he asked at last, indistinctly.

Then, in one gush, I related what I knew, what I had done, and how, the appearance of things having altered, it seemed almost as if it were Yvonne de Galais who had sent me to him.

He was now dreadfully pale.

During all this narrative—which he listened to in silence, with head sunk between his shoulders in the attitude of one who is taken by surprise and cannot tell how to defend himself, whether to hide or run away—I remember that he interrupted me only once. I was telling him, amongst other things, that all the Sand Pit had been pulled down and that the old manor no longer existed.

'Ah!' he said, 'there you are' (as if he had watched for a chance of justifying his behaviour and the despair into which he had sunk). 'There you are: there is nothing left . . .'

To end my tale, as I felt convinced that the assurance of such an easy course would sweep away what remained of his grief, I told him that a country outing had been arranged by my Uncle Florentin, that Mademoiselle de Galais was coming to it on horseback, and that he himself was invited. . . . But he appeared completely put out and continued silent.

'You must at once cancel your journey,' I said with impatience. 'Let's go and tell your mother.'

And, as we were going downstairs together: 'That country outing? . . .' he asked with some hesitation. 'Must I really come? . . .'

'My dear good chap,' I replied, 'what a question to ask!'

He looked like a man who is pushed forward against his will.

Downstairs, Augustin gave Madame Meaulnes to un-

derstand that I would stay for lunch, dinner, and the
night, and that he himself would hire a bicycle next day
and go with me to Vieux-Nançay.

'Oh! very well,' she said with a nod, as if this news
confirmed all she thought.

I sat down in the little dining-room under the illustrated calendars, the chiselled daggers, and the leather
bottles from the Sudan which a brother of M. Meaulnes,
who had been in the marines, had brought home from
his distant travels . . .

Augustin left me there alone for a moment before the
meal, and in the next room, where his mother had prepared his luggage, I heard him tell her, in a slightly lowered voice, not to unpack his trunk—as his journey was
perhaps only delayed . . .

chapter 5. THE COUNTRY OUTING

I had trouble to keep up with Meaulnes along the
road to Vieux-Nançay. He rode like a racer. He did not
push up any of the hills. His unaccountable hesitation
of the previous day was followed by a feverish nervousness and an eagerness to hasten our arrival which rather
frightened me. At my uncle's he showed the same impatience and seemed unable to be interested in anything
until about ten next morning, when, settled in the carriage, we were ready to start for the river.

It was the end of August; the summer was drawing
to a close; the empty sheaths of the yellowing chestnut
trees were beginning to litter the white roads. The drive
was not long. The Guelders, the farm close to the spot
we were making for on the banks of the Cher, was
scarcely more than two kilometres beyond the Sand Pit.
Now and again we came across other guests also driving,
and even young fellows on horseback, whom Florentin
had boldly invited in M. de Galais' name. . . . An attempt had been made, as of old, to bring rich and poor
together, squires and peasants. Thus it was we noticed
Jasmin Delouche coming on his bicycle, for he had, some
time back, made the acquaintance of my uncle through
Baladier the forester.

'There's the fellow,' said Meaulnes, spotting him,
'who had the key of the whole thing while we were
searching as far as Paris. It is maddening!'

And each time he looked at him his bitterness in-
creased. Delouche, who on the contrary considered he
deserved our full gratitude, rode very near to our carriage as escort, right to the end. He had clearly taken
pains with his toilet, without much result, and the end

of his threadbare jacket rubbed the mud-guard of his
machine.

But in spite of the constraint he put upon himself to
be agreeable, his old-looking face never succeeded in
pleasing. It made me feel a kind of vague pity for him.
But on whom would I not have had pity that day? . . .

I never recall that country outing without an obscure
regret—a stifling uneasiness. I had looked forward to the
day with so much joy. . . . Everything appeared so perfectly contrived to make us happy. But so little happiness
came of it! . . .

Yet how beautiful were the banks of the Cher!
Where we stopped, the hill sloped gently down to the
riverside, and the land was divided into small green
meadows and willow groves separated by fences like so
many tiny gardens. On the other side, the river had steep
banks cut out of rugged grey hills; and on the most distant of these you could make out romantic country seats,
each with a turret rising from the firs. Now and again,
in the far distance, was heard the barking of the pack
of hounds at the Château de Préveranges.

We had reached this spot through intricate little lanes
thick with sharp flints or else full of sand—lanes which,
near the river, springs changed into streams. As we went
by, wild brambles caught at our sleeves. And at one
moment we plunged into the cool darkness at the bottom of ravines, while the next, owing to a break in the
hedges, we were bathed in the clear light of the whole
valley. Then, farther out on the other bank, as we approached, a man hanging onto the rock was with slow
movements setting ground lines for fishing. Heavens!
what a beautiful day it was!

We settled on a grass plot, a clearing in a copse of
silver birches. It was like a wide lawn of fine turf and
seemed to offer room for endless games.

The horses were unharnessed and taken to the farm.

Then we began to unpack the food—right in the wood
—and to set up on the grass the small folding tables my
uncle had brought.

Just then volunteers were required to go to the entrance of the adjoining road to keep watch for the late
comers and show them where we were. I at once offered
myself; Meaulnes followed me, and we posted ourselves
by the suspension bridge at the junction of many lanes
and the road leading from the Sand Pit.

There we had to wait, walking up and down, talking
of the past, trying as best we could to divert our
thoughts. One more carriage arrived from Vieux-Nançay
with some unknown peasants and a tall girl decked with
ribbons. Then nothing more, or rather three children in
a donkey cart, the children of the former gardener at
the Sand Pit.

'I seem to recognise them,' said Meaulnes. 'I feel
sure these are the kids who got hold of my hands, that
first evening of the fête, and took me in to dinner . . .'

But at that moment the donkey refused to go and the
children jumped down to pull at the beast, poking and
whacking him as hard as they could; then Meaulnes,
much put out, pretended he had made a mistake . . .

I asked them if they had come across Monsieur and
Mademoiselle de Galais on the road. One replied that
he did not know, the other, 'I believe so, sir.' So we were
no better off.

At last they walked down towards the lawn, some pulling the donkey by the bridle, others pushing behind. And
we turned back to wait. Meaulnes kept his eyes fixed on
the bend of the Sand Pit road, watching with a sort of
terror for the approaching vision of the girl he had once
so much sought. A strange and almost ludicrous nervousness clutched at him and vented itself on Jasmin. From
the small hillock on which we had climbed to survey
the road, we could see, on the lawn down below, a group

of guests amongst whom Delouche was trying to cut a
fine figure.

'Look at that idiot holding forth!' Meaulnes said to
me.

And I replied, 'Leave him alone. He does the best he
can, poor chap.'

Meaulnes would not stop. Some distance away a hare
or a squirrel must have come out of the thicket. Jasmin,
to show off, pretended to chase it.

'Look at that! He's running now! . . .' said Meaulnes,
as if that beat everything in cheek.

And this time I could not keep from laughing:
Meaulnes, too, but only for a moment.

After another quarter of an hour:

'Suppose she does not come? . . .' he asked.

I replied, 'But she promised. Try and be patient!'

He resumed his watch. But at last, unable to put up
any longer with this unbearable delay, he said:

'Listen. I'm going down to the others. I don't know
what fate is now against me: but if I stay here, I feel
sure she will never come—that it is utterly impossible
she will presently appear at the end of this road.'

And he went away towards the lawn, leaving me alone.
I walked some hundred yards along the road to kill time.
And at the first bend I saw Yvonne de Galais riding
side-saddle on an old white horse, so frisky this morning
that she was obliged to pull the reins to prevent him
trotting. M. de Galais, in silence, painfully walked on
foot by the horse's head. On the way they had most
likely taken turns in using the old mount.

Seeing me alone, the girl smiled, jumped nimbly to
the ground, and, giving the reins to her father, came
towards me while I hurried up to her.

'I am pleased at finding you alone,' she said. 'For I
wouldn't show old Bélisaire to any one but you, and I
don't want to put him with the other horses. He's too
ugly and too old, for one thing, then I always fear he

might get hurt by the others. Yet he's the only one I dare to ride, and when he's dead, I shall never go on horseback . . .'

In Mademoiselle de Galais as in Meaulnes I felt, beneath this charming animation and this grace which seemed so peaceful, something impatient and almost anxious. She talked faster than usual. In spite of a rosy flush on her cheeks, there was an intense pallor here and there round her eyes, on her forehead, in which all her trouble was manifest.

We agreed to tie Bélisaire to a tree, in the little wood near the road. Old M. de Galais, still not saying a word, produced the halter from the holster and tied up the animal—rather low, so it seemed to me. I promised to send presently from the farm hay and oats and straw . . .

And Mademoiselle de Galais arrived on the lawn just as I picture her in former days, walking towards the shore of the lake, when Meaulnes saw her for the first time.

Taking her father's arm and with her left hand holding aside the flap of the long cloak that wrapped her round, she drew near the guests with her usual expression, at once so serious and so childlike. I walked by her. All the guests, who had scattered about or were playing farther out, stood up and gathered to welcome her. There was a brief moment of silence while every one gazed as she approached.

Meaulnes had mingled with the group of young men and nothing marked him out from amongst his companions except his height; yet there were others almost as tall. He did nothing to draw attention to himself, making no gesture, taking no step forward. I could see him, dressed in grey, standing motionless, and, like every one else, keeping his eyes fixed on the beautiful girl advancing. At last, however, with an unconscious and uneasy gesture, his hand went over his bare head as if amongst the well-brushed heads of his companions, to hide his own, so rough, and with hair cropped like a peasant's.

Then the group gathered round Mademoiselle de Galais. She was introduced to the girls and boys she did not know . . . My friend's turn was soon to come and I felt as anxious as he could be. I was preparing to make the introduction myself.

But, before I could say anything, the girl advanced towards him, with surprising assurance and gravity:

'I recognise Augustin Meaulnes,' she said.

And she held out her hand to him.

Newcomers drew near almost at once to greet Yvonne de Galais and the two young people found themselves parted. By some wretched accident they were not put together for lunch at the same little table. Yet Meaulnes seemed to have recovered confidence and courage. I was isolated between Delouche and M. de Galais and more than once from this distance I saw my friend wave his hand to me.

It was only towards the end of the evening, after boating on the neighbouring pond, games, bathing, and chatting had started everywhere, that Meaulnes found himself again in the girl's presence. We were sitting on some garden chairs which we had brought, talking with Delouche, when Mademoiselle de Galais, deliberately leaving a group of young people amongst whom she seemed bored, made her way towards us. I remember that she asked us why we were not boating on The Guelders lake as the others were.

'We had a few goes this afternoon,' I replied; 'but it's rather dull and we soon tired of it.'

'Well! why shouldn't you go on the river?' she said.

'The current's too strong, we might get carried away.'

'We want a motor-boat,' said Meaulnes, 'or that steamboat there used to be.'

'We no longer have it,' she said in a rather low voice. 'We've sold it.'

And there was a moment's awkward silence.

Jasmin seized this opportunity to declare that he was going to join M. de Galais.

'I shall manage to find him,' he said.

Strangeness of fate! These two, so completely dif-

ferent, were delighted with each other, and had hardly
parted company since the morning. M. de Galais took
me aside for a moment, towards evening, to tell me that
I had in Delouche a friend full of tact, deference, and
fine qualities. He had even perhaps entrusted to him the
secret of old Bélisaire's existence and of the horse's hiding-place.

I was planning also to withdraw, but I felt the two
young people so ill at ease, so worried in each other's
presence, that I thought it prudent to remain.

But all this discretion on Jasmin's part, all this precaution on mine, served little purpose. These two talked,
but invariably, with an obstinacy of which he must have
been unaware, Meaulnes always came back to the marvels of the old days. And each time the poor tortured
girl had to repeat to him that everything was gone: the
old queer and oddly shaped house rased to the ground;
the lake drained and filled with earth; and the children
in their charming costumes dispersed for ever . . .

'Ah!' Meaulnes would simply say with despair and as
if each of these disappearances showed him to be right
and the girl or myself wrong . . .

We were walking side by side . . . I vainly tried to
create a diversion from the sadness which was coming
over all three of us. For again Meaulnes, with one abrupt question, would give way to his haunting idea. He
asked information about everything he had seen of old:
the little girls, the driver of the old berlin, the ponies of
the race.

'. . . Are the ponies also sold? So, there are no longer
horses on the estate? . . .'

She replied that there were none. She did not speak
of Bélisaire.

Then he conjured up the things in his bedroom; the
chandeliers, the tall looking-glass, the old broken lute.
. . . He inquired about all this with unwonted eagerness,
as if he wanted to convince himself that nothing sur-

vived of his fine adventure, and that the girl would not
bring back to him one piece of wreckage which could
prove that they had not both lived in a dream—as the
diver brings up from the bottom of the sea mere pebbles
and seaweeds . . .

Mademoiselle de Galais and I could not refrain from
smiling sadly; then she decided to explain to him:

'You will never see again the beautiful mansion that
M. de Galais and I had arranged for our poor Frantz.
We spent our lives doing as he wished us. He was such
a strange, charming boy. But everything vanished with
him on that evening of the betrothal that never came off.
M. de Galais had then already lost his fortune without
our knowing. Frantz was in debt and his former friends
—getting news of his disappearance—at once brought
us their claims. We became poor. Madame de Galais
died, and in a few days we lost all our friends. Could
Frantz come back—if he is not dead—and find again his
friends and his fiancée, and the interrupted wedding
take place—then perhaps everything would be as of old!
But can the past come to life again?'

'Who knows?' said Meaulnes thoughtfully. And he
put no more questions.

We were walking, all three of us, without noise on
grass that was short and ever so slightly touched with
yellow. Augustin had close to him on his right the girl
whom he had thought for ever lost. Whenever he asked
one of his cruel questions, her charming and troubled
face would slowly turn towards him as she answered;
and once, while speaking, she gently placed her hand on
his arm in a gesture full of trust and surrender. Why
was Admiral Meaulnes there like a stranger, like some
one who has not found what he was looking for and for
whom nothing else has any interest? Three years earlier he might not have been able to bear this happiness
without terror, without madness, perhaps. But whence

came this emptiness, this remoteness, this powerlessness
to be happy which now possessed him?

We were approaching the little wood where M. de
Galais had that morning tied up Bélisaire; the sun, now
declining, lengthened our shadows upon the grass. On
the far end of the lawn we heard the voices of the little
girls and others playing games—voices mellowed by distance to a happy buzz; and we remained silent in the
marvellous quiet; then we heard some one singing on
the other side of the wood, from the direction of The
Guelders, the farm by the river. The voice was young
and distant, and belonged to some one taking cattle to
water: the tune was rhythmic as a dance, but the man
sang it with a drawl and dragged it as though it were
some old sad ballad:

> *My shoes are red . . .*
> *Good-bye, my lover!*
> *My shoes are red . . .*
> *Good-bye for ever! . . .*

Meaulnes had raised his head to listen. It was ac-
tually one of the tunes which the belated peasants had
sung that last evening of the fête at the nameless manor,
when everything had fallen to pieces. Nothing but a
memory—the most wretched memory—of those beautiful days which would return no more.

'Do you hear that?' said Meaulnes in a subdued voice.
'Oh! I am going to see who it is.' And thereupon he
dashed into the little wood. Almost at once the voice
was silent; one heard for a moment longer the man
whistling to his beast still farther away—then nothing
more . . .

I looked at the girl. Pensive and dismayed, she kept
her eyes fixed on the copse where Meaulnes had just
disappeared. How many times, in later days, was she not
to look thus pensively at the gap through which Admiral
Meaulnes was vanishing for ever!

She turned towards me.

'He's not happy,' she said sorrowfully.

She added: 'And perhaps I can't do anything for him? . . .'

I hesitated to reply, fearing that Meaulnes, who must have reached the farm in an instant and was now coming back through the wood, might hear what we were saying. I was, however, on the point of encouraging her; of advising her not to mind being rather blunt with the tall boy; that most likely some secret tormented him which he could never confide to her or any one of his own accord—when suddenly a cry came from the other side of the wood; then we heard a thudding, as of a horse furiously pawing the ground, and the noise of wrangling in broken sentences . . . I understood at once that an accident had happened to old Bélisaire and I ran towards the place whence the uproar came. Mademoiselle de Galais followed me from afar. At the other end of the lawn our movement must have been noticed, for directly I entered the copse, I heard the shouts of people hurrying to meet us.

Old Bélisaire, tied up too low, had caught one of his forefeet in the halter; he had not moved until M. de Galais and Delouche, in the course of their walk, had come near him, then frightened, upset by the unusual oats given him, he had begun to struggle furiously; the two men had tried to free him, but so clumsily that they had only succeeded in further entangling him, at the risk, too, of dangerous kicks. It was then that Meaulnes, on his way back from The Guelders, had chanced upon the group. Furious at so much bungling, he had pushed the two men aside, almost knocking them into a bush. He had freed Bélisaire cautiously but very deftly. Too late, though; the damage was done; the horse appeared to have strained a tendon or else to have broken something, for he drooped his head dismally and kept one of his legs held up under his belly; he was trembling all over; his saddle, too, was half off his back. Meaulnes was stooping to feel the leg and examine it and said nothing.

When he looked up, nearly every one had gathered around, but he saw no one. He was red with anger.

'I would like to know,' he called out, 'who tied him up like this! And left his saddle on all day! And who dared to saddle so old a horse, scarcely fit for the lightest gig.'

Delouche was about to say something—to take the blame upon himself.

'Shut up! It's your fault. I saw you tugging at his halter like a fool to get him loose.'

And bending down again he began rubbing the horse's leg with the palm of his hand.

M. de Galais, who so far had said nothing, made the mistake of attempting to come out of his reserve. He stammered:

'Naval officers are accustomed to . . . My horse.'

'Oh! He's yours, is he?' said Meaulnes, a little calmer, but very red, turning his head towards the old man.

I thought he was going to change his tone, to apologise. He paused a moment. And then I saw that he took a bitter, despairing pleasure in aggravating the situation, in smashing everything for ever, as he said with insolence:

'Well, I shouldn't boast of it, if I were you!'

Some one suggested: 'Perhaps cold water . . . If we bathed it at the ford.'

'This horse must be taken away at once,' said Meaulnes, without replying, 'while he can still walk—and there's no time to be lost! He should be put in the stable and never taken out again.'

Several young fellows immediately offered themselves. But Mademoiselle de Galais at once thanked them. Her face on fire and ready to burst into tears, she said goodbye to every one and even to Meaulnes, who, utterly abashed, dared not look at her. She took the animal by the reins as one catches hold of somebody's hand, more to feel close to him than to lead him . . . The late summer wind was so mild on the Sand Pit road that it seemed like May, and the leaves in the hedges quivered in the south wind . . . We saw her set off thus, her arm partly out of her cloak, and holding in her slim hand the thick leather rein. Her father walked painfully by her side . . .

Sad end to the evening! Little by little everybody picked up his belongings and the picnic things; chairs were folded, tables taken down; the carriages, loaded with luggage and guests, went away one by one while hats were raised and handkerchiefs waved. We were the last to go with my Uncle Florentin who, like us, was silently brooding over his sad and great disappointment.

Then we drove swiftly off in our well-hung carriage behind our beautiful chestnut. The wheels grated on the sand as we took the corner, and soon Meaulnes and I, who sat at the back, saw the cross-road which old Bélisaire and his owners had taken slowly disappear.

Then my friend, the last person in the world to cry, turned suddenly towards me and his face was twisted by the coming of irresistible tears.

'Stop, will you?' he said, placing a hand on Florentin's shoulder. 'Don't bother about me. I'll come back by myself on foot.'

He put a hand on the mud-guard of the carriage and vaulted to the ground at one leap. He turned back, to our consternation, and started running: he ran right back to the lane we had just passed, the lane leading to the Sand Pit. He must have reached the manor by the avenue of firs he had followed in the old days when, like a tramp hiding in the thicket, he had heard the mysterious conversation of the unknown beautiful children.

And this was the evening on which, sobbing, he asked Mademoiselle de Galais to marry him.

chapter 7. THE WEDDING DAY

A Thursday, early in February, a fine icy Thursday evening with a high wind blowing: somewhere about half-past three or four . . . Near the villages, clothes have been hung on hedges since midday and are drying in the strong breeze. Children, tired of playing, sit by their mothers asking for the story of their wedding days. In every house the dining-room fire brightly lights up what seems an altar of shining toys.

Any one who does not wish to be happy has only to climb up to the attics to hear till evening the whistle and moan of shipwrecks; or he can go out on the road for the wind to flap back his scarf on his mouth as in a sudden warm kiss which will make him weep. But for him who loves happiness there stands, by the side of a muddy lane, the Sand Pit house which my friend Meaulnes has just entered with Yvonne de Galais who has been his wife since midday.

The engagement had lasted five months. It had been a peaceful time, as peaceful as the first meeting had been full of excitement. Meaulnes had often come to the Sand Pit during those days, either on his bicycle or driving. At least twice a week, as she sat sewing or reading by the window overlooking the moor and the firs, Mademoiselle de Galais would suddenly see his tall hurrying shadow move behind the curtain, for he always comes that roundabout way, up the drive he once came by. But this is the only allusion—a tacit one—which he makes to the past. Happiness seems to have lulled his strange anguish.

Some trivial happenings have marked these five quiet months. I have been appointed teacher at the little ham-

let of Saint-Benoist-des-Champs. Saint-Benoist is not a
village, but only a few farms scattered about the countryside, with the schoolhouse standing completely isolated on the side of the road some way up a hill. I lead a
very solitary life; but going across the fields it takes me
only three quarters of an hour to reach the Sand Pit.

Delouche lives now with his uncle who is a builder at
Vieux-Nançay. He will soon be the head man. He often
comes to see me. Meaulnes, at the request of Mademoiselle de Galais, is now very nice to him.

All this explains why we are there rambling about
together, towards four in the afternoon, when all the
wedding people have already left.

The ceremony was held at midday as quietly as possible, in the old chapel of the Sand Pit, which was not
pulled down and stands partly hidden by firs, on the
slope of the adjoining hill. Meaulnes' mother, M. Seurel
and Millie, Florentin and the others went off in their
carriages after a hurried lunch. Jasmin and I alone remained.

We are taking a stroll along the woods behind the
Sand Pit house, by the side of a wide expanse of land,
the site of the manor now destroyed. Without owning
to it and without knowing why, we are filled with anxiety.
We try in vain to divert our thoughts and beguile our
uneasiness during this wandering walk, by attracting one
another's attention to the forms of hares and the small
sandy furrows where rabbits have been scratching . . . to
a trap set in the wood . . . or to the trail of a poacher
. . . But we always come back hauntingly to the edge of
the copse from where the silent and closed house can be
seen . . .

The wide window which looks on the firs opens onto a
wooden balcony invaded by unruly grass bending under
the wind. A light, as of a burning fire, is reflected on the
panes of the window where from time to time a shadow
is seen to pass. Silence and solitude are all around: in

the neighbouring fields, in the kitchen garden, in the farm which alone remains of the old outhouses. The farm hands have gone to the village to celebrate the happiness of their master and mistress. From time to time the wind, heavy with a mist which feels almost like rain, comes to damp our faces, and brings us the remote phrases of a piano. Out there, in the closed house, some one is playing. I stopped a moment to listen in silence. It is at first like a trembling voice which, from afar, scarcely dares to sing its joy . . . It is like the laughter of a little girl who, in her room, fetches all her toys out and displays them to her sweetheart . . . It also brings to my mind the shy pleasure of a woman who, having gone to put on a beautiful dress, comes back to show it and is not yet sure it will please . . . This air which I do not know is also a prayer, an entreaty to happiness not to be too cruel, a bowing of the head and as it were a falling on the knees before happiness . . .

The thought comes to me: 'At last they are happy. Meaulnes is there close to her . . .'

And to know this, to feel sure of it, is sufficient to bring perfect satisfaction to the simple child that I am.

But just then, while thus dreaming, and my face wet from the wind crossing the moor as if by sea-spray, I feel some one touch me on the shoulder.

'Listen!' says Jasmin in a low voice.

I look at him. He beckons to me not to move; and he too, with bent head and knitted brow, stands listening.

Hou-ou!

This time I have heard. It is a signal—a call on two notes, high and low—which I once heard of old . . . Ah! I remember: it is the cry of the tall comedian as he hailed his young companion from the school gate. It is the call to which Frantz made us swear to answer no matter where or when it came. But what can he be wanting here to-day, that fellow?

'It comes from the big fir wood on the left,' I say in half whispers. 'Most likely a poacher.'

Jasmin shakes his head: 'You know quite well it's not,' he says.

Then lower: 'They have both been in these parts ever since this morning. About eleven I came unawares upon Booby keeping a lookout in a field close to the chapel. He took to his heels when he spotted me. Perhaps they've come a long way on their bikes, for he was covered with mud halfway up his back . . .'

'What are they after, I wonder?'

'I don't know. But we must certainly send them off. They must not be left to prowl about here. Else all the mad tricks will begin again.'

I am of the same opinion without owning to it.

'The best would be to join them,' I say, 'to see what they want, to make them listen to reason . . .'

So, stooping under the branches, we slowly and silently make our way across the copse as far as the big fir wood from where, at regular intervals, rises this prolonged cry, which is not in itself uncanny, yet seems to us an evil omen.

In this part of the wood where the eye roams between

regular rows of trees, it is difficult to take any one by surprise or walk any distance without being seen. We make no attempt at it. I post myself at one corner of the wood, Jasmin goes to the opposite corner, thus allowing each of us to command, from the outside, a view on two sides of a rectangle and to let neither of the bohemians escape without hailing him. These arrangements being made, I begin to play my part of peace messenger and call out:

'Frantz! . . . Frantz! Have no fear. It's only me, Seurel; I want to talk to you . . .'

There is a moment's silence; I am about to call again when from the very heart of the wood and rather too far for my eyes to reach, a voice orders: 'Stay where you are; he'll come to you.'

Gradually from between the tall firs, which in the distance look closely set together, I discern the outline of the young man approaching. He seems to be covered with mud and is badly dressed; trouser clips are tight round his ankles, an old midshipman's cap fits closely on his hair which is too long. I can now see his face, so much thinner . . . He looks as if he had been crying.

Coming towards me resolutely: 'What is it you want?' he asks insolently.

'And yourself, Frantz, what are you doing about here? Why come and disturb those who are happy? What are you asking for? Tell me.'

Questioned thus point-blank, he blushes slightly, stammers, and only replies: 'But I am not happy; I am so wretched.'

Then he breaks into bitter sobs, his head in the bend of one arm; he is leaning against a tree. We had taken a few steps in the wood, the spot is perfectly quiet. Even the sound of the wind is hushed by the tall firs bordering the wood. Amongst the rows of trunks the noise of the stifled sobbing of the young man echoes and dies out.

I wait until he grows calmer, and, placing a hand on his shoulders, say:

'Frantz, you'd better come with me. I'll take you to them. They'll welcome you as a lost child now found, and all this will be at an end.'

But he would hear nothing; in a voice subdued by tears, miserable, angry, obstinate, he started once again: 'And so Meaulnes won't be bothered with me? Why does he not answer when I call? Why can't he keep his word?'

'Oh! come on, Frantz,' I replied, 'these fantastic child-like days are over. Don't disturb with mad whims the happiness of those you love; of your sister and Augustin Meaulnes.'

'But he alone can save me, you know that well. He alone can find again the trail I am looking for. These last three years, now, Booby and I have been knocking about France without any success. My one hope left was in your friend. And he does not answer my call. Hasn't he got his love back? Why can't he think of me? He must begin to think of me. Yvonne will let him go . . . She's never refused me anything.'

He turned towards me a face where tears had traced dirty streaks in dust and grime, the face of an old-looking child, worn-out and beaten. His eyes were circled with freckles, his chin badly shaved; his hair, too long, trailed over his dirty collar; with hands in his pockets he stood shivering. He no longer was, as of old, a princely child dressed in tatters. Yet at heart, most likely, he was more of a child than ever: fantastically imperious and then all at once in despair. But these childish ways were now intolerable in a young man already looking more than grown up . . . Formerly there was so much youthful pride about him that all the madness in the world was right for him. But now one was at first tempted to pity him for having failed in life, then to reproach him for absurdly acting the romantic young hero, as I

saw that he persisted in doing . . . And finally I could
not help thinking that our handsome Frantz with the
beautiful love story had most likely taken to stealing
for a living, just like his companion Booby . . . So much
pride had ended in this!

'What if I promise,' I said at last, having thought it
out, 'that in a few days Meaulnes shall start on a search
all for your sake? . . .'

'He will be successful, won't he? You are sure of it?'
he asked with chattering teeth.

'I believe so. Everything comes easy to him now!'

'And how shall I know? Who will tell me?'

'You will come back here in exactly a year from to-
day, at this same time: you will then find the girl you
love.'

And saying this I am thinking not of disturbing the
newly married couple, but of making inquiries through
Aunt Moinel and myself hastening to find the girl.

The bohemian looked straight at me with really wonderful trustfulness. Just as if he were fifteen!—the age
one could easily have taken us to be at Sainte-Agathe, on
the evening of the sweeping of the classrooms, when we
three took that terrible childlike oath.

Despair gripped him once more when he felt obliged
to say: 'Very well, we must go.'

He looked with an evident pang at the surrounding
woods which he was about to leave again.

'In three days from now,' he said, 'we shall be on the
roads of Germany. We've left our caravans a long way
off. And for the last thirty hours we've ridden without
a stop. We thought to get here in time to take Meaulnes
away before the wedding and search with him for my
fiancée, as he once looked for the Sand Pit Manor.'

Then again, falling back to his terrible childishness:
'Call your Delouche back,' he said, going away; 'meeting
him would really be too dreadful.'

Gradually, in between the firs, I watched until I saw

his grey outline disappear. I called Jasmin and we resumed our watch. But almost at once, farther out, we spotted Augustin closing the shutters of the house, and we were struck by his strange behaviour.

chapter 9. HAPPY PEOPLE

Later on I came to know in minute detail what had
happened out there . . .

From early in the afternoon Meaulnes and his wife,
whom I still call Mademoiselle de Galais, had been left
entirely by themselves in the drawing-room at the Sand
Pit. All the guests having gone, M. de Galais had opened
the door, letting the high wind moan for a second all
through the house, then he had set off towards Vieux-
Nançay, not to be back until dinner, in time for locking
up and giving orders at the farm. No noise from outside
now reaches the young people, only the leafless branch
of a rose tree tapping against the window-pane on the
side of the moor. Like two passengers in a drifting boat,
the two lovers, in the winter gale, are left alone with
happiness.

'The fire is almost going out,' said Mademoiselle de
Galais, and she tried to take a log out of the chest.

But Meaulnes hurried to put the wood on the fire
himself. He then took the hand the girl had put out, and
they stood there facing one another as if stifled by some
great news which could not be uttered.

The wind swirled by with the noise of an overflowing
river. From time to time, as on the window of a train, a
drop of rain left a slanting streak across the pane.

Then the girl suddenly stole away. She opened the
passage door and disappeared with a mysterious smile.
Augustin was for a moment left alone in semi-darkness
. . . The tick-tick of a small clock recalled the dining-
room at Sainte-Agathe . . . He no doubt thought: 'So
this is the house so much sought after; the passage once
so full of whispers and strange encounters . . .'

It is at this moment that he must have heard—Mademoiselle de Galais told me later that she also heard it—the first call of Frantz close to the house.

It was in vain then that the young woman showed him all the marvels with which she was burdened: the toys she had played with as a little girl; all the photographs of herself as a child; as a *vivandière*, herself and Frantz on their mother's knee, and such a pretty mother . . . then all that was left of her sedate little dresses of childhood: 'even this one which I was still wearing just before you came to know me, at the time, so I believe, you must have arrived at the Higher Elementary School at Sainte-Agathe . . .' Meaulnes no longer saw anything or heard anything.

Once, however, he appeared to grasp again the idea of his extraordinary, inconceivable happiness.

'You are here,' he said dully, as if merely to say it made him dizzy—'you are moving close to the table and your hand for a moment rests on it . . .'

And again: 'Mother, when she was young, would lean forward slightly like you, when speaking to me . . . And when she sat at the piano . . .'

Then Mademoiselle de Galais proposed to play before night came. But it was growing dark in that corner of the drawing-room and they had to light a candle. The pink lamp-shade accentuated the rosy flush which on the girl's face was a sign of great anxiety.

Out there, at the edge of the wood, I began to hear the trembling song brought by the wind, but soon broken into by the second call of the two mad fellows who had come nearer to us through the firs.

For a long time Meaulnes listened to the girl, while he looked silently out of the window. More than once he turned towards the sweet face, now so frail and anxious. Then he came near to Yvonne de Galais and lightly placed one hand on her shoulder. She felt, close to her

neck, the gentle pressure of the caress to which she
should have been able to respond.

'Night is falling,' he said at last. 'I am going to close
the shutters. But do not stop playing . . .'

What took place then in that mysterious and wild
heart? I often wondered and only came to know when
it was too late. Unknown remorse? Inexplicable mis-
givings? Fear of seeing this unheard-of happiness, to
which he clung so closely, soon vanish from between his
hands? And then the terrible temptation at once and
for ever to dash to the ground this marvel he had con-
quered? . . .

He went out slowly and silently after having once
more looked at his young wife. From the edge of the
wood we saw him first close with some hesitation one of
the shutters, then look vaguely our way, close another,
and suddenly run off at full speed in our direction. He
reached us before we could think of better concealment.
He noticed us as he was going to jump over a small
hedge recently planted and enclosing a meadow. He
changed his course. I recall that he looked haggard, like
a hunted beast . . . He attempted to retrace his steps
and climb over the hedge on the side of the brook.

I called him: 'Meaulnes! . . . Augustin! . . .'

But he never even turned his head. Then, feeling sure
that this alone could hold him back: 'Frantz is here,' I
called out. 'Stop!'

He at last stopped. Out of breath and without giving
me time to be ready with what I ought to say: 'He's
here!' he said. 'What's he wanting?'

'He's wretched,' I replied. 'He came to ask your help
in looking for what he has lost.'

'Ah!' said he, lowering his head. 'I guessed that much.
I tried in vain to drown that thought . . . But where is
he? Tell me quick.'

I told him that Frantz had just gone and that he
certainly could not be caught now. It was a great shock

to Meaulnes. He hesitated, walked ahead two or three steps, then stopped. He appeared in the depths of uncertainty and grief. I related to him what I had promised in his name to Frantz. I said that I had arranged a meeting with him a year hence at the same place.

Augustin, so calm usually, was now in an extraordinary state of impatience and agitation.

'Ah! why did you do that!' he said. 'Of course I can save him. But it must be at once. I must see him, speak to him; he must forgive me, that I may make amends for all . . . Otherwise I can no longer show my face out there . . .'

And he looked towards the Sand Pit house.

'Well,' I said, 'just for a childish promise you made you are now going to wreck your happiness.'

'Ah! if it were only that promise!' he exclaimed. And thus I knew that something else was binding the two men together, though I could not guess what it was.

'In any case,' I said, 'it's now too late. They are on their way to Germany.'

He was about to reply when a face, dishevelled, tortured, haggard, appeared between us. It was Mademoiselle de Galais. She must have run, for her face was wet with drops of sweat. She must have fallen and hurt herself, for her forehead was scratched above the right eye and blood was caked in her hair.

It has sometimes happened to me, in the poor districts of Paris, to witness a couple which one thought happy, united, and honest, suddenly bring their quarrel into the street to be separated by the intervention of the police. The scandal had broken out all at once, no matter when, just as they sat down at dinner, before the Sunday walk, when keeping the little boy's birthday . . . and now everything is forgotten and smashed. The man and the woman in their quarrel are no more than two pitiful fiends, while the children in tears rush up to them, hugging them closely, begging them to keep quiet and not to fight.

Mademoiselle de Galais, coming thus close to Meaulnes, put me in mind of one of those children, those poor distracted children. I believe that, had all her friends, all the village, all the world been looking on, she would have rushed forward all the same, she would have dropped on us in the same way, dishevelled, tearful, her face dirty.

But when she once understood that Meaulnes was really there, that this time, at all events, he would not forsake her, she placed her arm under his and could not help laughing amidst her tears as would a child. They said not a word to each other. But, as she had pulled out her handkerchief, Meaulnes took it gently from her hands; with care and precaution he wiped away the blood from the girl's hair.

'We must now go in,' he said.

And in the bracing high wind which lashed at their faces that wintry evening I left them to go back together, he helping her by the hand at awkward places, she smiling and hastening—towards the home they had for a moment forsaken.

I had to remain shut up in the school during the whole of the following day, a prey to dull anxiety, feeling but little reassured by the happy ending to yesterday's scene. Immediately after the hour of 'private study' which follows afternoon school, I made my way to the Sand Pit. Night was falling when I reached the avenue of firs leading to the house. The shutters were already closed. I feared to intrude by coming at so late an hour the day after a wedding. So I prowled about close to the edge of the garden and in the neighbouring fields for a long while, hoping all the time to see some one come out of the closed house . . . But my hopes were in vain. Nothing stirred, not even in the adjoining farm. And I had to go home, haunted by the gloomiest forebodings.

This uncertainty lasted on next day, a Saturday. In the evening I made haste to get my cape, my stick, a piece of bread to eat on the way, and reached the Sand Pit to find everything closed up there just as the day before . . . A little light on the first floor; but not noise, not a movement . . . At the farmhouse, however, I now noticed, from the yard, the front door left open, the fire burning in the great kitchen, and I heard a noise of voices and footsteps as is usual at supper time. This reassured me without telling me much. I could not say anything to these people nor ask them anything. And I went back to resume my watch, to wait in vain, thinking at any moment to see the door open and the tall form of Meaulnes emerge.

It was only on Sunday, during the afternoon, that I resolved to pull the bell at the Sand Pit. While I was making my way up the bare hills, I heard in the distance the church bells ringing for vespers on that winter Sunday. I felt lonely and distressed. I do not know what sad foreboding overwhelmed me. And I was only partly surprised when, in answer to my ring, M. de Galais appeared alone and spoke to me almost in whispers: Yvonne de Galais was in bed with a high fever; Meaulnes had been obliged to leave on Friday morning to go on a long journey; no one knew when he would come back . . .

And as the old man, very embarrassed, very sad, did not ask me to come in, I at once said good-bye to him. The door shut and I remained on the doorstep for a moment, my heart torn, my mind in chaos, watching without knowing why a branch of dead wistaria which the wind swayed in a beam of sunshine.

Thus the secret remorse, which Meaulnes had carried within him since his stay in Paris, had ended by proving too strong. My big friend had been forced in the end to let go of the happiness to which he had clung so obstinately.

Every Thursday and Sunday I came to ask news of Yvonne de Galais until the evening when at last, being convalescent, she sent word for me to come in. I found her sitting by the fire in the drawing-room with its low wide window looking on the grounds and the woods. She was not pale as I had imagined she would be, but on the contrary feverish, with bright red patches under the eyes and in a state of extreme agitation. Though she still seemed very weak, she was fully dressed. She hardly spoke, but said each sentence with extraordinary animation as though she were longing to convince herself that happiness had not yet vanished . . . I have no memory of what we said. I remember only that, with some hesitation, I came to ask when Meaulnes would be back.

'I don't know when he will come back,' she replied quickly.

There was entreaty in her eyes and I refrained from
asking more.

I often went to see her. I often talked to her by the
fire in that low drawing-room where night came quicker
than anywhere else. She never spoke about herself or
her hidden grief. But she never tired of making me relate
in all its details our schoolboy life at Sainte-Agathe.

She listened to the tale of our youthful troubles with
a grave, tender interest, almost maternal. She showed
no surprise at anything, not even at our most daring,
most dangerous childish pranks. This thoughtful tender-
ness which she had inherited from M. de Galais, had
not been exhausted by her brother's deplorable adventures. The only lament to which the past prompted her
was, I think, at not having been enough her brother's
true friend, for on the day of his great disaster he had
not dared to tell her more than any one else, and he had
thought himself for ever lost. And, after all, it was indeed a heavy task the young woman had assumed—a
perilous task that of seconding a mind as madly fantastic
as was her brother's; an overwhelming task when it was
a matter of joining one's lot with so adventurous a spirit
as my friend Admiral Meaulnes.

One day she gave me the most touching, I could almost say the most mysterious proof of this faith she kept
in her brother's childish dreams, and the care she took
to preserve at least some fragments of the dream in
which he had lived up to his twentieth year.

It was during a desolate evening of April, very much
like autumn. For nearly a month we had enjoyed a softly
premature spring and, accompanied by M. de Galais,
the dear woman had again resumed the long walks she
was fond of. But that day, the old man being tired and
myself free, she asked me to go with her in spite of the
threatening weather. The storm—rain and hail—caught
us more than two kilometres away from the Sand Pit as

we walked by the lake. Under the shed where we sought
shelter from the never-ending shower, the wind was icy
cold, and we stood close to one another, lost in thought
in front of the darkened landscape. I still picture her,
wearing a soft neat dress and looking pale and worried.

'We must go back,' she kept saying. 'We've been gone
so long. What might not have happened?'

But to my surprise, when at last it became possible to
leave our shelter, the young woman, instead of turning
back towards the Sand Pit, went on her way and asked
me to follow her. After a long walk we reached a house
I did not know, standing by itself at the side of a rutted
lane which must have led towards Préveranges. It was
a small private house with a slate roof, only marked out
from the type usual in the district by its isolation and
remoteness.

Any one watching Yvonne de Galais would have believed the house belonged to us and that we had left it
during a long absence. She stooped to open the small
iron gate, and she made haste to inspect anxiously the
lonely spot. A big yard, overgrown by weeds where children seemed to have come to play during the long dragging evenings at the end of winter, was hollowed out by
the rain. A hoop was soaking in a puddle. The heavy
shower had left only trails of white gravel in the small
gardens which the children had bestrewed with flowers
and peas. And we at last discovered, huddled together
against the step of one of the damp doors, a whole brood
of chickens quite drenched. Most of them were dead
under the stiffened wings and the crumpled feathers of
the mother.

The dear woman, fronted by so pitiful a sight, gave a
stifled cry. She bent down, disregarding water and mud,
pulled out the live chickens from the dead, and wrapped
them in a fold of her cloak. Then we went into the
house, of which she had the key. Four doors opened
out of a narrow passage into which swept a gust of wind.

Yvonne de Galais opened the first door on our right and
made me go into a dark room, where, after a moment of
uncertainty, I made out a tall looking-glass and a small
bed covered with a red silk eiderdown, in peasant fashion. As for her, having for a moment searched in other
parts of the dwelling, she came back with a flat basket
filled with down, which she delicately slipped under the
eiderdown. And while a languid ray of sunshine, the first
and last of the day, made both our faces paler and the
dusk more gloomy, we stood there, frozen and worried,
in this strange house!

From time to time she would look inside the feverish
nest, taking away another dead chicken to prevent it
causing the death of the others. And each time it seemed
to us that something, perhaps a gust of wind through
the broken panes of the attic, perhaps the mysterious
sorrow of unknown children, was silently lamenting.

'This was Frantz's house when he was little,' my companion at last said to me. 'He'd wanted a house all his
own, far from every one, in which he could go to play,
enjoy himself and live just as he pleased. Father had
found this fancy so extraordinary, so funny, that he
hadn't refused. And whenever it pleased him, on a
Thursday or Sunday, no matter when, Frantz would go
and live at his house like a man. Children of the neighbouring farms used to come to play with him, help him
with housekeeping, work in the garden. It was a wonderful game! And at night time he was not afraid of sleeping alone. As for us, we admired him so much, we never
once thought of being anxious.

'Now, the house is empty,' she went on with a sigh;
'it has been so for a long time. M. de Galais, altered by
age and grief, has never done anything to trace my
brother or call him back. And what could he have done?
But I often pass this way. Little peasant children, from
hereabout, come to play in the yard as in the old days.
It pleases me to pretend they are Frantz's old friends;

that he himself is still but a child and that he will soon
come back with the fiancée of his choice. These children
know me so well. I play with them. That brood of chicks
was ours . . .'

It had needed this shower and this childlike dismay to
induce her to confide to me the great grief of which she
had never spoken, her deep regret at having lost a
brother so mad, so charming, so much admired.

And I listened to her, not knowing what to reply, my
heart heavy with suppressed sobs . . .

Then, having closed the doors and the gate and replaced the chickens in their wooden hutch at the back
of the house, she sadly took my arm and I led her home.

Weeks and months went by. Days now of the past!
Lost happiness! This girl who had been the fairy, the
princess, the mysterious love dream of our youth, it was
now my lot to take by the arm, finding the necessary
words to soften her grief, while my friend had run away.
What can I now say of these days, of these evening
talks after school-hours on the hill of Saint-Benoist-des-
Champs, of these walks during which the one thing we
ought to have discussed was the only one concerning
which we were resolved to keep silent? The only memory I have preserved, though already dimmed, is that of
a beautiful face grown thinner, of two eyes whose lids
slowly lower when they look at me, as if already they
contemplate only an inner world.

And I remained her faithful companion—in this long
wait we never spoke of—during a whole spring and a
whole summer such as will never be again. Many a time
we went back to Frantz's house during an afternoon. She
would open the doors to air the rooms, so that nothing
should be mouldy on the young couple's return. She
tended the partly wild fowls which had their home in
the poultry-yard. And on Thursdays and Sundays we

helped to keep going the games of the neighbouring village children, whose laughter and shouts in this lonely spot made the small forsaken house appear more empty, more deserted than ever.

August, the holiday month, took me away from the Sand Pit and the dear woman. I was booked to go to Sainte-Agathe for my two months' leave. I once again saw the bare playground, the shelter, the empty classroom. . . . Everything spoke of Admiral Meaulnes and was filled with the memory of our youth now past. During those long mellowing days, I shut myself in the record room or the deserted classroom as I used to before Meaulnes' arrival. There I read, wrote, and recalled the past. . . . Father was often away jack-fishing. Millie, in the drawing-room, played the piano or sewed as of old. . . . In the absolute silence of the classroom torn green paper wreaths, jackets off prize books, clean blackboards, reminded me that the year was over, that the prizes were given, and that everything awaited autumn, the new school year and fresh endeavour—and here I kept brooding over the fact that our youth was likewise ended and that happiness had failed: and I awaited the return of the school year at the Sand Pit and Augustin's home-coming which perhaps would never be. . . .

There was, however, one piece of good news I could tell Millie when she insisted on questioning me about the bride. I dreaded her questions, and her way, at once very innocent and very shrewd, of causing you sudden embarrassment by putting her finger on your most secret thoughts. So I checked all inquiry by announcing that the young wife of my friend Meaulnes was expecting to become a mother in October.

As for me, I recalled the day when Yvonne de Galais had made me understand this great news. There had been a moment of silence; I had felt a youth's uneasiness,

and to be rid of it, I had said at once without thinking
—realising only too late all the tragedy I was thus stirring
up, 'You must be very happy?'

But she, without reservation or regret, neither remorse nor ill-will, had replied with a beautiful smile,
'Yes, very happy.'

This last week of the holidays, which was usually the
best and most romantic, a week of heavy rain when fires
begin to be lit and which I generally spent shooting at
Vieux-Nançay, in the black damp fir woods, I made
ready to return directly to Saint-Benoist-des-Champs.
Firmin, Aunt Julie, and my girl cousins at Vieux-
Nançay would have asked too many questions to which
I did not want to reply. So I gave up, for once, the joy of
spending eight good days shooting in the country, and
went back to my school-house four days before term began.

I arrived before night in the playground, which was
littered with brown leaves. My driver went away and I
entered the stuffy, echoing dining-room, where I sadly
undid the parcel of provisions Mother had prepared for
me . . . Then, restless and anxious, I hurried through a
light meal, took my cape and started on a feverish walk
which led me straight to the boundaries of the Sand Pit.

I had no wish to intrude on the very first evening of
my arrival. Yet, more daring than in February, after a
walk around the estate, where Yvonne de Galais' window alone showed a light, I climbed over the garden
fence at the back of the house and in the gathering
dusk sat on a bench near the hedge, happy merely to be
so close to what thrilled and troubled me more than anything else in the world.

Night approached. Fine rain began to fall. With
bowed head I watched my shoes getting wet in the rain
and shining—paying them no heed. Darkness slowly enclosed me, and the cool of night, without troubling my

reverie. I dreamed sadly and tenderly of the muddy
lanes at Sainte-Agathe on such a September evening; I
pictured the square full of mist, the butcher boy whistling on his way to the pump, the lights of the café, the
waggonette and its merry occupants under a shield of
open umbrellas, arriving at Uncle Florentin's at the end
of the holidays . . . And I was sadly saying to myself,
'What good is all this happiness if my friend Meaulnes
cannot be there, nor his young wife . . .'

It was then I raised my head and saw her two steps
away. Her shoes made on the sand a slight noise which
I had mistaken for raindrops from the hedge. Her head
and shoulders were wrapped in a big shawl of black wool
and the fine rain was like powder on the hair over her
forehead. She must have seen me from her bedroom
window, which looked onto the garden, and had come
down to me. In the old days Mother used thus to worry
about me, hunting me up to say, 'You must come in,'
but beginning herself to enjoy the night walk in the rain,
she would only say, very gently, 'You will catch cold!'
and remain by me for a long talk. . . .

Yvonne de Galais held out a burning hand; then she
gave up the idea of taking me indoors, and sat down on
the mossy, rusted bench at the end which was not too
wet, while I remained standing, one knee on the bench,
and stooped to catch what she was saying.

She at first scolded me in a friendly way for having
thus shortened my holidays.

'But I had to come back as soon as I could,' I replied,
'to keep you company.'

'The fact is,' she said, almost in whispers and with a
sigh, 'I am still alone. Augustin has not come back . . .'

Taking this sigh to express regret, an implied reproach,
I began slowly to say: 'So many mad schemes in so beautiful a mind! Perhaps the love of adventure stronger
than anything . . .'

But she interrupted me. And it was there, that very

evening, that for the first and last time she spoke to me of Meaulnes.

'Do not talk like this, François Seurel,' she said gently, 'you are my friend. It is only we—it is only me, who am guilty. Think what we did . . . We've said to him: "Here's happiness; here's what you've looked for during all your youth; here's the girl who was the aim of all your dreams!" How could anyone thus pushed into happiness not be seized with misgiving, then fear, then terror! How could he have resisted the temptation of running away!'

'Yvonne,' I said softly, 'you knew quite well you were that very happiness, that very girl . . .'

'Ah!' she sighed. 'How could such an arrogant thought ever have entered my head? It is that thought caused all the trouble. I had said to you, "Perhaps I can't do anything for him." And in my heart I was thinking, "He has searched for me so long and I love him so, I am bound to make him happy." But when I saw him by my side, with all this fever and anxiety, his mysterious remorse, I understood that I was but a helpless woman like others. "I am not worthy of you," he kept repeating when daylight came at the end of our wedding night. And I tried to comfort him, to reassure him. But nothing could quiet his anguish. Then I said: "If you must go, if I have come to you at a moment when nothing can make you happy, if you must leave me for a time so as to come back later, after having found peace, I myself ask you to go . . ."'

In the dusk I saw that she had raised her eyes towards me. It was a sort of confession she had made to me and she was anxiously waiting for my approval or condemnation. But what could I say? Certainly, within me, I pictured the Admiral Meaulnes of old, so clumsy, so awkwardly shy, that he would rather be punished than make excuses for himself or ask permission which would naturally have been granted. No doubt Yvonne de Galais should have shaken him out of this, and, taking his head

in her hands, have said to him: 'What do I care what
you did! I love you; are not all men sinners?' No doubt,
with all her generosity and her willingness to sacrifice
herself, she had been greatly in the wrong in thus throwing him back on the road to adventure . . . But how
could I condemn so much kindness, so much love! . . .

There was a long moment of silence during which,
both deeply stirred, we could hear the rain drip in the
hedges and beneath the branches of the trees.

'So he went away in the morning,' she went on. 'There
was no longer anything separating us. And he kissed me,
like a husband leaving his young wife for a long journey . . .'

She got up. I took her feverish hand in mine, then her
arm, and we walked up the avenue, now plunged in
darkness.

'Yet, did he ever write to you?' I asked.

'Never,' she replied.

And then the thought came to us both of the adventurous life he was at this moment leading on the roads
of France or Germany; so we began to speak of him as
we had never done before. Forgotten details, old recol-
lections came back to our minds while we slowly walked
to the house, at each step coming to a long stop, the
better to exchange our memories . . . And for a long
time—as far as the garden-gate—I heard in the night the
gentle, low voice of the young wife; and I too was caught
up in my old enthusiasm and never wearied of talking
to her, with deep friendship, of him who had forsaken
us . . .

School was to begin again on the Monday. On Saturday evening about five, a woman from the farm appeared in the playground where I was busy sawing wood for the winter. She came to tell me that a little girl was born at the Sand Pit. The confinement had been difficult. At nine in the evening, the midwife from Préveranges had been called. At midnight the horse had been once more harnessed to fetch the Vierzon doctor. He had had to use forceps. The little girl's head was injured and she screamed much, but appeared likely to live. Yvonne de Galais was at present prostrate, but she had suffered and struggled through with extraordinary courage.

Immediately I left my job, ran in to change my coat, and, content on the whole with the news, followed the good woman as far as the Sand Pit. With great care I climbed up the narrow wooden stairs leading to the first floor, anxious not to wake either of the patients. And there M. de Galais, tired but happy, made me go into the room where the cradle, draped in curtains, had been provisionally installed.

I had never been in a house on the very day a baby had been born. How quaint, mysterious, and good it seemed to me! It was such a beautiful evening—a true summer evening—that M. de Galais had not hesitated to open the window which looked on the yard. He leaned by my side on the window-sill and told me the story of the night in full detail but happily, and as I listened I became vaguely conscious of someone from a strange country now present in the room with us . . .

Then under the curtains the stranger began to cry, a

shrill, prolonged cry . . . And M. de Galais said in a
soft voice, 'It's that wound on the head makes her cry.'

Mechanically he began to rock the bundle of curtains,
and you felt he had been doing this ever since morning,
acquiring the habit at once.

'She has already laughed,' he said, 'and she takes hold
of one's finger. But you've not seen her yet?'

He opened the curtains and I saw a little face, red and
puffed, the top of the head was pear-shaped and de-
formed by the forceps.

'That's nothing,' said M. de Galais; 'the doctor says
it will set itself right . . . Give her your finger, she'll
hold on to it.'

I was there, discovering an unknown world. My heart
was full of a strange joy I had never felt before.

M. de Galais cautiously peeped in at the young
mother's door. She was not asleep.

'You can come in,' he said.

She lay prostrate, her feverish face in the midst of her
unloosened fair hair. She held out her hand to me, smiling in a tired way. I congratulated her on her daughter.
And in a voice that was a little hoarse and unusually
harsh—the harshness of one just back from a fight, 'Yes,
but they have injured her so!'

I had to go soon after, not to tire her.

The next day was a Sunday, and in the afternoon I
hurried almost cheerfully to the Sand Pit. On the front
door was pinned a notice which stopped my hand on its
way to the bell.

Please do not ring

I did not guess what it referred to. I knocked quite
loud. I heard, inside, muffled steps hastening. Someone
I did not know—it was the doctor from Vierzon—
opened the door.

'Well! What's the matter?' I said quickly.

'Hush! Hush!' he replied in a low voice, and troubled. 'The little girl nearly died in the night. And the mother's very ill.'

Completely disconcerted, I followed him on tiptoe up to the first floor. The little girl, asleep in her cradle, was dreadfully pale and white, like a little dead child. The doctor thought he would save her. As for the mother, he could not tell . . . He gave me long explanations as to the one friend of the family. He spoke of congestion of the lungs, embolism. He was doubtful, he could not be sure . . . M. de Galais came in, frightfully aged in two days, haggard and trembling.

He took me into the bedroom, scarcely knowing what he was doing:

'She must not be alarmed,' he said in a low voice; 'the doctor says we must assure her that all is well.'

Extremely flushed, Yvonne de Galais lay with her head thrown back as on the previous day. Her cheeks and forehead were dark red; at times her eyes became distended as happens to one who is suffocating; she was fighting death with untold courage and sweetness.

She could not speak, but she held out a burning hand with such friendliness that I nearly burst into tears.

'Well, now! Well, now!' said M. de Galais loudly, with terrible cheerfulness that resembled madness. 'You see, she doesn't look too bad for an invalid!'

And I did not know what to reply, but kept in mine the hand, so terribly hot, of the dying young woman . . .

She tried to make an effort to say something, to ask me I know not what; she turned her eyes to me, then towards the window as if to make me understand I must go and fetch someone . . . But then a dreadful fit of suffocation came upon her. Her beautiful blue eyes, which but a moment before had called me so tragically, distended, her cheeks and forehead darkened, and she struggled gently, endeavouring to the end to restrain her terror and despair. Doctors and women hurried to her

help with a flask of oxygen, towels, and bottles, while
the old man bending over her was shouting in his rough
and shaky voice—shouting as if she was already far away
from him: 'Don't be frightened, Yvonne. It's nothing.
No need to be afraid!'

Then the crisis passed. She managed to breathe a little, yet she continued to be half suffocated, her eyes
white, her head thrown back, still struggling, but unable,
even for a moment, to look at me or to speak, to emerge
from the abyss into which she had already sunk.

. . . And as I was entirely useless, I made up my mind
to go. I could no doubt have stayed a moment longer,
and at this thought I feel overwhelmed by terrible remorse. But how could one tell? I still hoped. Still tried
to convince myself death could not be so near.

When I reached the edge of the firs, behind the house,
that last look of Yvonne de Galais towards the window
came back to my mind, and I scanned with the attention
of a sentry or a man-hunter the depths of that wood
from which Augustin had come in former days and into
which he had fled this last winter. Alas, nothing stirred.
Not one suspicious shadow; not a branch that moved.
But at length, out there, towards the lane coming from
Préveranges, I heard the faint sound of a bell; soon a
child in a red *calotte* and black overall appeared at the
bend, a priest was following him . . . And I walked away
fighting back my tears.

School was to start next day. At seven o'clock there
were already two or three boys in the playground. I
hesitated a long while before coming down, before showing myself. And when I appeared at last, unlocking the
door of the mouldy classroom which had been closed for
two months, what I most dreaded happened: I saw the
biggest of the boys leave a group of youngsters playing
under the shelter and advance towards me. He came to

tell me that 'the young lady at the Sand Pit had died at nightfall on the previous evening.'

Everything turns to confusion, everything mingles with this grief. It seems to me now that never again shall I have the courage to start school. Only to cross the playground is an effort which will break me up. Everything is painful, everything is bitter, now that she is dead. The world is empty, holidays ended. Ended the long country drives, ended the mysterious fête . . . Life is again the burden it was of old.

I tell the children there will be no school this morning. They go away in small groups to carry the news to others about the country-side. As for me, I take my black hat, a mourning coat I have, and start wretchedly towards the Sand Pit.

I am in front of the house we had sought three years ago! It is in this house that Yvonne de Galais, Augustin Meaulnes' wife, died yesterday evening. A stranger would take it for a chapel, so great is the silence which has settled since yesterday on this desolate spot.

So this is what this beautiful morning of the new school year, this treacherous autumn sun which glides under the branches, had in store for us. How could I fight against hideous revolt and a blinding flood of tears! We had again found the beautiful girl. We had won her. She was my friend's wife and I myself loved her with that deep, secret friendship which is never told. I used to look at her and be happy like a little child. I might one day have married another girl, and she would have been the first to whom I should have confided the great secret news . . .

Yesterday's notice has been left close to the bell on one side of the door. The coffin has already been brought into the hall downstairs. In the room on the first floor, it is the child's nurse who greets me, relates to me the end, and gently pushes the door ajar . . . She is there. No more fever nor struggle. No more flush nor waiting.

Nothing but silence, and, framed in cotton wool, a hard face, unsensitive and white, a dead forehead from which the hair rises thick and stiff.

M. de Galais, crouched in one corner with his back to us, is there in his socks, searching with tragic obstinacy amongst a confusion of drawers he has pulled out of a cupboard. Now and again he takes out of them some old and already faded photographs of his daughter, and sobs shake his shoulders like a burst of laughter.

The funeral is for midday. The doctor fears the rapid decomposition which sometimes follows on an embolism. This is why the face, as well as the whole body, is surrounded by cotton wool soaked in carbolic.

The last toilet has been made—she had been dressed in her beautiful frock of dark blue velvet bespangled with little silver stars, its fine but old-fashioned leg-of-mutton sleeves flattened and folded under; but at the moment of bringing up the coffin it is found that there is not room to turn it in the very narrow corridor. It will have to be hauled up through the window from the outside, by means of a rope, and be lowered again in the same way . . . It is then that M. de Galais, still bent over these ancient things amidst which he searches for some lost tokens, suddenly steps in with terrifying impetuosity.

'Rather than allow such a dreadful thing to be done,' he says, in a voice broken by tears and anger, 'I will take her myself in my arms and carry her down . . .'

And he would do as he says at the risk of fainting halfway and crashing down with her!

Then I offer myself, deciding on the only possible course of action; with the help of a doctor and a nurse, placing one arm under the back of the stretched-out dead woman, the other under her legs, I gather her against my breast. Seated on my left arm, her shoulders resting on the right one, her drooping head uplifted under my chin, she weighs terribly against my heart. I walk down slowly step after step along the stiff flight of stairs, while in the room below all is being prepared.

My arms soon ache with fatigue. At each step, with this load on my breast, I am more out of breath. Clinging to the inert and heavy body, I lower my head towards the head of her I carry. I breathe heavily and her fair hair enters my mouth, dead hair with a taste of the earth. This taste of earth and of death, this weight on my heart, that is all that is left to me of the great adventure and of you, Yvonne de Galais, the woman so long sought—so loved . . .

chapter 13. THE COMPOSITION TEST BOOK

Not long afterwards, old M. de Galais took to his bed in the house full of sad memories, where women spent the day rocking and soothing a small ailing baby. He passed away peacefully in the first severe weather, and I found it hard to keep back my tears at the bedside of this charming old man whose kindly indulgence and fantastic whims, joined to those of his son, had caused our whole adventure. He fortunately died in complete oblivion of all that had happened, and indeed in almost absolute silence. As for a long time he had had neither relatives nor friends in this part of France, he chose me for his sole legatee until the return of Meaulnes to whom I was to account for everything, if he ever came back . . . And so I lived henceforth at the Sand Pit. I no longer went to Saint-Benoist except for school, starting early in the morning, eating at midday a lunch prepared at the farm, which I warmed up on my stove, and coming back in the evening after 'private study.' I was thus able to keep by my side the child whom the maids from the farm tended. Above all I added to my chance of not missing Meaulnes if ever one day he returned to the Sand Pit.

Besides, I had not lost hope of finding at last, in a piece of furniture or a drawer at the house, some paper, some indication, which would convey intelligence of his movements during his long silence of the previous years —and perhaps thus I might be able to grasp the reason of his flight or at all events to find some trace of him . . . I had already searched in vain through innumerable closets and cupboards; I had opened in the storerooms quantities of boxes of all shapes, which I found full of bundles of old letters and yellowish photographs of the Galais family, or else overflowing with various millinery trimmings: flowers, aigrettes, feathers, and old-fashioned birds. Out of these boxes came a strange faint perfume, the scent of faded things, which would suddenly awaken in me, for the whole day, memories and regrets, and stop my search . . .

At last, one day home from school, I unearthed in the attic a small old-fashioned trunk, very low and long in shape, covered with pig-hide half eaten through, which I recognised as Augustin's school trunk. I upbraided myself for not having begun my search there. I easily forced the rusted lock. The trunk was crammed full of books and exercise-books from Sainte-Agathe. Arithmetics, studies in literature, sum-books, goodness knows what! . . . Greatly moved rather than curious, I began to rummage amongst all this, reading over again the dictations I still knew by heart, as we had recopied them so many times: 'The Aqueduct,' by Rousseau, 'An Adventure in Calabria,' by P. L. Courier; 'A Letter of George Sand to her Son.'

There was also a 'Composition Test Book.' This surprised me a little, as such books usually remained at school, the pupils never taking them home. It was a green exercise-book, faded at the edges. The name of the pupil, Augustin Meaulnes, was written on the cover in a beautiful round hand. I opened it. By the date of the tests, April, 189. . I realized that Meaulnes had started it only a few days before leaving Sainte-Agathe. The first pages were kept with religious care, as was the rule when one set work down in the composition book. But there were only three pages written, the others were blank, and this explained why Meaulnes had taken it away.

I was there on my knees, brooding over these practices and petty rules which had loomed so large during our youth, while my thumb skimmed the pages of the un-

finished book causing them to open. And it was thus I
discovered writing on other sheets. After four blank
pages it started again.

It was still Meaulnes' writing, but a hurried hand, ill-
shaped, scarcely legible, forming small, unequal para-
graphs separated by blank lines. In places there was only
an unfinished sentence. Sometimes a date. From the
first line I came to the conclusion that there might be
information concerning Meaulnes' past life in Paris, indications of the trail I was looking for, and I went down
into the dining-room to use the daylight in perusing this
strange document. It was a clear rough winter day. Sometimes the bright sun would cast the shadows of the cross-
bars of the window on the white curtains, then a sudden
squall would throw an icy shower against the panes. And
it was at this window, in front of the fire, that I read
these lines which explained so many things to me and of
which I give here the exact copy . . .

'I passed once more under her window. The panes are always dusty and whitened by the double curtain behind. Should Yvonne de Galais open it now, I have no longer anything to tell her, since she is married . . . What's to be done now? How live? . . .

'*Saturday, February* 13. I met by the river that girl who gave me news in the month of June and who used, like me, to wait before the closed house . . . I spoke to her. While she walked, I noticed, from the side, the slight blemishes in her face: a little line by the lips, a little hollowness in the cheeks, and powder a little thick on her nostrils. Turning suddenly, she looked me full in the face, perhaps because her full-face was prettier than her profile, and said abruptly: "You do amuse me. You remind me of a young man who made love to me once at Bourges. I was engaged to him . . ."

'Moreover, at night, on the deserted wet pavement reflecting the light of a street lamp, she suddenly came close and asked me to take her with her sister to the theatre that evening. For the first time I observed that she was dressed in mourning, in a woman's hat far too old for her young face, and that she carried a long thin umbrella like a cane. And as I was quite close to her my nails got caught in the front of her dress . . . I do not jump at her suggestion. She is cross and immediately wants to go away. And now it is I who hold her back and beg her. Then a workman, passing in the dim light, says in a low voice, bantering: "Don't you go, little girl. He'll do you a mischief!"

'And we stopped there, both of us, embarrassed.

'*At the theatre*. The two girls—my friend, whose name is Valentine Blondeau, and her sister—have come in cheap scarves.

'Valentine is in front of me. Every moment she turns round, restlessly as though inquiring what I want of her. I, near her—well, I feel almost happy; each time I reply with a smile.

'All round us there were women wearing dresses that were too low. And we joked about them. She smiled at first, then said, "I must not laugh at them: my dress is too low, too." And she wrapped her scarf round her. As a matter of fact, under the square of black lace, you could see that in her hurry to change her dress she had rolled back the top of her simple chemise that was working up.

'There is something poverty-stricken and childish about her. She has a curious suffering and adventurous look which attracts me. Near her, the only person in the world who could give me news of the people of the manor, I never stop brooding on my strange past adventure . . . I wanted to ask fresh questions about the little house in the boulevard. But she, in her turn, put such troublesome questions to me that I did not know how to reply. I feel that henceforth we shall, both of us, be dumb on that subject. And yet I know, too, that I shall see her again. What's the good? Why? . . . Am I now doomed to dog the steps of every person who carries with him the faintest, most distant whiff of my foiled adventure? . . .

'At midnight, alone in the deserted street, I ask myself what meaning this new strange story has for me. I walk by houses like cardboard boxes in a row, in which a whole people sleep. And all of a sudden I remember a

decision I had taken a month or so ago: I had resolved
to go there by night, about one in the morning to go
right round the house, to open the garden-gate, to enter
like a thief and to search for some indication which
would help me to find the lost manor, to see her again,
merely to see her again . . . But I am tired, I am hungry.
I, too, hurried to dress for the theatre and I have had no
dinner . . . However, I remain a long time seated, much
disturbed in mind, on the edge of my bed before lying
down, a prey to vague remorse. Why?

'They did not want me either to see them home or
to know where they lived. But I followed them long
enough to know. I know they live in a little street which
leads into the neighborhood of Notre-Dame. But at
what number? . . . I guessed they were dressmakers or
milliners.

'Valentine, without telling her sister, made a plan to
meet me on Thursday at four in front of the theatre we
had been to.

' "If I'm not there to-morrow," she said, "come on
Friday at the same time, and Saturday, and so on, every
day."

'*Thursday, February* 18. I went to wait for her, in a
high wind foretelling rain. You said to yourself all the
time, "It'll end by raining." . . .

'I walk along in the twilight of the streets with a
weight on my heart. A drop falls. I fear a downpour: a
storm would keep her from coming. But the wind rises
again and the rain still keeps off. Above in the grey
afternoon sky—now grey and now ablaze with light—a
great cloud must have yielded to the wind. And I am
here on the earth, miserably waiting . . .

'*In front of the theatre.* I am certain, after a quarter of
an hour, that she won't come. From where I stand on
the embankment I keep watch on the stream of people

passing over the bridge, the way she ought to be coming.
I follow with my eyes all young women in mourning
whom I see approach and almost feel a kind of gratitude
for those who, when nearest to me, have resembled her
the longest and made me hope . . .

'*An hour's wait*. I am tired. At nightfall a policeman
takes a rough to the station near by and the rough hurls
all the filthy insults he knows at him. The policeman
is furious, pale, dumb . . . In the passage he begins to
strike, then he closes the door to beat the wretched man
in peace . . . This terrible thought comes to me: "I have
renounced paradise and am now stamping my feet at
the gates of hell."

'To ease my restless mind, I leave the place and make
for the little narrow street, between the Seine and Notre-
Dame, where I almost know where they live. I walk to
and fro alone. Now and again a servant or housewife
comes out in the fine rain to shop before night . . . Nothing here for me and I go away . . . I walk through the
clear rain which keeps the night back, up to the square
where we ought to meet. There are more people than
before—a black crowd . . .

'Suppositions—despair—fatigue—I cling to the thought
of to-morrow. To-morrow at the same time I shall come
back and wait for her. And I am in a great hurry for
to-morrow to come. I look forward with weariness to the
evening to-day and then to the next morning which I
must go through somehow with nothing to do . . . But
surely this day anyhow is practically over? . . . By the
fire, in my room, I hear them shout the evening papers.
Without any doubt, from her house hidden somewhere
in the town near Notre-Dame, she is hearing them cried,
too.

'She . . . I mean: Valentine.

'That evening, which I wanted to skip, weighs strangely

upon me. While the hours advance, while the day is soon to end—and I should like it ended—there exist men who have trusted all their hope to it, all their love and their last strength. There are dying men, others threatened by ruin, who would all like to-morrow never to come. There are others for whom remorse will dawn with to-morrow. Others who are so tired that this night will never be long enough to give them the rest they need. And I, I who have wasted to-day, how dare I summon to-morrow?

'*Friday evening.* I had thought to write, "I have not seen her again." And everything would have been finished.

'But when I reached the corner of the theatre at four o'clock—there she was! Slight and solemn, wearing black, but with powder on her face and a little collar which made her look like a naughty Pierrot. A look at once doleful and malicious.

'She comes to tell me that she wants to leave me at once, that she will never come any more . . .

'And yet at nightfall here we still are, the two of us, slowly walking, one close to the other, on the gravel path of the Tuileries. She tells me her story, but tells it in so involved a manner that I understand it badly. She says "my lover" in speaking of the man to whom she had been engaged, but whom she did not marry. She does so purposely, I think, to shock me and to keep me from attaching myself to her.

'Here are some of her phrases which I write down against my will:

' "Don't you trust me an atom," she says; "I always get into scrapes."

' "I've seen a good bit of life, quite on my own."

' "I upset the man I was engaged to. I left him because he admired me too much; he saw me only in

imagination, never as I was. I'm full of faults. We should
have been very unhappy."

'Every moment I catch her trying to make herself out
worse than she is. I think that she wants to prove to herself that she was right in doing the stupid thing she
speaks of, that she has nothing to regret and is not
worthy of the happiness which was offered her.

'Another time:

' "What I like about you," she said, giving me a long
look—"what I like about you—and I can't know why
—are my memories . . ."

'Another time:

' "I still love him," she said, "more than you think."

'And then suddenly, abruptly, sadly: "Well, what do
you want? Do *you* love me? Are *you* going to propose
to me?"

'I muttered something. I don't know what I replied.
As likely as not I said, "Yes." '

Here this sort of journal stopped. There began rough
drafts of letters, illegible, scribbled, scratched out. Pre-
carious betrothal! . . . The girl, at Meaulnes' request,
had left her job. He had busied himself with preparations for the wedding. But for ever clutched at by the
desire to continue the search, to set out again on the
tracks of his lost love, he must doubtless have disappeared on several occasions; and in his letters, with tragic
embarrassment, he tried to justify himself to Valentine.

Then the journal began again.

He had noted memories of a stay they had both made somewhere in the country: I do not know where. But, strange to say, from this moment, perhaps from a feeling of secret modesty, the journal had been kept in such a broken, irregular manner, scribbled down so hurriedly, that I have been obliged to go over it again myself and rewrite all this part of his story.

June 14. When he awoke early in the morning in the bedroom of the inn, the sun lit up the black curtain's red design. Farm labourers were drinking their morning coffee in the inn parlour and talking in loud voices. They were put out, in a rude and kindly way, about one of their employers. Doubtless Meaulnes had been hearing this restful noise for a long time in his sleep, for he took no notice at first. The curtain figured with grapes reddened by the sun, the morning voices rising to the silent bedroom, all this mingled with the one impression of waking up in the country at the beginning of delightful summer holidays.

He got up, knocked lightly on the door into the next room without obtaining a reply and opened it a little, noiselessly. Then he saw Valentine and understood where his feeling of peace and happiness came from. She was asleep, quite still and silent: you could not hear her breathe: she slept as a bird might sleep. For a long time he watched this child's face with the shut eyes, this child's face that was so peaceful you could not wish it to waken or ever be troubled.

She made no other movement to show she was no longer asleep than to open her eyes and look at him.

As soon as he was dressed, Meaulnes came back to the girl.

'We are late,' she said.

And she immediately became like a housewife in her home.

She tidied the rooms, brushed the clothes which Meaulnes had worn the day before and, when she came to the trousers, was quite upset. The bottoms of the legs were covered with thick mud. She hesitated, and then, with careful precaution before brushing them, began to scrape off the first coat of mud with a knife.

'That's just what the boys do at Sainte-Agathe,' Meaulnes said, 'when they have taken a toss in the mud.'

'Oh! Mother taught me that,' Valentine said.

. . . And such was exactly the helpmate that the sportsman and peasant which Admiral Meaulnes was might have wished for previous to his mysterious adventure.

June 15. At the dinner at the farm where they were invited, much to their annoyance (thanks to friends who introduced them as husband and wife), she behaved as shyly as a young bride.

Candles had been lighted in two stands, and one was put at each end of the white linen-covered table, as at a quiet country wedding. Faces in that dim light, when people looked down, were hidden in shadow.

On the right of Patrice (the farmer's son) sat Valentine, then Meaulnes, who remained gloomy and silent to the end of dinner, though he was the one they generally addressed. Ever since he had resolved, in order to check gossip, to pass Valentine off for his wife in this deserted village, regret and remorse tore at him. And while Patrice was playing the host like a proper squire, Meaulnes kept thinking: 'By rights, I should be presiding at my own wedding feast this evening, in a low dining-room like this, a lovely room I know well.'

Valentine, close to him, timidly refused everything that was offered her. You would have said she was a peasant girl. At each fresh offer she looked at her friend and seemed to want to hide against him. Patrice had been vainly insisting for a long time that she should empty her glass, until at last Meaulnes leaned towards her and said gently: 'You must drink, dear little Valentine.'

Then she meekly drank. And Patrice smilingly congratulated the young man on having such an obedient wife.

But both of them, Valentine and Meaulnes, remained silent and thoughtful. For one thing, they were tired; their feet were soaked in the mud of their walk and felt frozen on the newly washed kitchen flagstones. And then the young man was forced from time to time to say: 'My wife, Valentine, my wife . . .'

And every time he heavily pronounced the word, before these unknown peasants in this dark room, he felt that he was doing a wrong.

June 17. The afternoon of this last day began badly.

Patrice and his wife went for a walk with them. Little by little the two couples became separated, among the rough slopes covered with heather. Meaulnes and Valentine sat down in a little copse amongst some junipers.

The wind brought drops of rain: the weather was lowering. The evening, it seemed, had a bitter taste, the taste of such gloom as love itself could not dispel.

They stopped there, for a long time, in their hiding-place, crouched under branches, talking little. Then the weather lifted. It became fine. They believed, now, that all would be well.

And they began to speak of love. Valentine talked and talked . . .

'This,' she said, 'is what the man I was engaged to promised me, like the child he was: we should immediately have a home like a thatched cottage hidden away in the country. It was all ready, he said. We were to arrive as though returning from a long journey on the evening of our wedding day, about the time that night comes. And along the roads and in the courtyard, and hidden in bushes, unknown children would have a fête to welcome us, shouting, "Long life to the bride!" What nonsense, isn't it?'

Meaulnes listened, speechless and anxious. There came back to him the echo of sounds once heard before. And in the voice of the girl as she told this story, there seemed the tone of vague regret.

But she feared that she had hurt him. She turned towards him with warmth and kindness: 'All I have I want to give to you,' she said, 'something which has been more precious to me than anything . . . and you shall burn it!'

Then, looking straight at him, anxiously, she produced a small packet of letters from her pocket and handed them to him, letters from the man to whom she had been engaged.

Ah! instantly he recognised the fine handwriting. Why had it not occurred to him sooner! It was the handwriting of Frantz, the bohemian, which he had once seen on the despairing note left in the bedroom at the manor . . .

Now they were walking along a narrow lane, between daisies and grasses lit by the slanting rays of the sun at five in the afternoon. Meaulnes was so stupefied that he could not yet grasp the extent of the disaster which all this meant for him. He read because she asked him to read. Childish, sentimental, pathetic words and phrases . . . Such as, in the last letter:

'. . . Ah! *you have lost that little heart, unforgivable little Valentine. What's going to happen to us? At any rate I am not superstitious . . .'*

Meaulnes read, half blinded by regret and anger, his face motionless but pale, and he shuddered. Valentine, uneasy to see him like this, looked to find what page he was at and what so bothered him.

'Oh! that's a jewel,' she explained quickly—'a jewel he gave me and made me swear to keep always. That was one of his mad ideas.'

But she managed only to exasperate Meaulnes.

'Mad!' he said, putting the letters in his pocket. 'Why repeat that word? Why not have wanted to believe in him? I knew him; he was the most wonderful fellow in the world!'

'You knew him!' she cried at the pitch of excitement. 'You knew Frantz de Galais?'

'He was my best friend; he was my brother-in-arms, and now I've taken the girl he was engaged to from him! —Ah!' he went on, in fury, 'what mischief you've done us, you who would believe in nothing! You're the cause of it all. It's you who've mucked it all, mucked it all . . .'

She wanted to speak to him, wanted to take his hand, but he repulsed her brutally.

'Go away! Let me be!'

'All right,' she said, her face hot, stammering and half crying, 'if that's it, I shall indeed go.—Make my way back to Bourges with my sister. And if you don't come and find me—you know, don't you, that father's too poor to keep me—well, I shall go right back to Paris. I shall tramp the streets as I've done once already; and I shall become a bad girl for certain, I know I shall, as I've no job any more . . .'

And she went off to find her belongings to catch the train, while Meaulnes, not even watching her go off, kept walking on anywhere.

The journal broke off again.

Rough drafts of letters followed once more, the letters of a man undecided and at his wit's end. Back at La Ferté d'Angillon Meaulnes wrote to Valentine, apparently to reaffirm his resolve never to see her again and to give her the precise reasons for it, but in reality, perhaps, so that she could reply. In one of these letters he asked her what, in his first distress, he had not even dreamed of asking her: Did she know where the manor was, the manor that had been so searched for? . . . In another, he begged her to make it up with Frantz de Galais. He would set himself to find him again . . . All the letters of which I saw the rough drafts could not have been sent. But he must have written two or three times without receiving any reply. It must have been a time of fierce and miserable struggle for him, in complete isolation. As the hope of ever seeing Yvonne de Galais again had vanished, he must have felt his great resolution weaken little by little. And from the pages which I shall presently give—the last in the journal—I imagine that he must have hired a bicycle one fine morning at the beginning of the holidays and gone to Bourges to visit the cathedral.

He started out early by the lovely road through the woods, inventing, as he went along, any number of reasons for appearing before the girl he had thrown over, without loss of dignity and without asking her to make it up.

The last four pages which I have been able to put together give the narrative of this journey and of this last mistake . . .

August 25. After a long search he found the house of
Valentine Blondeau on the other side of Bourges, at the
far end of the new suburbs. A woman on the doorstep
—Valentine's mother—seemed to be waiting for him.
She was a good housewife in appearance, heavy, shabby,
but still good-looking. She watched him come with curiosity and when he asked, 'Are the Misses Blondeau at
home?' she explained gently and kindly that they had
gone to Paris on August 15. 'They forbade me to say
where they were going,' she added, 'but their letters will
be forwarded from their old address.'

As he pushed his bicycle back along the little garden,
he thought: 'She's gone . . . All is over as I wanted . . .
I've driven her to this. "I shall become a bad girl for
certain," she said. And I've pushed her into it! I've
ruined the girl Frantz was engaged to!'

And he kept saying to himself in a low voice like a
madman, 'So much the better! So much the better!'
knowing quite well that it was really 'So much the
worse!' and that under the eyes of that woman, before
reaching the gate, he was going to stumble and fall on
his knees.

He never thought of luncheon, but stopped at a café
in which he wrote a long letter to Valentine, only to cry
aloud, only to get rid of the despairing cry which choked
him. His letter kept repeating endlessly: 'You could!
. . . You could! . . . You could stoop to this! . . .
You could ruin yourself like this!'

Officers were drinking near him. One of them was
noisily telling a story about a woman which could be
heard in snatches: 'I said to her . . . you ought to know

me . . . I play with your husband every evening!' The others laughed and turning round spat behind the benches. Meaulnes, pale and dusty, watched them as a beggar might. He imagined them holding Valentine on their knees.

For a long time he rode round the cathedral on his bicycle muttering, 'As a matter of fact, I really came to see the cathedral.' You could see it rise on the deserted square, enormous and indifferent, at the end of every street. These streets were narrow and filthy as the alleys that surround village churches. Here and there hung a red lantern, sign of a house of ill fame . . . Meaulnes felt his utter misery in this unclean, vicious quarter, nestling, as in old times, under the buttressed walls of the cathedral. There came over him a peasant's fear, a loathing for this church of the town, where vices are sculptured on the cornices, which is built among evil places and has no remedy for the purest sorrows of love.

Two girls passed, street walkers, their arms round one another's waists, and looked at him boldly. From disgust or for fun, to avenge his love or to destroy it, Meaulnes followed them slowly on his bicycle, and one of them, a wretched girl whose thin yellow hair was held up at the back in a false chignon, gave him a rendezvous for six o'clock in the Garden of the Archbishop's Palace —the very garden in which Frantz in one of his letters had arranged to meet poor Valentine.

He did not say no, realising that he would have left the town far behind by that time. And she stopped a long while at her low window over the sloping street, making vague signs to him.

He hurried to regain the road.

Before leaving, he could not resist the mournful wish to pass for the last time before Valentine's house. He gazed at it and was able to gather food for sorrow. It

was one of the last houses in the suburb and the street
became a road from that place . . . In front a sort of
empty plot made something like a little square. No one
was at any of the windows, no one in the yard or anywhere. Only a dirty powdered girl passed along the wall,
dragging two little boys in rags.

There had Valentine passed her childhood, there she
had begun to look at the world with her confident, wise
eyes. She had worked, stitching, behind those windows.
And Frantz had gone by to see her, to smile at her, along
this very street. But now nothing remained, nothing . . .
The sad afternoon dragged on and Meaulnes knew only
that somewhere, this very day, the melancholy place she
would never come to again was passing before the mind's
eye of Valentine, now ruined.

The long ride ahead of him must have remained the
last succour against his woe, his last enforced distraction
before being plunged into its depths.

He went away. By the side of the road, and amongst
the trees at the edge of the water along the valley, delicious farmhouses showed their pointed gables with
green trellises. Down there, no doubt, on the lawns, girls
were pensively talking of love. You could imagine souls
down there, beautiful souls . . .

But for Meaulnes at that moment there existed but
one love, that unsatisfying love which had just been
buffeted so cruelly, and the girl among all girls whom he
ought to have protected and kept safe was precisely the
girl whom he had just sent to her ruin.

A few hurried lines of the journal informed me that
he had planned to find Valentine again, at all costs, before it was too late. A date, in the corner of one page,
led me to believe that this was the long journey for which
Madame Meaulnes was making preparations when I
came to La Ferté d'Angillon to upset everything.

Meaulnes was noting down his memories and projects in the deserted 'Town Hall' one fine morning at the end of August—when I had pushed open the door and brought him the great news which he had ceased to expect. He had been caught, checked by his old adventure, without daring to do anything or confess anything. Then remorse began and regret and grief, sometimes stifled, sometimes emerging in triumph, until his wedding day on which the cry of the bohemian in the fir wood reminded him dramatically of his young manhood's first oath.

He had hastily scribbled in this same composition test book a few words, at dawn, before going away (with her permission—but for ever) from Yvonne de Galais, his wife since the previous day:

'I am going. I must follow the tracks of the two bohemians who came yesterday to the fir wood and have gone on bicycles toward the east. I shall not come near Yvonne de Galais again until I can bring back with me and install in "Frantz's house," Frantz and Valentine married.'

'This manuscript, which I began as a secret journal and which has become my confession, is to be the property, if I do not come back, of my friend François Seurel.'

He must have hastily slipped the exercise-book under the others, relocked his old small schoolboy trunk and disappeared.

EPILOGUE

Time passed on. I lost hope of ever seeing my friend again, and the days went by mournfully in the village school and sadly in the deserted house. Frantz never came to meet me at the place I had arranged, and anyhow Aunt Moinel had long since forgotten where Valentine lived.

The only happiness of the people at the Sand Pit soon became the little girl whom they had been able to save. At the end of September, she showed herself to be a sturdy and pretty child. She was nearly a year old. She pushed chairs along quite by herself, gripping the rungs, and trying to walk, not minding tumbles, and she made a clatter which woke long remote echoes in the empty house. When I held her in my arms, she would never let me give her a kiss. She had a shy, and at the same time charming way of wriggling to get free and pushing my face away with her little open hand, while shouting with laughter. With all her gaiety, with all her childish violence, you would have said that she was on the way to scatter the gloom which had weighed on the house since her birth. I would sometimes say to myself, 'Without any doubt, in spite of this shyness, she will be a little my child.' But once again Providence decided otherwise.

One Sunday morning at the end of September, I got up very early, even before the woman who was the little girl's nurse. I was to go fishing by the Cher, with two men from Saint-Benoist and Jasmin Delouche. Villagers from the neighbourhood often met me in this way for poaching expeditions, tickling trout at night, fishing with nets in prohibited waters . . . On holidays all through the summer time we left at dawn, and did not come back till noon. It was the way most of these men gained a living. As for me, it was my one pastime, the only adventure which recalled the doings of our set in former days. And I ended by really liking these jaunts, these long hours of fishing by the riverside or amongst the reeds of the pond.

That morning, then, I was down at five-thirty, in front of the house in a little shed that leaned against the wall which separated the English garden of the Sand Pit from the kitchen garden of the farm. I was busy disentangling my nets which I had thrown down in a heap the previous Thursday.

It was not quite day: it was the dawn of a beautiful morning in September; and the shed from which I was hurriedly getting my tackle was half in darkness.

There I was silent and busy when suddenly I heard the iron gate opening and a footfall on the gravel path.

'Ha! ha!' said I to myself. 'Here come these fellows sooner than I thought. And here am I, not ready yet! . . .'

But the man who came into the courtyard was un-known to me. He was, so far as I could distinguish, a great bearded fellow dressed like a sportsman or a poacher. Instead of coming to find me where the others knew that I always was at the time we had arranged to meet, he went straight to the front door.

'Good!' I thought; 'it's a friend of theirs whom

they've invited without telling me and they've sent him
on ahead to explain.'

The man gently played with the latch of the door,
making no noise. But on coming out I had fastened the
door behind me. He behaved in the same way at the
kitchen door. Then he hesitated a moment and turned
towards me a troubled face, made clear in the half light.
And it was only then that I recognised Admiral
Meaulnes.

For a long moment I remained where I was, terrified,
in despair, suddenly gripped again by all the grief which
his return awakened. He had disappeared behind the
house, had walked round it, and returned, hesitating.

Then I approached him and without saying a word I
threw my arms round him, sobbing. Immediately he understood:

'Ah!' he said in an abrupt voice. 'She's dead, is that
not so?'

And he stood where he was, upright, deaf, motionless,
and terrible. I took him by the arm and gently led him
towards the house. It was day now. At once, so that the
hardest task should be accomplished, I made him mount
the stairs which led to the death chamber. As soon as he
was in, he fell on his knees by the bed and for a long
time kept his head buried in his arms.

At last he rose with bewildered eyes, swaying, not
knowing where he was. And still guiding him by the
arm, I opened the door by which this room communi-
cated with that of the little girl. She had awakened of
her own accord—while her nurse was downstairs—and
had boldly sat up in her cot. One could just see her
surprised face turned towards us.

'Here is your daughter,' I said.

He started and looked at me.

Then he seized her and lifted her up in his arms. He
could not see her well at first because he was crying.
Then, a little to divert this great emotion and this flood

of weeping, holding her tightly against him all the while on his right arm, he turned his lowered head to me and said:

'I've brought them back, the other two . . . You must go and see them in their house.'

And indeed, when I went early in the morning, thoughtful and almost happy towards the house of Frantz which Yvonne de Galais had once shown me empty, I saw from the distance, sweeping the doorstep, a sort of young housewife with a turned-down collar, an object of curiosity and excitement to several little cowherds in their Sunday clothes on the way to mass.

Meanwhile the little girl became annoyed at being squeezed up, and as Augustin, his head on one side to conceal and check his tears, continued not to look at her, she gave him a great slap with her little hand on his bearded, wet mouth.

This time the father lifted his daughter on high, jumped her up on his outstretched arms, and looked at her with a kind of smile. She was pleased and clapped her hands . . .

I had stepped back a little to see them better. Rather let down and yet wonder-struck, I realised that the little girl had at last found in him the playfellow she had been dimly expecting . . . Admiral Meaulnes had left with me one joy; I felt that he had come back to take it away from me. And already I could imagine him at night, wrapping his daughter in his cloak and setting out with her for new adventures.

THE END

ANCHOR BOOKS

FICTION

THE ANCHOR ANTHOLOGY OF SHORT FICTION OF THE SEVENTEENTH CENTURY—Charles C. Mish, ed., AC1

BANG THE DRUM SLOWLY—Mark Harris, A324

THE CASE OF COMRADE TULAYEV—Victor Serge, A349

CHANCE—Joseph Conrad, A113

COME BACK, DR. CALIGARI—Donald Barthelme, A470

THE COUNTRY OF THE POINTED FIRS—Sarah Orne Jewett, A26

DREAM OF THE RED CHAMBER—Chin Tsao Hseueh, A159

THE ENGLISH IN ENGLAND—Rudyard Kipling; Randall Jarrell, ed., A362

ENVY AND OTHER WORKS—Yuri Olesha; trans. by Andrew R. MacAndrew, A571

HALF-WAY TO THE MOON: New Writings from Russia—Patricia Blake and Max Hayward, eds., A483

HEAVEN'S MY DESTINATION—Thornton Wilder, A209

A HERO OF OUR TIME—Mihail Lermontov, A133

IN THE VERNACULAR: The English in India—Rudyard Kipling; Randall Jarrell, ed., A363

THE LATE MATTIA PASCAL—by Luigi Pirandello, trans. by William Weaver, A479

LIFE OF LAZARILLO DE TORMES—W. S. Merwin, trans., A316

A MADMAN'S DEFENSE—August Strindberg, trans. by Evert Sprinchorn, A492b

THE MASTERS—C. P. Snow, A162

REDBURN: HIS FIRST VOYAGE—Herman Melville, A118

THE SECRET AGENT—Joseph Conrad, A8

THE SHADOW-LINE AND TWO OTHER TALES—Joseph Conrad, A178

THE SON OF A SERVANT: The Story of the Evolution of a Human Being (1849–1867)—August Strindberg; trans. by Evert Sprinchorn, A492a

THE TALE OF GENJI, I—Lady Muraski, A55

THREE SHORT NOVELS OF DOSTOEVSKY: The Double, Notes from the Underground and The Eternal Husband, A193

UNDER WESTERN EYES—Joseph Conrad, ed. and introduction by Morton Dauwen Zabel, A323

VICTORY—Joseph Conrad, A106

THE WANDERER—Henri Alain-Fournier, A14

WHAT MAISIE KNEW—Henry James, A43

THE YELLOW BOOK—Stanley Weintraub, ed., A421

YOUTH, HEART OF DARKNESS and END OF THE TETHER—Joseph Conrad, A173

CLASSICS AND HUMANITIES

THE AENEID OF VIRGIL—C. Day Lewis, trans., A20

A BOOK OF LATIN QUOTATIONS—Compiled by Norbert Guterman, A534

THE ECLOGUES AND GEORGICS OF VIRGIL—In the Original Latin with Verse Translation—C. Day Lewis, A390

FIVE COMEDIES OF ARISTOPHANES—Benjamin Bickley Rogers, trans., A57

FIVE STAGES OF GREEK RELIGION—Gilbert Murray, A51

GREEK TRAGEDY—H. D. Kitto, A38

A HISTORY OF ROME—Moses Hadas, ed., A78

THE ILIAD, THE ODYSSEY AND THE EPIC TRADITION—Charles R. Beye, A521

THE ODYSSEY—Robert Fitzgerald, trans., illustrated by Hans Erni, A333

SAPPHO: Lyrics in the Original Greek with Translations by Willis Barnstone, A400

SIX PLAYS OF PLAUTUS—Lionel Casson, trans., A367

SOCRATES—A. E. Taylor, A9

SOPHOCLES' OEDIPUS THE KING AND OEDIPUS AT COLONUS: A New Translation for Modern Audiences and Readers—Charles R. Walker, A496